# Nine Lives

# John Morritt

Published in 2012 by New Generation Publishing

**www.newgeneration-publishing.com**

 **New Generation Publishing**

# Chapter 1

It was a chilly October afternoon at Stamford Bridge with Chelsea leading two-nil, with only ten minutes left to play. Ed pulled his jacket tighter around him to stave off the cold breeze and marvelled at the hardy Newcastle supporters to his left. He had heard that anyone from Tyneside in possession of a coat was considered a poof, but going topless just to dispel any doubts regarding their masculinity seemed to be a little over the top. The game itself was one of the best Ed had been to in years. It was end to end and both teams were playing good quality football. Chelsea needed the points to keep level with Manchester United at the top of the table and Newcastle needed the points to edge away from the relegation places into mid-table obscurity.

Ed was only there because it was Matt's birthday and he had bought him a pair of tickets for the top of the West stand, as he lacked imagination and couldn't think of anything else to buy him. He'd jumped up and down and cheered every kick. He had suggested that the referee needed a trip to Specsavers and questioned his parentage, along with the rest of the forty-thousand-plus crowd, and informed the linesman that he didn't know the rules and clearly didn't know what he was doing. However, it was all a front. The truth was, he didn't care one way or the other what the score was or even who won for that matter. He hoped he was putting up a good pretence and that his melancholy mood wasn't spoiling Matt's birthday. Deep down the final whistle couldn't be soon enough for Ed and when it did blow, he gave his biggest cheer of the afternoon.

The reason for Ed's sombre mood was his girlfriend, Laura. Laura was perfect in every way, bar one. She was without doubt the most beautiful woman he had ever met and had a figure most women would die for. She had deep brown eyes that Ed could stare at all day and a smile that still made his heart skip a beat, even after six months of being together. Despite this, she was the most natural and unassuming person he had ever met. She even had a mother that cooked like an angel. What more could a man want? The only problem was that she was disabled, after a car knocked her off her bike. After enduring months of non-invasive treatment, the last resort was surgery. However, removing the benign tumour that was crushing her spinal cord was a high risk. The operation could be complete success or could leave her paralysed for life.

Ed knew that the day would come and they had spoken about it at length, many times. Obviously, he wanted Laura to make a full recovery and get back to leading a normal life. Equally, if surgery failed, he had told her it would make no difference. He loved her and he would stand by her, regardless of the outcome. However, two weeks ago and completely out of the blue, Laura had told him she didn't want to see him any more. She had been given a date for surgery, although she wouldn't tell him when it was, only that she didn't want to see him until afterwards. Her reasoning for this was that she didn't want Ed to feel obliged to stay with her and said it wasn't fair for her to ruin his life. Since then she hadn't returned his calls, emails or letters, and it was tearing him apart. She could be on the operating table right now and he wouldn't know. Ed just wanted to be there for her, but it wasn't to be. He was worried sick and missing her more than he thought possible. The last two weeks had been two of the worst weeks of his life.

'Right, where to now, Matt? Kebab and a few beers, just like the old days?' Ed said, trying to sound enthusiastic but falling short of the mark.

'You sure you're up for it? You've had a face like a slapped arse all day. What's the problem? Not still thinking about Laura?'

'That obvious, is it?' he replied, giving his friend a weak smile.

'Just a lot. Look, I'm sure it's only temporary. Once she's got the operation out the way, she'll welcome you back with open arms. Now, cheer up you miserable bastard. We're supposed to be celebrating. It's not every day I get to be thirty-four.'

'You're probably right. Come on. Let's go, while you're still young enough to enjoy a few beers.'

'You're forgetting something important here. You're only a few months younger than me.'

'Yeah, but I look a lot younger,' Ed joked.

'I'm taller and better-looking though,' Matt informed him. Ed had no argument for that.

'I'm richer though,' Ed said as a last resort.

'And I can't argue with that. But if you wanted to be as good looking as me, you'd have to spend most of your millions on plastic surgery and you'd still be a short-arse,' Matt said triumphantly.

'Five Foot Ten isn't short. It's only two inches shorter than you,' Ed replied indignantly. He had always been a little touchy about his height.

'Come on. Let's get those kebabs, I'm bloody starving,' Matt replied. Ed could tell Matt wanted to change the subject and knew the last thing his friend needed was him sulking, on top of feeling sorry for himself. Matt put a hand on Ed's shoulder and pushed him towards the exit, Ed praying that a kebab and a couple of pints would cheer him up.

They finally managed to extract themselves from the stadium and headed towards Fulham Broadway tube station, along with the rest of the capacity crowd. They stopped off for a king-size doner kebab and large chips before joining the horde, eager to get home. They eventually squeezed into the third train that came along and spent the next ten minutes up close and personal with their fellow supporters. Ed was glad it was only a couple of stops to Earl's Court, where they would change for the Piccadilly line. The guy he was pushed up against didn't smell too good and was altogether a little too moist for Ed's liking. Fortunately the Piccadilly line was not as crowded, but all the same Ed was glad to be out at street level, breathing fresh air - or what passed as fresh air in central London.

After a couple of unfulfilling pints in a crowded chrome and mirror wine bar, they decided to head off the beaten track and avoid the crowds of tourists trying to get a few drinks in before attending a show. By chance, although Ed suspected Matt knew exactly where they were heading, they wandered into Soho. The streets here were even filthier, littered with fag butts, chewing gum, freebie newspapers and fast food packaging. Whoever said the streets of London were paved with gold was very much mistaken; they were paved with shit. Ed thought the whole area had a tacky feel about it - from the neon signs advertising girls, live shows and films, to the scantily-clad girls touting for customers in the doorways - but also found it fascinating. It was as he was gazing at the neon signs, like a moth attracted to a light bulb, that he nearly walked into a young girl who wasn't there a minute ago. On second glance, he realised she wasn't so young and was probably around mid to late twenties, maybe even older.

'Sorry,' Ed said, giving her a smile, and made to walk around her.

'Fancy a drink and a good night's entertainment?' she asked, indicating to the entrance to a club behind her.

'Thanks, but I don't do clip joints. What makes you think I want to pay fifty quid for a pint, have some girl sit on my lap and charge me another two hundred, and then have a burly bouncer frog march me to a cash point and fleece me?'

She smiled at him and replied, 'It's not a clip joint. It's a respectable club, offering lap-dancing and pole-dancing and no funny stuff. The beer's reasonably priced and it's not watered down. It's free entry before ten o'clock, too. You should give it a go. I'm sure you'll enjoy it.'

'Respectable, you say? Just like all the others along this street. No thanks.'

She wrinkled her nose up at the mention of the other clubs. 'No, this one really is. Trust me. Twenty quid for a lap-dance. More, if you want a private dance and you can check the price list if you don't believe me about the price of the beer. God, you're a cynical bugger aren't you?' she said, smiling.

Ed looked at Matt, who shrugged and walked over to the entrance to study the price list and seemed satisfied it was genuine.

'Seems to be OK and I can't see you being marched off by a bouncer. I'd like to see him try, anyway. Come on, one pint - and if it's crap, we'll go somewhere else,' Matt said.

'You're the birthday boy, it's your choice,' Ed replied, as they followed the woman down the steps into the club.

# Chapter 2

It wasn't quite a squalid as Ed was expecting and it did look relatively respectable. There was a bar along the left hand side and a stage in front of them with two poles and a large seating area, which was only a third full. It seemed the credit crunch was even hitting the perverts in their pockets. They chose a seat a little way back from stage and near the bar; not wanting to look like dirty old men leering by the front of the stage, but close enough to do just that. Thoughts of being ripped off soon evaporated after a couple of minutes of watching two girls cavorting around the poles. This was just what Ed needed as a distraction to take his mind off Laura, although he did feel slightly guilty, but soon got over it.

The woman who had enticed them in appeared at their table, minus her coat and wearing an outfit that, folded, could have comfortably fitted into a matchbox.

'Hi, I'm TJ. What can I get you to drink?' she said, smiling broadly.

'Two pints of lager please. I'm Matt,' he replied, mentally undressing her.

'I'm Ed and I'll have the same,' Ed said, giving her one of his best grins, trying not to dribble.

TJ returned a few minutes later, with four pints. Ed gave her a twenty pound note and didn't get any change. Not that he expected any, but he got a nice smile. Ed was actually enjoying himself. The club, despite his earlier reservations, appeared at face value to be friendly and so far he hadn't been ripped off, although five quid a pint was a bit steep. The pole-dancers constantly coming round for tips before going on stage was slightly annoying, especially as both he and Matt were running out of pound coins. In fact, the only downside was the group of lads to their right who were a bit loud and generally boisterous. One even had a beard, which was a complete faux pas as far as Ed was concerned. Beards were for old men, tramps or woodwork teachers, not for young men in their twenties. How anyone could think it was a good look was beyond him.

Matt was fidgeting about like a bored child. The reason for his agitation was a buxom girl with long dark hair and large, silicon-enhanced breasts who, in Matt's opinion, seemed to be taking far too long in making her way to his side of the room. Obviously a very popular girl, if you liked that type of thing.

'Hi, want a dance?' TJ asked, looking at them both.

'No thanks,' Ed replied.

'Suit yourself,' she replied, a little put out.

'No thanks. I'm waiting for her,' Matt replied, pointing at the dark-haired girl.

'He likes the large, plastic breast look,' Ed informed her. 'Tell you what, Matt, have this one on me. Call it an extra birthday present. You look like you might explode if you don't get something soon. Do your worst, TJ.'

TJ was good. She was wearing the shortest, tightest gold spandex shorts Ed had ever seen and a tiny white bikini top that allowed for a lot of movement. He sat there, mesmerised, as she gyrated and draped herself all over Matt, who sat there open-mouthed and wide-eyed. TJ had to remind him of the house rules on more than one occasion, by pointing to a large sign on the wall that said no touching the dancers. Matt was clearly having problems with this and TJ spent more time wagging her finger at him than she did jiggling her breasts at him.

'That was bloody awesome,' Matt said, turning to Ed when it was over.

'It looked it, and you've got somewhere special to hang your coat now!' he replied, looking at Matt's crotch. 'TJ, I think I've changed my mind.'

Ed sat on his hands, and looked up as TJ stepped across and began her routine. It was a variation on the dance she had just performed on Matt and equally erotic. TJ gyrated and cavorted around him with a feline grace that made his heart pound. She stared at him with smouldering eyes and pouted seductively throughout. Ed had to remind himself she was just doing her job. He managed to keep his hands firmly wedged under his thighs, but the temptation to touch her was overwhelming. The two bouncers seemed more interested in the dark-haired girl with the plastic breasts than TJ, so he could probably have gotten away with a furtive touch. Good manners and a lot of willpower won over his caveman urges. That, and the fact that the bouncers were big bastards.

'Glad you changed your mind?' she asked him when it was over, all too quickly for Ed's liking.

'Yep. Looks like I've got somewhere to hang my coat as well, now,' he said, with a grin so big it threatened to split his face in two.

'I'll be back later if you want another one.'

'One's enough. I only packed one spare pair of pants today,' he said, handing her a fifty pound note for the two dances. 'And keep the change.'

'I intended to,' she said, smiling and walking off slowly and seductively to the next table.

Matt and Ed sat there grinning at each other and watching the dancers up on the stage. Both agreed it was a good decision to come to the club and the perfect end to a day out. OK, Ed felt like a dirty old man, despite the fact that there wasn't an old man in a raincoat anywhere to be seen. There was, however, something just a little bit sordid about the place; but once he pushed those thoughts to one side, he had to admit that he was bloody enjoying himself. Matt was clearly enjoying himself and was almost bouncing around in his seat, trying to take in everything at once, not wanting to miss a thing.

Ed was distracted by TJ gyrating over the guy with the beard, who couldn't keep his hands to himself. TJ seemed to be getting annoyed as he pawed over her and tried to kiss her. The bouncers hadn't intervened and it was beginning to look as if it might get out of hand. Ed was bristling and Matt had noticed.

'Ed, just leave it to the bouncers and don't get involved. I know what you're like.'

'I can't, look at him. It's bloody winding me up. You know me. I can't turn a blind eye. It's not in my nature.'

When Beardy grabbed her breast and tried to put his hand down her shorts, it was the final straw for Ed. He stood and walked over to the next table and glared at Beardy, who glared back, defiantly.

'Why don't you give her a break and just let her get on with her job?' Ed said angrily.

'Why don't you fuck off and mind your own business?' he spat back.

'Look, just because you've got hairs around your lips, there's no need to act like one. Try and show the lady a little respect.'

Beardy seemed to take exception at Ed inferring he was a cunt. TJ wriggled out of his grip and moved away. Beardy stood up and Ed realised he was a lot bigger than he first thought. Ed was five foot ten and the guy standing before him was at least six foot and looked a lot broader standing, than he did sitting. Not that that bothered him, it just meant he had further to fall. Beardy took a couple of steps forward and stood a few inches in front of Ed and sneered down at him, before pushing him back. Ed moved back to where he was and grinned back, before smashing him in the mouth with a powerful right hook. Blood spurted from his mouth as his lips split and he fell to the floor. Ed glared at his two friends, defying them to try anything.

'I wouldn't if I were you. He's bloody lethal when he's pissed off,' Matt said, leaning over to the guy nearest him. This seemed to make his mind up, and he sat there placidly. TJ gave Ed an amused smile, then stared over his shoulder and frowned. Ed turned just in time, as one of the burly bouncers came racing up to him and launched a roundhouse at him. Ed blocked it easily and followed up with a right and left jab to his stomach and finished with a kick in the balls, after which he dropped to the floor, clutching his gonads. TJ smiled broadly at him and put her hand over her mouth, suppressing a laugh. Ed gave her a shrug and turned to go back to his table. Unfortunately, his path was blocked by the second bouncer who was wielding a baseball bat - which, judging by the dents and nicks in it, had seen quite a bit of action.

Ed backed away, until he was up against the bar. He quickly glanced left and right, as the barman swiftly removed everything off the counter, in case Ed picked up a glass or bottle and used it as a weapon. The bouncer slowly approached, slapping the baseball bat into the palm of his hand, rather melodramatically, Ed thought. By now, the whole club was watching them and Ed felt rather foolish, but didn't think that apologising and walking off was going to be an option.

The bouncer stood at arm's length in front of Ed, with a look of pure hatred in his eyes. Quick as a flash, he brought the bat over his shoulder and swung it down, aiming for Ed's head, with a cry of 'Motherfucker!'

Ed, just as quickly, ducked down below the level of the bar as the baseball bat crashed against it, making the entire bar shudder. Ed was glad the beer he'd consumed hadn't impaired his reflexes. Wasting no time, he rose and threw his left arm out on top of the baseball bat, to thwart any further attempts at taking his head off. In the same fluid movement he launched an upper cut to the bouncer's chin, putting his entire body weight behind it. When his fist connected, the bouncers head snapped back and his eyes glazed over. He wobbled a little before falling down onto his arse and hitting the back of his head on the table behind.

A slow hand-clapping from his right got his attention. Ed turned and looked straight at a man he judged to be in his late fifties or early sixties. He had steel-grey hair, swept back off his forehead, and was wearing an equally grey suit. He reminded Ed of someone but he couldn't think who.

'That was impressive. I was watching you on the CCTV,' he said in a voice that was as gravelly as Orson Welles with laryngitis. Ed wasn't sure how to respond to that so just shrugged. The two men behind him looked mean. The bouncers had been big and scary. These two looked mean and cruel, the sort of men that would torture cute, furry animals just for fun. The one on the left was taller, around six foot one, with short black hair and pointed features, which reminded Ed of a weasel. The other was slightly shorter, with thinning hair and a little on the chubby side, with small eyes that never stayed still. Ed was immediately distrustful of both of them.

'I'm Johnny Gold. I own this place,' the grey haired man in the suit announced, walking forward with his hand outstretched.

'Ed Case,' he replied, wincing at the vice like grip he received when he shook his hand.

Johnny laughed. 'Ed Case? Either your parents had a serious sense of humour or you're taking the piss. Is that really your real name?'

'About as real as Johnny Gold is,' Ed said, annoyed at the slur.

'Fair point. It's actually John Goldstein but that a bit overtly Jewish, don't you think?'

Ed shrugged again. 'The nose is still a bit of a giveaway,' Ed said before he could stop himself, and smiled back sheepishly. 'It's actually James Case but everyone calls me Ed,' he added quickly, hoping he would forget the insult about his oversized hooter.

'I can see why. What do you do for a living, Ed?'

'Not a lot. I buy property, do it up and sell it for a few quid profit.'

'I could use someone like you. How do you fancy a couple of weeks' work?'

'No thanks. Thanks for the offer, though.'

'I'll pay top dollar.'

'I don't need the money.'

'Rubbish, we all need money. I've got plenty but I still want more. Look, why don't you and your friend take a seat and enjoy the rest of the night, on the house, as my guests? Here's my card, have a think about it. I'll even get TJ to keep you company for the night. How's that sound?'

'It's very generous of you, but I don't think it'll be a good idea working with these two. I haven't exactly made two new best friends, have I?' he replied, pointing at the two bouncers he'd just laid out.

'Don't worry about them. They'll do as they're told. Muscle like that is two a penny round here. Just sit down, enjoy the evening and give me a call when you've changed your mind,' he said, with certainty that he would. With that, Johnny turned and left with his two nasty-looking associates following in his wake.

Ed tried to shake hands with the two bouncers but was snubbed, as he expected. Beardy and his two friends sloped off, giving Ed a wide birth as Ed wandered back over to his table.

'You just can't help yourself, can you?' Matt said, once Ed had sat down.

Ed smiled and took a few gulps of lager. 'I thought that bouncer was gonna take my head off there. Not sure if I ducked in time or my knees gave out in fright. Still, no harm done.' Matt shook his head in despair. He was more than used to Ed's antics.

TJ walked over to them carrying two pints of lager and set them down on the table. She smiled, walked back to the bar, picked up her own drink and rejoined them.

'You're a bit of a dark horse, aren't you?' she said, addressing Ed who shrugged and smiled back at her. 'I suppose I should thank you,' she said and kissed him gently on the cheek.

'Do you get a lot of idiots like that, treating you like a piece of meat?'

'It happens occasionally but usually it's the bouncers who sort it out. Those two on tonight are particularly useless, though. I can't see them lasting too much longer after that. Johnny doesn't suffer fools lightly. Anyway, why did you decide to take matters into your own hands?'

Before Ed had a chance to answer, Matt interjected 'He does it all the time. Thinks women belong on pedestals and should be treated like princesses. I've lost count of the number of times he's done that, in the twenty-odd years I've known him.'

'Really? And I thought chivalry was dead.'

TJ looked as though she was going to say more, but looked over Ed's shoulder and frowned. Ed and Matt both turned to look and saw that the dancer Matt had been leering over all night was approaching, much to his delight.

'Want a dance?' she asked Matt, who was nearest.

'You bet!' Matt replied, almost childlike.

She was good, very good, if the smile on Matt's face was anything to go by.

'That's Pandora,' TJ whispered to Ed. 'She's Johnny's favourite and a right prima donna. We don't get on.' Ed nodded in acknowledgement.

When Pandora had finished, leaving Matt breathless with sweat beading on his brow, she turned and asked Ed if he wanted a dance.

'No thanks. I had one earlier from TJ. One's enough for me.'

Pandora gave TJ a look of contempt. 'I'm much better than her. I've made more men come in their trousers than you've had hot dinners. Are you sure?'

'Really?' Ed replied, looking at Matt, who gave him an embarrassed look and reddened. 'That's a matter of opinion. I thought TJ was much better. Anyway, I'm silicon intolerant.'

'You're an arrogant bastard, aren't you?' she spat back.

'I can do smug, condescending, conceited and patronising, too. Would you like me to explain those to you, or do you want to get back to me on that?' Ed said smiling.

'You're also a real arsehole.'

'Well, at least I can say mine's real,' Ed replied. He could see TJ suppressing a smile as Pandora stormed off, clearly unhappy.

'You certainly know how to make friends! I thought you put women on a pedestal?' TJ said with a smile.

'The smug cow deserved that. And in answer to your question, I do put women on a pedestal. However, my friends always come first. I'm not normally that

16

rude to the opposite sex.' TJ seemed pleased to be considered a friend.

'Pity you're not going to take Johnny up on his offer, I could use a friend like you around the place. Why aren't you? You said you haven't got a full-time job as such.'

'Too much hassle. I'd have to make arrangements for the dog and to be honest, the thought to coming to London every day for a fortnight doesn't really appeal to me.'

TJ studied him for a few moments before replying. 'Wife or girlfriend wouldn't approve, is that it?'

'No wife and... or girlfriend. Just a dog.'

'Why don't I believe you?'

'Because you find it so hard to believe a good-looking bugger like me hasn't got a girlfriend?'

'No. It was because you hesitated. Come on, what's the story?'

'If you're going to start crying in your beer again, I'm off to the gents,' Matt chipped in, before leaving.

'I've sort of been jilted,' Ed started, and felt compelled to add more as TJ stared at him. 'She's in a wheelchair and is due to have an operation that will either mean she walks again, or spends the rest of her life in a chair. She told me she doesn't want to see me until afterwards, so that I don't feel trapped and obliged to stay with her. She thinks she might be ruining the rest of my life. Not that it will, because I'll stay with her whatever the outcome is. I'm worried sick and missing her like mad and she doesn't return my calls or emails and it's pissing me off.'

'So, why don't you just go round and see her? That way she doesn't get a choice.'

'I promised I wouldn't and a promise is a promise. I always keep my promises. She'll contact me once the operation's over. Whenever that is.'

'She's a lucky girl. Do you have a photo of her?' she asked, which surprised Ed. He wasn't sure why, but deep down knew that he had immediately stereotyped her as being an empty-headed blonde, whose only qualification was getting her tits out for the lads. Perhaps she was but at least she was friendly, which was more than could be said for Plastic Pandora. Ed fished out his wallet and handed it to TJ, who studied the photo.

'Pretty girl.'

'I know. I couldn't believe my luck when we got together. Beauty, brains and a mother that cooks like an angel. What more could a man want. What about you - husband, boyfriend, string of boyfriends?'

'Ha ha, very funny. In my job. What do you think?' she said bitterly.

Ed shrugged. 'There's a bloke down the pub I know, who empties bins for a living. It doesn't mean he likes what he does or lives like a pig, although he does hum a bit sometimes, especially on a hot day. No different with your job.'

'It's completely different. Believe me, I've been doing this job long enough to know. Would you get into a relationship with someone who did this job? No.'

Ed studied her. She was pretty with natural, thick blonde hair, cut into a long bob, which perfectly framed her small face. Her lips were full and enticing. Ed could imagine kissing them, and smiled. TJ was staring at him with her kind eyes, waiting for an answer.

'I don't know, is the honest answer. I think I'd have trouble coping with it. I think I'd be permanently jealous, thinking of you cavorting with all those men every night, even though it is only a job.'

'Exactly! And jealously would lead to abuse. I've been there before, so now I don't bother.'

Ed realised he had hit a nerve and tried to recover the situation. 'I think that's a bloody waste.' he replied and meant it. 'Why don't you give it up?'

'Hello. Wake up and get with the real world. Give up, just like that and do what? Wait for some tall, dark and handsome millionaire to come and sweep me off my feet and worry that he'll find out about my past?'

'Millionaire?' Matt replied taking his seat. 'I'm surprised you told her that!'

'Told me what?' TJ replied, looking at Matt, confused.

'He's a millionaire,' he replied, pointing at Ed. 'That is what you're talking about, right?' Ed raised his eyes skyward in despair as TJ stared at him.

'Are you?' she said surprised.

'Yes. I inherited a bit of money when my parents died. I bought some shares and forgot all about them. One day, I remembered and cashed them in. That money, plus redundancy money and what I already had, amounted to just over three million quid.'

'Lucky you. I mean, it's a shame about your parents but it must be nice having all that money. It's no wonder you haven't got a job. Well, not a proper job. You know what I mean,' she said, slightly embarrassed.

'Believe me, it doesn't make you happy. Don't get me wrong, I'm not unhappy - well, not now - but it took me a long, long time to come to terms with it. In fact, it was only really very recently that I did.'

'Well, at least it hasn't turned you into a grade-one arsehole,' she said, giving him a huge smile. If it wasn't for the house rules, Ed would had leaned over and snogged her face off. Instead he said 'Thanks,' and wandered off to the gents.

TJ watched him go and smiled, deciding he had a nice bum. 'How long have you two known each other then, Matt?' she asked.

Matt scratched his head and thought about it. 'It must be about twenty-seven or twenty-eight years. Since we started going to school. He's got the money, I've got the looks,' he replied.

TJ thought about it and decided he was probably right. Ed intrigued her. 'He seems like a nice bloke, and he's certainly not ugly.'

'He's not my cup of tea but yeah, he's a nice bloke. Considering the amount of money he has, he's still down to earth and it hasn't changed him. Not bad when you consider what he's been through. He's not had an easy life.'

'Are you going to elaborate on that?' TJ asked, a little intrigued. Matt coughed and turned his head slightly to watch Ed returning from the toilets.

Once he arrived at the table, he looked at his watch and suggested to Matt it was time to head off so that they could get the train home, which made TJ laugh.

'A millionaire and you travel by train, that's interesting. Have you been lying to me?'

'No, of course I haven't. Blame Matt. He gives me a bollocking if I start spending money on him. He can be a right pain in the arse. Believe me, I'd much rather make a night of it and get a cab home.'

Once they had put their jackets on, Ed pulled out his wallet and looked at the contents and handed TJ two hundred and fifty pounds, which was just about all he had left.

'You don't have to pay me. Johnny said it's on the house.'

'I know, but I've enjoyed your company. Call it a thank you and compensation for loss of earnings. I'm sure you could've made much more than that in the time we've been talking.'

TJ shrugged, kissed him on the lips and gave him a hug. 'Why don't you change your mind? You've no job, you're bored and missing your girlfriend. It'd be a laugh and it would only be for a couple of weeks. Go on, you know you want to.'

'Leaving without saying goodbye?' boomed the gravelly voice of Johnny from behind. Ed turned and stared at the hard face of Johnny Gold. 'Well, are you going to take me up on my offer? I really could do with someone with your talents on board for a couple of weeks. What about it?' he asked, stretching out his hand.

Ed hesitated, before shaking the outstretched hand. It was a moment of hesitation that he would regret for a very long time. One that would threaten his very existence and everything he cared about.

# Chapter 3

On the journey home Matt sat on the train in silence, clearly brooding over Ed's decision to take Johnny up on his offer, which was confirmed when Ed broached the subject. Matt thought he was a dodgy bastard and Ed was mad taking the job, even if it was only for a couple of weeks, to help him out of a tight spot with manpower. Ed argued that nothing could possibly go wrong. He would turn up on Monday morning and get briefed on what was expected, growl at a few punters when they over stepped the mark and come home again, simple!

Ed made arrangements on Sunday with the neighbours to look after Fat Boy, his ageing Golden Retriever and constant companion for the last ten years. He had told them he was doing a friend a favour and working in his club for a couple of weeks. Due to the late hours, he would pick Fat Boy up around breakfast time and bring him back again late morning. Julie and Mark didn't mind and the kids were thrilled to bits to have the dog to play with. Not that he played a lot these days. The years were creeping up on him and sleep was now his favourite pastime.

At nine-thirty on Monday morning he was sitting in the armchair, waiting for his lift to arrive. Johnny had insisted he send a driver for Ed on his first day, which was fine by Ed. Years of commuting had put him off trains and the thought of driving through central London didn't hold much appeal. However, if the lift was only a one off, he would drive in each night, on account of not having much choice. The club shut at two in the morning and the last train was around midnight but driving was preferable to the train. Besides, he doubted he would be able to persuade too many cabbies to take him back to home at that late hour. If they refused to go south of the river, he had no chance getting to Hertfordshire.

The door bell chimed dead on ten and Ed opened the door to an angry-looking thug who, without announcing himself, walked back down the drive and got behind the wheel of a black BMW. Ed walked down the drive and, without thinking, opened the rear passenger door and made to get in.

'In the front. I'm not a fucking chauffeur!' he barked. Ed closed the door and sat in the front passenger seat.

'I'm Ed,' he said, extending his hand to the driver.

'Obviously, or I wouldn't have knocked on your fucking door. Would I?'

'You have a point,' Ed conceded. 'But do you have a name?'

'Barry,' was the one word reply. Clearly, he was a man of few words. Whether this was due to ignorance or he just lacked the ability to communicate, Ed didn't know and didn't care. He just hoped that everyone else at the club wasn't going to be such hard work, or the next two weeks were going to be a right barrel of laughs.

The drive was completed in utter silence, with the exception of a few choice expletives from Barry. Ed didn't realise just how many cunts, wankers and pillocks there were driving or walking in London. Ed tried a few more times to engage in conversation but only received a few grunts in reply, and gave up trying. It was with great relief that they pulled up into the yard at the back of the club.

Quite why Ed was feeling apprehensive was a mystery to him. It wasn't like his mortgage depended on it, as he didn't have one. He didn't think it was anything to do with not having worked for anyone but himself for over three years, since taking redundancy.

23

So what was it? Matt thought Johnny was a right dodgy bastard and the whole thing stank of trouble. Was that the reason? Ed would have to admit that it was playing on his mind a little, but shrugged it off and followed Barry inside.

They entered through the back entrance into a dimly-lit narrow corridor with equally narrow staircases on the left and right, about halfway down. Barry turned and walked up the right-hand one, Ed following close behind. Barry knocked on the solitary door at the top of the short flight of stairs and entered, without waiting for a reply. Barry departed and left Ed to watch Johnny finish his telephone conversation. He put Johnny in his mid-fifties but it was difficult to tell. He had a deeply lined, well-lived-in face, which was also deeply tanned, giving him a Mediterranean look. This was either through too much time on a sun-bed or plenty of holidays in the Costa Brava. Or, Ed decided as an afterthought, from his Jewish origins. He didn't strike Ed as a sun-bed type of person so decided it was the Costa Brava - he looked that type.

'Welcome on board,' Johnny said in his gruff voice, extending his hand, which Ed shook and felt like checking his ring was still in place afterward. 'I suppose I'd better get you a uniform. I see you've got the black trousers and sturdy shoes on, like I said. Are they steel toecaps?'

'They are. You didn't say, and that's all I had. I didn't have time to buy a new pair.'

'Nice touch. Unnecessary, but nice,' Johnny said, almost proudly. Ed was unsure why he felt a little intimidated by this man. It wasn't like him at all. Normally Ed wasn't worried by anyone, but there was something about Johnny. He shuddered inside and silently admonished himself for his stupidity.

'Right, try this for size,' Johnny said, throwing a T-shirt in a plastic bag at him. Ed took it from the bag and held it up. It was black with the club name Johnny's emblazoned across the front in Day-Glo green italics, with a matching border. Ed pulled his jumper over his head and pulled the T-shirt on.

'Looks good. Tuck it in, though. I don't like scruffy bastards. It's a good fit.'

'Do I get to keep it?' Ed said, just for want of something to say.

Johnny nodded and lifted the phone, and asked whoever was on the other end to send TJ up. Ed turned around and noticed a bank of four television screens mounted on the wall, facing the desk that Johnny sat behind.

'Impressed?' Johnny asked, startling him.

'Yeah, I suppose so. I recognise the stage and the bar area, but not the other two.'

'They're the private rooms, where you go if you want a private dance. Good little earners. As it's a private dance, we don't have any security in there with them but we need to keep an eye on what's going on. There are some right sick bastards out there. Let's just say, we've had a couple of incidents in the past. Nasty business, so I got this lot installed. That's how I saw your little show on Saturday. It's on tape if you want to see it?' Ed declined the offer with a shake of his head.

'Do you get much trouble, generally?'

'Not really. One or two idiots who have a few too many and try to cop a feel of the dancers or try to get on stage. Generally, everyone is well-behaved.'

'In that case, why do you need me?'

Johnny gave a hoarse laugh. 'Good question. Suspicious little sod, aren't you? As it happens, I'm a bit short-staffed. I saw you on the screen and thought you'd be perfect. That's it, don't look so worried.'

A light tap on the door and TJ entering stopped Ed from replying.

'TJ, I think you're acquainted with Mr Case. Can you do the honours and show him around the place. Oh, and introduce him to the girls, then hand him over to Jim, there's a good girl.'

TJ gave him a warm smile and led him back down the staircase. At the bottom she turned around, stretched up, kissed him on the cheek, giving him a big hug for good measure, and welcomed him to the club. Ed smiled broadly; it felt good. The staircase opposite led to the two private rooms, both containing a double bed and table and chairs - very unimpressive but no doubt sufficient. Ed thought it was a little sordid, especially as he knew Johnny would be watching everything that went on behind closed doors and getting it all down on video. Not very nice, and not exactly what Ed would call private.

They descended the steps and walked towards a pair of swing doors at the end of the short corridor. These opened out into the main bar, with the toilets on the right as they entered. Ed was glad to be back in familiar surroundings. Johnny's office and the dingy, narrow corridors were a bit claustrophobic and oppressive. They walked past the bar, where Barry was filling up the shelves, and headed towards the stage, where they exited through another door marked Private. This led to another corridor with staff toilets to the left and a small canteen area to the right. In front of them was an unmarked door, which TJ pulled him through by the arm.

There were four girls in there, of varying shapes and sizes and all absolutely stunning. They all turned and stared at him, which was slightly unnerving. Three, including Pandora, were scantily-clad, ready to start work, and another, sporting a long blonde ponytail, was wearing just a tiny G-string. She also had a collagen-enhanced pout and looked like she could suck a golf ball through a hundred feet of garden hosepipe. Ed realised he was staring and made a conscious effort to blink and smile at everyone.

'This is Ed. He's our newest member of the security team,' TJ said by way of introduction. Ed smirked at being described as the newest member of the security team, when he thought he was a bouncer. She then introduced the four girls. The girl with the pout was called Debbie, and she made no attempt to cover up her breasts - but why should she? He would see them often enough on stage over the next couple of weeks. There was a petite oriental girl called Suzanne who gave Ed a bored look and went back to applying her make-up. Next was Sarah who had long dark hair and the greenest eyes Ed had ever seen. Finally there was Pandora, who stared daggers at Ed, giving him a look that could curdle milk.

'Security,' Debbie sneered 'You don't look like you could punch your way out of a paper bag!' The others tittered and cackled at her jibe.

'Mothercare is down the road, but being a bouncer there might be a bit much for you,' Sarah quipped, to more laughter. Ed wasn't too bothered. Being underestimated was often an advantage.

'Give him a break, will you!' TJ said, coming to his defence. 'He laid out Paul and Andy on Saturday night and from what I saw, he's better than half of the bouncers we've currently got.' That seemed to quieten his critics.

'They were a couple of faggots anyway. I could've seen those two off. You don't exactly make me feel safe. You don't even fill your T-shirt,' Pandora added. TJ gave her a scowl.

'I think TJ likes you, Ed. You want to watch yourself with her. The old ones are always the worst,' Suzanne added cattily.

'Good,' Ed replied, giving them what he hoped was a winning smile. 'Anyway, it's nice meeting you all,' he added and walked out, with TJ still clinging onto his arm. He hadn't noticed until Suzanne had said but TJ was a little older than the others. On closer inspection she looked to be around her late twenties, possibly even early thirties, whereas the others were probably late teens or early twenties. Not that it really mattered. She still looked good and went in and out in all the right places. What other qualifications did you need?

'Nice bunch. It's good to see that you all get on so well.'

'Oh yeah, like a house on fire. They can be so bitchy, I'm sorry about that. I'll take you to see Jim. He's OK but can be a bit prickly, depending on how bad his hangover is.'

'I can't wait,' Ed replied.

Jim was bloody miserable. One look at his bloodshot eyes and Ed knew that last night had been a good one. The grazed knuckles stood out vividly on his huge hands, a sure sign that someone had crossed him. The absence of any other battle scars told Ed that whoever it was came off worse. Jim eyed him suspiciously, almost smirking at him.

'Right, Ed. I'm Jim Curtis and I'm in charge down here. This is Spike. We call him that for obvious reasons.'

'I guess that must be the haircut. Either that, or he has a humorously shaped penis?' Ed replied, making Jim laugh. Spike just glared at him.

'And this is Dave Carter.'

Ed regarded his new workmates. All were hugely muscular and filled every inch of their black T-shirts. At five foot ten Ed was about average height, but was of a wiry build, and was dwarfed by these three. Jim was the tallest and had a film-star, lantern chin, covered in thick stubble. His hair was dark brown and cropped close to his scalp. His nose had been broken at some point and his pale blue eyes were cold and humourless. Spike had jet-black hair gelled into short spikes, and appeared to be the youngest of the three. He didn't look to be too bright but Ed surmised that it wasn't a necessary qualification. Dave was the shortest and not much taller than Ed at five foot eleven. He had short brown hair and, unlike Spike, looked quick-witted and intelligent. Ed didn't particularly like the look of any of them. Jim and Spike didn't seem to give a toss about Ed and gave him nothing more than a cursory glance. Dave on the other hand glared at Ed, with an intent that Ed found unsettling.

'There isn't much of you, is there?' Jim stated, 'But I saw the video of you from Saturday night so I know you can handle yourself. I know Johnny was impressed too, so welcome to the show.'

Ed shook everyone by the hand and, as expected, it was the usual macho game of 'Let's see who can squeeze hardest.' Ed lost all three rounds and was thankful that no bones were broken.

'As I said earlier,' Jim continued, 'down here, I run the show. Spike is number two so when I'm not around, you do what he says. Then comes Dave but it's unlikely either me or Spike will be out at the same time. Then it's you, and you know what that makes you?'

'I get it. Bottom of the food chain, and it's not a problem. I'm only here for a couple of weeks,' Ed replied, with a shrug.

'Correct! Don't forget that and don't piss me off. I don't like being fucked around. People who do, only do it the once.' Jim gave him a long hard stare to press the point. Ed felt compelled to enter into a staring competition but thought it wouldn't be a good idea - at least not on his first day, anyway. Instead, he blinked and nodded then looked away, letting Jim win the battle of wills.

His duties, he was told, was to stand around and look mean. Politely advise the clientele to keep their hands to themselves and if that didn't do the trick, give them some physical abuse. In addition to that, it was anything Jim or Johnny told him to do. The club was closed on Sunday and that would be his day off. He could also choose one evening a week to take off so he elected for Wednesday, deciding that would be a nice mid-week respite from cracking heads.

It was only four o'clock and already Ed was bored. He'd been standing around for four hours and hadn't had to do a single thing. He hadn't even had to berate a punter, let alone thump one, not that there had been many punters. The idea of thumping anyone didn't exactly appeal to him anyway. Having experienced the thrill of a lap-dance, he knew how tempting it was to join in. He'd only managed to keep his hands to himself by sitting on them. It was a relief when Jim walked up to him and told him to take a break and go get something to eat, before the rush started.

Ed found a sandwich shop just around the corner and was shocked at the prices, especially the coffee. The thought of being ripped off made the slightly plastic-tasting sandwich even less enjoyable, and the black coffee taste all the more bitter. He was standing in the canteen area, staring out the open door, as Pandora walked past. She stopped and stared at him. Ed gave her his friendliest smile, despite not really liking her, and got the middle finger for his trouble. Working at Johnny's was a laugh a minute and he was having serious regrets about accepting the job.

Almost as soon as he had he washed the last mouthful of dry, bland sandwich down with his weak, overpriced coffee, Jim walked in and told him to get his skinny little arse out there. Just for a change, he would be standing at the end of the bar, adjacent to the stage. His duties were to stop anyone getting on stage, entering the staff-only area behind him and sorting out anyone touching. Ed could manage that, just as long as he managed to stay awake. Even the pole dancing was beginning to lose its appeal and he had already memorised the dance moves of each of the girls; so much so, he could probably get up there and do a routine himself.

Ed was trying hard not to stare too long in any one direction - namely Suzanne, gyrating suggestively around the chrome pole on stage - when TJ walked up to him.

'You look bored.'

'I'm working on being mean and moody. Move along please, madam, or I'll lose concentration,' he replied, trying to sound happy and failing miserably. TJ looked at him and smiled as Ed carried on with his mean and moody look, which was more I'm bored and I don't want to be here. TJ put her hands on his chest, pressed against him and rubbed her leg up and down his thigh, before snaking down his body and dropping to her knees. Her hands dragged down his torso and stopped on his hips. She then lunged forward and bit the front of his trousers.

'That did the trick. You look much better smiling.'

'Great, how can I look mean and moody with a hard-on? If there's lipstick on my trousers, I'm sending you the bill,' he said, smiling back at her. TJ blew him a kiss and wandered off to find another punter in need of a dance. Ed held on to the memory for the remainder of the day, on account of it being the only highlight of the entire day.

Ed looked at his watch for the umpteenth time. It was just after half past one and he was beginning to wonder how he was going to get home. Jim was walking by and Ed stopped him to ask if a lift home was available, as he got a lift in. The reply, which included the words go forth and multiply and we're not running a taxi service, seemed to indicate that it wasn't. Great, no trains and no car, which meant he had to persuade a cabbie to venture outside the boundaries of central London. Of course, anyone who has ever tried to get a cab late at night knows that all cabbies are descendants of the crew of Christopher Columbus who believed the world was flat. Cabbies have a similar belief, only the world ends at Walthamstow.

Salvation came in the form of TJ, who seemed to be his only ally in the place.

'Still here? I thought you would have gone ages ago.'

'So did I,' Ed said flatly. 'Now I've got to offer a taxi driver a huge cash incentive to take me home, which might be interesting.'

TJ studied him. 'You can sleep on my couch if you like, or wait there until you can get a train. I don't fancy your chances of getting a cab. Don't worry, I don't bite!' she added, after seeing the look on Ed's face. 'Up to you, but it's the best offer you'll get tonight.'

# Chapter 4

TJ's flat was in Southwark. From the outside it looked like a fleapit but inside it was tastefully decorated in neutral colours. The living room was small and cosy and had just enough room for a two-seater sofa with a coffee table in front of it, a small dining room table and chairs, an old-fashioned sideboard and a large plasma screen television in the corner. TJ poured them both a glass of red wine and set them down on the coffee table.

'I'm off to slip into something more comfortable,' she told him, making him laugh. 'What's so bloody funny about that?'

'It sounds like a cliché from a bad porn film, that's what. I've got visions of you coming back out in a see-through negligee and leaning seductively against the door frame.' TJ smiled and shook her head. A few minutes later she returned wearing a pale grey lightweight sweatshirt with matching shorts. It was obvious that she had nothing on underneath, as her breasts jiggled beneath her top as she walked towards him. It was the first time he had seen her not wearing her stiletto heels and she looked diminutive and very cute, Ed thought, as she sat down next to him on the sofa.

'There's no need to look so bloody relieved. Just because I work in a Soho club, it doesn't mean I'm a tart,' she chided him.

'That was my surprised look. It's the first time I've seen you not wearing your work outfit and you still look great. Cheers,' he said, raising his glass.

'Are you flirting with me?'

'I am. Sorry,' Ed replied meekly.

'Don't be. Unless you didn't mean it,' she replied, staring at him with narrowed eyes, trying to detect a lie.

Ed gave her his would I lie to you? look and grinned, which she seemed satisfied with.

They made small talk about Ed's first day. TJ tried to reassure him it would get better and that the people at the club were just naturally suspicious of newcomers; after a few days they would warm to him. Ed wasn't so sure. He only had two weeks and doubted in that time they would be even slightly tepid.

'Tell me about yourself,' she asked. 'Give me your life story.'

'OK. It won't take long. I was born thirty-three years ago. Went to school and got three A-levels. Got a job in London working in a finance department, moved into sales and became a sales manager. Parents died when I was twenty-five and left me some cash. Ex-girlfriend came back on the scene and thought she was marrying into money. When she found out she hadn't she had a string of affairs and died shagging her latest bit on the side, when his van went down a gully and burst into flames. I went off the rails a little bit and tried to commit suicide. Got over that and found out I was a millionaire and spent the next three years trying to come to terms with it. Met Laura six months ago, and that's about it.'

'Christ, you've not had it too good, have you? Matt said as much on Saturday night.'

Ed smiled. 'Matt's got a big mouth. You're lucky. I left out the bad bits. So what's your story, then?'

'I was born thirty-six years ago. I never knew my father and my mother died when I was ten, so I went to live with my grandmother in Bermondsey. She died when I was twenty-two and left me a little money; nothing life-changing like your inheritance, but enough to put a fairly large deposit on this place. Work-wise, I never really settled anywhere and spent years temping. One of my friends at work suggested taking a pole-dancing course, just for a bit of fun, and I really enjoyed it. Some time after this, I was on a hen night and had a few too many. One of the girls I was with dared me to get up on the stage in the nightclub we were in and show her what I could do. I did and was asked by the nightclub owner if I fancied doing a few regular spots. I thought it would be a good laugh and the money was better than temping, so when I got an offer of doing it full time, I jumped at it and have been doing it ever since.'

'Thirty-six, eh? I thought you were a bit older than the other girls in the club but would have put you more in your late twenties. I'm surprised.'

'Flattery will get you everywhere,' she said, with a mischievous smile. 'So, any breakthrough with Laura?' TJ asked, surprising him.

'You've got a good memory.' TJ shrugged. 'As it happens, no. I've phoned, I've emailed and sent her a few texts and got bugger all response. Obviously, I just said it was a club and didn't go into details. Maybe, I should have. It might have got a reaction. It's just so frustrating.'

'At least you have a relationship of sorts. You're the first member of the opposite sex I've had through the door in two years.'

'Really, that surprises me. Does it bother you?'

'Of course it does. Wouldn't it bother you?'

'I went three years after my wife died. Up until I met Laura, to be precise, and yes it did. I had bollocks like watermelons. It was just nice to go out for a meal with someone again. You can't really go with a mate. It's a bit gay, don't you think? Different for women but two blokes, it just doesn't look right. So, what do you miss most?'

'Apart from the obvious?' she replied, giving Ed a look that sent his heart racing. 'Being taken out to dinner, and this. Just sitting, talking and snuggling up to someone on the sofa.' Her gaze fixed on Ed again as she said this and she smiled at him, coyly. Ed picked up on the hint, opened his arms, and smiled back. TJ slid the short distance across the sofa, put an arm round his back, rested her head on his chest and sighed contentedly. It felt good to Ed and he slipped his own arm over her back, resting his hand on her hip, which felt even better. He could feel his pulse quickening and had to remind himself he had Laura, as TJ's other arm was dangerously close to his crotch. 'Thanks. This is nice,' she told him, wriggling into a more comfortable position. 'You're not very comfortable to snuggle up to,' she told him.

'I guess I was built for speed, not comfort. Sorry.'

'Maybe I'll find out one day?' she said, quietly into his chest.

'Are you flirting with me, now?' He felt TJ give a small shrug.

'I might be. Do you have a problem with that?'

'When's your next day off?' he asked, changing the subject quickly, wanting to avoid answering. Right now he didn't have a problem with it, and things could easily get out of hand. The last thing he wanted to happen was to cheat on Laura.

'Wednesday and then Sunday, obviously, as the club is shut on Sundays, in case nobody told you.'

'Good. I'm on a half-day Wednesday and supposedly finish at five. How about I take you to dinner?'

'Why?' she asked, surprising him.

'I like going out for dinner and so do you, and because I'd like to. Call it a thank you for being the only person at the club who's been nice to me.'

TJ looked up at him, smiled and kissed him on the cheek. 'Perfect. Have you got anywhere in mind?'

'Yes, somewhere posh and expensive, so put your glad rags on. Unless you have somewhere you'd particularly like to go?'

'No. Anywhere posh and expensive is fine by me.'

'That's a date then,' he said, regretting using the word date, not wanting her to get the wrong idea. 'On one condition though - you tell me what TJ stands for,' he grinned.

'Tracy Jane but I've been called TJ by everyone for years. I hate being called Tracy, so don't, right!'

'OK.'

# Chapter 5

Wednesday morning, Ed was feeling a little better. TJ had fallen asleep with her head in his lap on Monday night and he hadn't the heart to disturb her. He had sat there until around half-past four, before gently laying her head down on the sofa. He fetched the duvet from her bed and laid it over her, before letting himself out and walking up to London Bridge, en route to Liverpool Street station, to catch the first train of the day.

After collecting Fat Boy from the neighbours and taking him for a walk, he got a couple of hours of sleep, before driving back into London for work. Tuesday had been as uneventful as Monday, although slightly busier. TJ had invited him back for a drink after work, which he had declined. The idea appealed to him, but the need for a good night's sleep was even more appealing. She gave him a look of such disappointment that he nearly relented. Sleep was the genuine reason, but also guilt played a part. Cuddling up with her on the couch on Monday night had left him feeling like he had somehow cheated on Laura, despite nothing happening. Ed felt that it could so easily have been different, certainly from his point of view. There was just something about TJ that he found attractive, apart from the obvious. Looks and figure aside, she was just a very warm and genuine person who Ed felt extremely comfortable with. So much so it worried him.

The day looked to be heading into the same routine as the last two days; Suzanne walked past him and gave him a contemptuous look, Debbie had just completely ignored him and Pandora had given him the middle finger, which he now came to expect. A look at his watch told him he only had three hours to go, as the last of the lunchtime crowd began to leave. The only punters remaining were three Asian men who had recently entered. All were wearing expensive-looking suits and were sitting in front of the stage, waiting expectantly. Pandora approached them with her exaggerated wiggle, and set their drinks down on the table in front of them. Ed couldn't hear what was being said but it was obvious from her flirting that Pandora was touting for work. The eager smiles and leers from the three Asians suggested she was in luck.

She began dancing as Suzanne took to the stage and began gyrating around the pole. Ed's eyes were flicking between the two of them. No matter how many times he saw them dance, it never became less appealing. Unfortunately, Ed was being paid to do a job and so he concentrated on Pandora, not that it was a difficult task. Despite the fact that he couldn't warm to her, she was very easy on the eye. The Asians were getting a little too keen for Ed's liking but he held back as Pandora seemed to be holding her own, admonishing them with a seductive wag of her finger or playfully smacking their hands as she moved them off her hips.

Ed didn't like the look of any of them. The man on the left appeared to be the youngest of the trio, perhaps no more than in his early twenties. His hair was short and gelled up into spikes, not unlike Spike's but it looked better on him, due to his expensive designer suit. The one on the right was a few years older and of a muscular build that filled every inch of his black suit. The man in the middle was in his forties and looked like he enjoyed the finer things in life, especially food. At some point he probably had a muscular build like the one on the right, but it had long since gone to seed.

It was becoming clear to Ed that things were getting very out of hand. The man in the middle had pinned Pandora to his lap, by holding her tightly by the crook of the arms. The other two were pawing at her breasts and thighs and trying to kiss her, laughing at her futile struggles. Ed walked over briskly and businesslike, to intervene.

'Come on gents, you know the rules, no touching,' he said firmly but politely. All three stared at him with hard eyes, almost daring him to exert his authority. 'Look, I'm pretty new here and no doubt my boss is watching on the CCTV, so give me a break and stick to the rules,' Ed added, trying a different tact.

'We're friends of Johnny's, so why don't you turn around and fuck off!' the man holding Pandora said, with such malice that Ed found it unsettling.

'I can't do that. House rules, and I'm being paid to make sure everyone follows them - even friends of Johnny's - so just let the girl go, and enjoy the stage show.'

'Asif, teach this prick a lesson in manners, will you,' the man in the centre who was still holding Pandora said. Asif, who was sitting to the left of him, gave a nod and an unfriendly smile and stood to face Ed. He took his jacket off and placed it neatly on his chair. Ed stood his ground and appraised Asif, who was about the same size and build as he was.

He got no further than that in his appraisal, as Asif lashed out with a vicious left hook. Ed saw it coming and took a step back, managing to avoid being hit. Asif smiled and renewed his attack, with a series of punches and Kung Fu style kicks, which again Ed either blocked or avoided. Ed smiled back and edged forward, just to intimidate his opponent and see what reaction he got. He was pleased when he noticed a glimmer of uncertainty in Asif's eyes and smiled more broadly, in order to gain the psychological advantage.

Asif was clearly rattled and Ed lashed out with a left hand jab, which glanced off his cheek. The man in the middle, who was still clinging onto Pandora - so tightly in fact, Ed could see his fingernails digging into the soft flesh on her arms - said something in a language Ed didn't understand. Whatever it was, it was to admonish Asif, who glanced nervously at him and nodded, before hurling another combination of punches and kicks at Ed. Most of these Ed easily blocked and those that did connect were lacking in power. Asif aimed another Kung Fu style kick at Ed and, fed up with sparring, Ed grabbed Asif's leg. Asif twisted but was unable to shake off Ed's grip, enabling Ed to kick him hard, between the legs. He dropped to the ground and Ed picked him up and punched him hard in the solar plexus, forcing the air out of him. As he was about to aim a blow to his face, the man in the middle shouted at him to stop.

Ed held his assailant by the hair and looked over towards the two seated men. Ed stared, blinked and looked again at the man holding Pandora, who had a gun in his hand, aiming it at Ed. Without thinking, Ed spun Asif round and gripped his neck in a stranglehold. Firstly to stop him from a further assault, and secondly to use his body as a shield, against the man holding the gun.

'Pandora, get up and walk towards me,' Ed barked. The man with the gun had lost interest in Pandora and made no attempt to stop her. Pandora cowered behind Ed, who wasn't sure what to do next.

'Put the gun away or I'll strangle the bastard,' Ed said, and tightened his grip to prove a point. The man didn't make a move but just stared intently at Ed. 'The only way you're gonna shoot me is through him and even you don't look that stupid, so put the bloody gun away.' Ed was pleased that his voice remained firm and steady, disguising the fact that he was on the verge of soiling his trousers.

'Mo, put the gun away. Ed, let go of Asif, please,' Johnny's gravelly tones commanded from behind Ed. Mo made a big show of putting it away and Ed released Asif, who slumped to the floor, gasping for breath.

'Take a break, Ed. Go and get a coffee or something, whilst I take my associates up stairs,' Johnny said, placing a firm hand on Ed's shoulder, squeezing it hard and painfully with one of his large hands. Ed tried not to show that it hurt, not wanting to show any weakness. He turned, nodded to Johnny, and walked out for some fresh air.

Ed was still shaking when he arrived back, and was sipping his coffee in the kitchen area. He hadn't signed up to having some bastard pull a gun on him and was beginning to have serious regrets about agreeing to work here, even if it was only for two weeks. He made up his mind he would tell Johnny he was going to leave before he left this evening. A shadow passed the door to the canteen and Ed looked up quickly, still very much on edge and shaken by the events earlier. Pandora was standing there, staring back at him. Ed gave her a nervous smile. He looked at her bare arms and noticed the red welts, standing out vividly against her pale skin. Rather than give him the middle finger and walk off, which was her usual greeting, she walked towards him and gave him a friendly smile.

'Look, I know we haven't exactly got off to the best of starts, but thanks for what you did earlier,' she said, sounding genuinely grateful.

Ed shrugged 'No problem. How are the arms? They look a little sore.' It was Pandora's turn to shrug. 'Who were those three guys?'

'Business associates of Johnny's - or in other words, local villains. This place may seem above-board, when you compare it to the other clip joints round here, but it's just a front. Johnny isn't as kosher as he likes to make out.' Ed nodded in agreement as Pandora continued. 'Tell me to mind my own business if you like, but you seem like a decent bloke. You're not like those other bastards out there, who expect certain perks for doing what you did. So why are you here?'

'So, the other bouncers expect a few free dances and a bit more, just to do their job and see off a few over-eager punters?' Ed asked almost rhetorically. Pandora nodded. 'Jesus. That explains why they all ignored TJ on Saturday, because she doesn't pay.' Again, Pandora nodded. 'In answer to your other question, I'm here because Johnny said he was short-staffed and saw what I could do. I'm only here for two weeks, although after today, it might not be as long as that. Johnny didn't seem too pleased earlier.'

'Do yourself a favour and get out as soon as you can, before you get sucked in and become as poisoned as the rest of them out there.' She kissed him on the cheek and gave him a worried smile and turned to leave.

'Pandora,' he called after her 'Thanks and sorry for being such a prick on Saturday night.' She turned, smiled again, and gave him the middle finger before disappearing.

Thinking that perhaps Pandora was warming to him cheered him up slightly. It didn't make him feel any different about working at Johnny's, but for now it made him feel a little better about it. It was short-lived. Ed had just finished his coffee and was about to leave, when Dave put his head round the door and gave Ed a menacing stare, before walking in and pulling the door to behind him. Whatever it was he wanted, it was personal. Ed was concerned that Johnny had sent him, for screwing up with his "Associates" earlier. He stared back at Dave as he advanced towards him, bracing himself for the violence that seemed inevitable.

'What the fuck are you doing here, Ed?' Dave asked in a calm even voice that Ed wasn't expecting.

'The same as you are, Dave. Just working and trying to do a job,' Ed replied, just as calmly.

'I don't trust you and I don't like you. There's something about you that doesn't stack up. You waltz in here on Saturday night, cool as you like, and kick ten shades of shit out of Andy and Paul - and just like that, Johnny takes you on. Who are you working for?'

'Dave. This is all bullshit and you know it. It's exactly as it seems. I'm working for Johnny and nobody else. You've obviously got a problem with me and to be honest, I don't give a shit. In two weeks, I'm out of here and you'll never see me again or vice versa. So you keep out of my way and I'll keep out of yours. OK?'

Dave walked up to Ed and poked him in the chest. 'I'm going to do some digging on you and find out who you are and who you're working for. Then, I'm gonna make sure you're history. Got it?'

Ed batted his finger away with the back of his hand and stood nose to nose with him. 'I wouldn't waste your time, Dave. There's nothing to find out. You're looking for a conspiracy theory that doesn't exist. So fuck off and find someone else to wind up, someone who gives a shit.' Ed took a step back and walked off, shoulder-barging him as he did. He half expected Dave to follow him and was relieved when he didn't. He'd had enough for one day. In fact, he'd had enough, period.

He had made up his mind to speak to Johnny and tell him it wasn't working out and he would be leaving. He was on his way to his office when Asif, Mo and the other Asian, whose name Ed didn't know, came through the doors accompanied by Johnny. Mo made a gun of his hand, pointed it at Ed, and pretended to fire it at Ed's head. Ed used to do the same thing as a kid, playing war with his friends, but this was altogether more menacing and chilled him to the bone. They all had their coats on, including Johnny, so now wasn't a good time. He would wait until tomorrow. Another day wouldn't make any difference.

# Chapter 6

The drive from Soho to Southwark was painfully slow, due to the rush hour traffic. The journey, which was only around three miles, took the best part of an hour to complete. Time wasn't a problem as the table had been booked for eight o'clock but it was mentally tiring, having to keep a watch for weaving motorbikes or cyclists and buses that pulled out at will, regardless of what was in the next lane. That, on top of the events of earlier in the day, meant he arrived at TJ's flat tense and on edge. He really wasn't in the mood for going out but he didn't want to cry off, as TJ had told him she was really looking forward to it.

TJ answered the door, wearing a little black dress that stopped a few inches above the knee, and she looked stunning. Her blonde hair was immaculate; not a hair out of place. Her make-up was subtle, a far cry from the battle paint she wore when she was at work. The overall effect left Ed lost for words. He didn't even want to begin to consider if she was wearing tights or stockings.

'You're a bit optimistic, aren't you? How long are you planning to stay for?' she said, eyeing his overnight bag.

'It's just a few toiletries. I thought I could grab a quick shower before we go, to wash the smell of sleaze and corruption off me,' he replied with a wry smile.

'Bad day, I take it?'

'Let me grab a shower and I'll tell you all about it. You look absolutely drop dead gorgeous, by the way. I'd better make it a cold shower.' It was clearly the right thing to say if TJ's smile was anything to go by.

'You don't scrub up too badly, either,' TJ said, as he walked into the living room in a dark charcoal grey suit and a matte black shirt underneath. Ed smiled at the compliment but still felt like the ugly duckling next to TJ. 'So, what's got under your skin today?'

'Just about everything. I'm going to tell Johnny tomorrow that I'm leaving. When I said I'd do two weeks work, I didn't expect to have one of the local Mafia pull a bloody gun on me!' TJ stared at him open-mouthed as Ed told her about his run in with Asif, Mo and the third man he now knew to be called Abdul. 'The only good thing is that Pandora seems to be warming to me.'

'That's a good thing?' she said, making Ed laugh.

They left the flat and walked arm in arm down to Blackfriars Road, where they hailed a black cab. Ed leaned though the window and told the cabbie where to go so that TJ wouldn't hear, wanting to keep it a surprise. When they pulled up outside the Ritz, she sat there open-mouthed in awe. Ed thought she was going to hyperventilate when the concierge, clad in his immaculate old-fashioned finery, opened the door for her and gave her a slight bow.

'This is very nice,' TJ said in almost a whisper. 'Do you come here a lot?' she asked, making Ed laugh again.

'To be honest, I'd prefer a good curry. Have you heard the expression, champagne taste but lager pockets? Well, I'm more champagne pockets and lager taste. I only booked the Ritz because I thought you might like it.'

'I'm just so lost for words. I love it. If I was rich, I'd come here every day!'

'Just don't look at the prices. Order what you want, not because it's cheap... or expensive,' Ed added as a jest.

Ed had never been to the Ritz and didn't know what to expect. He had a feeling it would be special but they were both blown away, by the sheer opulence the hotel exuded, and they hadn't even progressed any further than reception. The restaurant seemed even more extravagant in its decor, from the impossibly high ceiling, to the murals that adorned the walls. It was far better than anything Ed had expected and he was in total admiration of the place. TJ was equally impressed and sat down at the table, staring wide-eyed at her surroundings. Ed gave himself a mental pat on the back and a smug grin. If you wanted to impress a lady, this was the way to do it.

The food was superbly cooked and mouth-wateringly delicious, if a little rich for Ed's simple tastes. He had ordered the confit of salmon starter, with cannelloni of cucumber with smoked trout and apple and lovage puree. He didn't know quite what he ordered but it looked great and tasted fantastic. TJ had the lobster salad, which came with vegetables in a jelly and a vinaigrette sauce and, judging by the look on her face, it was to her liking. He had ordered a bottle of Chateau Margaux, which he normally got by the case on the internet at two hundred pounds a bottle and was a little shocked that they were charging just shy of six hundred. But he thought, what the hell, it was a one off. TJ's jaw nearly hit the floor when she looked at the wine menu and saw the cost, and shook her head in disbelief.

The conversation flowed, both avoiding talking about Johnny's, neither wanting to spoil the occasion by talking shop. TJ was great company, and for the first time in weeks Ed felt happy and thoroughly relaxed.

After the main courses had been and gone - Ed having had the grilled fillet of Aberdeen Angus and TJ opting for the fillet of beef, which came with oxtail ravioli and red wine sauce - they were both struggling. The waiter appeared and offered them the dessert menu and they both blew out their cheeks and shook their heads. However, they both ordered the caramelised apples in calvados sauce, with crème fraiche and cinnamon doughnuts. Neither of them had room after the first two courses but they sounded so mouth-wateringly good that neither of them could resist. Afterwards they both regretted their greed and sat back, wishing that they had more willpower. Ed wanted to undo the button on his trousers to give himself some breathing room but thought it might be a little out of place in such a fine establishment and didn't want to embarrass TJ.

'TJ, tell me to mind my own business, but why do you work at Johnny's? You're much better than that.'

She smiled at the compliment and thought about an answer. 'I've been doing it for so long, I don't know what else I could do,' she replied, almost apologetically.

'Rubbish! You're young - well, youngish - you're beautiful, and you've got your whole life ahead of you.'

'Look out everyone, cliché man has entered the building.'

'OK, I'll put it another way. You look much younger than thirty-six. You've got film star looks and figure and it's not too late for a career change.'

TJ stared at him thoughtfully and gave him a seductive smile. 'Are you trying to sweet talk your way into my knickers, by any chance?'

'Of course not!' Ed said, feigning hurt. 'I've got Rohypnol for that.'

'Well, you're doing OK without it,' she replied and blew him a kiss. It seemed to signal the end of that line of conversation, but Ed had a feeling that there was something left unsaid. He made a mental note to bring it up another time, to find out what she was hiding.

'So, who are those three Asian guys?' Ed asked, changing the subject.

'They're a lot of trouble so steer well clear of them. Although, it's probably a bit late for that, isn't it? They run a few clubs on the more seedy side of Soho, clip joints of the highest order. They also have a big share in the drugs market, illegal porn and, of course, prostitution.'

Ed nodded and, if he was asked, would say that he was now a little concerned. 'What about the other two guys who were in on Saturday night? I thought they looked a bit like coppers.'

'That's exactly what they are. Bent as they come and nasty as they come. Detective Inspector, Roger Blackthorn and Detective Sergeant, Mike Denton. They make your Asian friends look like pussycats. Johnny does a lot of business with them. Look, I shouldn't be telling you this, it's probably better that you don't know, but rumour has it they supply Johnny with drugs - the spoils of police raids. Trust me, they're the scum of the earth. For your sake, stay well clear.'

Ed nodded. 'What do you know about Dave? He seems to have a bit of a chip on his shoulder. He gave me a bit of a hard time earlier. Seems to think that I'm up to something or working for someone else and am trying to muscle in. On what exactly, I have no idea.'

TJ seemed surprised by this and looked at Ed thoughtfully before answering. 'I don't know too much about him. He's only been here a few months or so but seems to keep himself pretty much to himself. I've not had much to do with him, but then I don't have much to do with any of them. Perhaps he just doesn't like you?'

Ed gave a shrug and changed the subject. He didn't see Dave as being a real issue. He was just flexing his muscles to reaffirm the pecking order. 'I also hear that my fellow bouncers need paying, too. Although a certain person, not a million miles away from me

50

doesn't, which is why I had to step in on Saturday night,' Ed said raising a quizzical eyebrow.

'You don't miss much!'

'Pandora told me earlier, after my run in with the Asians. Good for you. Although, that does mean you owe me one.'

'What would you like?'

'The pleasure of your company tonight is payment enough,' Ed said in jest.

'Lay off it. Any more of that and I'll be sick and I'd feel guilty after what you're about to pay for this.'

'I thought we agreed to go Dutch?' Ed said with a grin.

'I'll pay you in kind,' she replied giving him a very seductive smile. If only, Ed thought.

After Ed had paid by credit card, they decided to walk back and headed down to the Embankment and towards Waterloo Bridge, hand in hand. The night was cool but not too chilly. The fresh air felt good and the exercise was certainly needed, after the mountain of food they had both eaten. The wind as they were walking over the bridge was bracing as it whipped along the Thames and TJ let go of his hand and put an arm around Ed's waist, almost snuggling into his body as they crossed. Ed placed an arm around her shoulder and pulled her in closer. TJ looked up at him and smiled and gave a contented sigh. In that moment, he knew that his planned conversation with Johnny about leaving would not happen, and he would stay the full two weeks as agreed.

'Are you coming in for a coffee?' TJ asked, once they had arrived back at her flat.

'Thanks, but I better get going.'

'You've got to come in for your bag so you might as well. Don't look so worried. I won't eat you,' she said, having seen the concerned look on Ed's face.

'It's not you I'm worried about,' he said with raised eyebrows.

'Well, if you try anything on with me, I'll knee you in the balls.'

'Really?'

TJ shook her head. 'I'll just get your bag,' she said and went inside. She returned a short time later and placed it on the floor, just outside the flat. 'Thanks for a lovely night. It's been a long time since I've been taken out for a meal. I'd forgotten how nice it is,' she said, looking up at him with her lovely blue eyes.

'You're welcome. Maybe we can do it again next week, before I finish at Johnny's?'

'As long as it's a curry and I'm buying.'

'Deal,' Ed replied. He bent down and kissed her on the cheek and gave her a hug. TJ was still holding on, long after Ed had released his grip. She looked up at him and gave him a sulky pout.

'Are you sure I can't tempt you with coffee?' Ed shook his head sadly. 'How about breakfast?' she asked, giving him another seductive smile.

Ed laughed. 'Goodnight, TJ.'

# Chapter 7

The long shifts at the club and lack of sleep were catching up with Ed by Friday evening. The last two days had been much the same routine as the previous three, namely long and tedious. His newfound Asian friends hadn't been seen since Wednesday, which was fine as far as Ed was concerned. Having a gun waved in your face was something he could well live without. DI Blackthorn and DS Denton put in an appearance on Friday morning and disappeared up to Johnny's office. Ed was down the far end of the bar, where he seemed to spend most of his time; but he noticed that Blackthorn carried a large silver briefcase and left without it, which was a little suspicious, he thought. Bearing in mind TJ's words of wisdom on Wednesday, he didn't dwell on it. Having made such good friends with the Asians, getting on the wrong side of two bent coppers was the last thing he wanted.

'Boss wants to see you,' Spike informed him.

'What for? Not in the shit, am I?' Ed asked.

'How the fuck should I know?'

'Fair point,' Ed said with a shrug and made his way up the stairs to Johnny's office.

Ed knocked and walked in, not waiting for a reply. 'You wanted to see me? Not in the shit, I hope?'

Johnny smiled. 'I don't think you made a good impression on Mo. I must admit, you've got some bollocks. I'll give you that. Do me a favour though - don't try that again.'

Ed shrugged and thought about saying nothing, but it went against his nature. 'They were being a bit rough with Pandora. What was I supposed to do, turn a blind eye?'

'That's exactly what you should've done. There are plenty of Pandoras out there, looking for work. My business associates are more important. Next time, walk away. You might even want to apologise to them next time they're in, but something tells me you're not the apologising type.'

Ed shrugged again. 'So apart from pissing off Mo and his merry men, how am I doing?'

'Good. You stick out like a dog's bollock but you're doing OK. You're a bit too clean-cut and you don't look like a bouncer. Try not shaving or something so you blend in a bit better. There's not much you can do about your physique, at least not in the short term. Maybe you should join a gym and bulk up a bit to fill that T-shirt.'

Ed laughed. 'Not exactly the worst appraisal I've ever had. I take it I'm not being sacked, then?'

Johnny reached into his jacket pocket, never taking his eye off him and Ed never taking his eye off Johnny. Johnny whipped his hand out and thrust it towards Ed, who tensed, making Johnny laugh. 'Your wages for the week,' he said smiling.

Ed took it and thanked him, folding the envelope in half and putting it in his pocket.

'Aren't you going to check it?' he said, which came out more like an order than a question.

'I wasn't going to. Do I need to?'

Johnny nodded and Ed took it out and opened the envelope and counted it. The envelope contained a thousand pounds in cash.

'Seems a bit generous and it's more than we agreed,' Ed said suspiciously. He quickly calculated that it equated to around eighty thousand gross, which seemed a little over generous just for a bit of bouncing.

'Like I said, you've done OK. I want you to think about staying on longer than two weeks. I need someone like you, with plenty of attitude and balls. Think about it.'

'I don't see why. You've got bigger and scarier blokes than me down there, with attitude and balls. Any mug can give someone a slap and kick them out the door if they don't play by the rules.'

'This is just the tip of the iceberg. There are bigger and better things than this, and you can be part of it. Think about it.'

Ed thought about it for all of a second. There was no way he was staying longer than the two weeks. If he was honest, it was only TJ that had stopped him having walked out already. The offer of bigger and better things didn't exactly fill Ed with any comfort. Bigger and better was just a nice way of saying illegal and dangerous. Ed nodded slowly, not knowing how to answer Johnny's question, hoping he didn't take that as his agreement. Not that Johnny noticed as he had his head down, looking at a ledger of some description. When he did look up, he frowned and said 'Why the fuck are you still here?' Ed took that as his cue to leave.

The evening was hotting up with the Friday night after work crowd. Ed had been warned that it could get a little fractious as the evening wore on. Too many city workers drinking after work on an empty stomach, and getting a little boisterous. Ed was kept busy but nothing that wasn't resolved with a reminder of the rules and a hard stare. He had been working on his tactics, having decided that the being nice approach wasn't working. If you were nice the punters saw you as a soft touch, especially as Ed was of a much slighter build than his fellow bouncers. Being blunt and aggressive seemed to have much more success.

At just before midnight, a very drunk punter staggered towards Ed, weaving his way to the gents. He thought about ejecting him but felt a bit sorry for him so left him to stagger. When Ed asked him if he was

OK, the drunk turned his head and nodded. Unfortunately, the act of turning threw him completely off balance and he staggered into Ed, who had to hold him up. The drunk smiled and threw up over his T-shirt. Ed marched him off the premise, any sympathy having long since evaporated. Jim and Spike thought it was highly amusing. Ed gave them a glare and the middle finger, and went to the gents to clean up.

The T-shirt was ruined and he had no other option to get another one from Johnny. He had been given five but the other four were at home, since he hadn't been given a locker to keep them in. He made a mental note to keep a spare in the car from now on. He knocked and walked into Johnny's office, which was empty. He tried the filing cabinet, where he had seen Johnny get his T-shirt on his first day but it was locked, so he sat down on Johnny's desk and waited. He glanced up at the four CCTV monitors and noticed that one was showing Johnny with Blackthorn and Denton, in one of the private rooms. The three of them were seated around a table, talking animatedly. Johnny reached down and retrieved a silver briefcase from his side and placed it on the table. Blackthorn opened it, nodded and closed it again. Ed couldn't see what was in it but assumed it was payment for the drugs they brought in, earlier in the day. He was still sitting on the desk swinging his legs when Johnny, Blackthorn and Denton walked in and stopped dead.

'What the fuck are you doing in here?' Johnny barked, eyeing him suspiciously.

'Some drunk threw up on me and I need a new T-shirt,' Ed said, surprised by the venom with which Johnny had asked.

'They're in the cabinet,' he said, nodding to the corner of the room.

'I know but it's locked. I tried it.'

56

Johnny took his keys from his pocket, opened it and threw him a T-shirt. 'How long have you been in here?'

'Only a couple of minutes. Thanks, I'll get back to work now.' Ed gave them a quick smile and left.

'I don't trust him, Johnny,' Blackthorn told him, as soon as the door closed behind Ed.

'Well, you checked the bastard out and told me he was clean.'

'I know, but I still don't trust him. Anyone who can fight like that and has a clean record makes me suspicious. His fingerprints are on file but that was just for elimination purposes, for some incident in Cornwall a few months back. Other than that, he's squeaky clean. You need to do something about him - he makes me nervous.'

'Don't worry about that. I've got a little surprise lined up for him. By next week, he'll either be with me one hundred percent or he'll be history.'

'Well, you better fucking make sure he is, or I will.'

Closing time was rapidly approaching and Ed was shattered. There were only one or two die-hard punters remaining, watching Debbie and Sarah up on stage, pole-dancing. Pandora was still touting for more dances, without success - either the remaining punters were content to watch the stage show or were out of cash, or both. Ed took the opportunity to grab a drink of water in the canteen. Just as he was leaving, TJ walked in and pulled the door to behind her and gave him a weary smile.

'You've been busy tonight. I wish I could say the same. I'm tired through doing nothing,' Ed informed her.

'Never mind, only one more day to go and you've got a day off. Any plans?'

'Sleeping and getting reacquainted with my dog, who thinks I've deserted him. What about you?'

'Same as you, really, unless you want to invite me over so I can buy you that curry?'

'I thought we were going to do that Wednesday. I really do need to catch up on some sleep. I'm bloody shattered.'

'Well, you can still do that,' she continued, enthusiastically and undeterred. 'You still have to eat and next week is your last week, so you can catch up with all the sleep you need then. Don't be such a boring old fart.' She gave him a sad look. Whether it was genuine or she was a good actress he couldn't tell, but it seemed genuine. It was enough to make him crack. God, he was so weak.

'OK then, a curry it is,' he said, giving her a tired smile.

'Good. I'll bring a few things with me and we can go straight from work.'

'Whatever you say, TJ. I get the feeling that you're not going to take no for an answer, regardless of what I say.'

'You're learning,' she replied smugly. She grinned broadly and hurried off towards the dressing room, leaving Ed grinning wearily.

# Chapter 8

The drive home on Saturday night was an effort. Ed's eyes were tired and gritty, which wasn't helped by the bright sodium lights of the city, which were on even at two-thirty in the morning. He was glad when he got on the motorway and left the bright lights behind him. It helped his eyes but did nothing to alleviate the tiredness he felt, which was absolute, despite having the window open and sucking deeply on the cold night air. TJ was beside him in the passenger seat, doing a fine impression of a nodding dog, her eyes rolling back in their sockets as sleep slowly overcame her. Ed looked away as just looking at her was making him even more tired. TJ had insisted that they leave separately as relationships of any sort between employees were frowned upon, as they could get in the way of business. TJ had left first and Ed picked her up on the corner as he exited the yard, at the rear of the club. Ed thought it a little strange as he didn't consider their friendship as a relationship and he only had a week left to work, but TJ seemed insistent, so he played along to keep her happy.

It had been a strange day. Pandora saying hello to him, and giving him what seemed to be a genuinely warm smile first thing in the morning, threw him off balance immediately. He barely managed to stutter hello back, much to her amusement. She didn't even give him the middle finger, which seemed to be an ongoing joke between them - or at least, he hoped it was a joke. It appeared that she was no longer bearing a grudge from their first meeting on Saturday night. Looking back, Ed decided he'd acted childishly and made a decision that he would try to be more tolerant. He might even buy her some chocolates as an apology but she would probably think he was soft and ridicule him, so perhaps he wouldn't.

Johnny summoned him to the office shortly after, and Ed wondered if Pandora knew what it was about and was just taking the piss. Johnny had asked him to keep an eye on Barry, who when he wasn't playing at being a chauffeur, worked behind the bar. Johnny thought he had been skimming, as the takings for the last week had been down. The way he squinted at Ed unnerved him. Did he think he had something to do with it? Takings down in the last week and Ed had been there a week. He didn't like it and didn't like the idea of spying on Barry, any more than the thought that he might also be under suspicion. Working at Johnny's was beginning to worry him but there was nothing specific he could put his finger on. There were the Asians who he had obviously made enemies of. Blackthorn and Denton were both crooked as they come, and he hadn't liked the way they looked at him while he was in Johnny's office looking for a T-shirt. He would make sure he kept out of their way. Johnny giving him double the wages they had agreed on puzzled him. Why would he do that, without an ulterior motive? His comments about bigger and better things seemed to carry sinister undertones. He also seemed far too sure that Ed would be staying on longer than the two weeks agreed. Ed didn't like it. Maybe he was just tired and his imagination was going into overdrive, but he couldn't help but think that it was going to culminate in disaster.

Ed pulled up onto the drive and braked hard, jolting TJ awake, thinking it would be funny. She stretched languidly and smiled at him, unaware of Ed's childish prank. Why was it, he thought, a woman could stretch and look sexy and alluring but a man just looked like a slob? Another of life's little mysteries he would never understand. He sprung the boot and retrieved TJ's overnight bag, which weighed more than one of the suitcases he would take on a week's holiday, and carried it inside.

'Tea, coffee, something stronger, or bed?' Ed asked.

TJ gave him what he could only describe as a leer. 'Bed,' she replied.

Ed carried her bag upstairs and deposited it in the guest room, hoping that she would take that as a hint. The idea of sleeping with TJ - or, more to the point, making love to TJ - appealed to him immensely, but Laura was always at the back of his mind. Having a conscience was a royal pain in the arse.

'This is your room. Through that door there is the en-suite,' Ed said indicating to the door on the left. 'Right, anything you need?'

'You,' she said walking up to him and embracing him. 'And a glass of water, please.'

'Coming up,' Ed said, prising TJ off him, smiling nervously.

When he returned with the water he couldn't see TJ, so set the water down on the bedside table, assuming she was in the bathroom, and headed across the landing to his own room. He switched on the bedside lamp and was greeted by TJ smiling up from under the duvet. 'Oh shit,' he said to himself, wondering how he was going to get out of this one. He was dreading something like this happening and was already feeling like he had cheated on Laura, and nothing had happened. Although, he could probably be arrested for some of the thoughts he'd had about what he would like to do with her. TJ wasn't slow to pick up on his obvious discomfort.

'Don't worry, I just want a bit of company and besides, I'm too exhausted for anything else.'

'I left your water in the guest room,' Ed said, immediately feeling stupid for saying it. TJ smiled and got out of bed and walked across the room naked to fetch it. 'Jesus Christ, TJ!'

'You've seen it all before, don't be such a prude!'

'I bloody well haven't seen it all before. Some of it, but not all of it.'

'Oh well, you have now,' she said, relishing his embarrassment. Ed was still standing there, fully clothed, when she returned.

'It won't be worth going to bed if you don't get in soon. Do you want me to help you get your clothes off?' she asked.

'No, I can manage,' he replied, flustered. He pulled off his T-shirt and stepped out of his trousers, with TJ staring at him, grinning broadly.

'That's a nice scar,' she said, looking at his thigh.

'Yeah, it's a knife wound and a long story, for another day,' he replied as he turned off the light.

'Do you always sleep in your pants?'

'Not usually, but then I usually don't have company.'

'Ed, take them off. I'm not going to seduce you. I've already told you, I'm far too tired.' Ed reluctantly pulled his pants off and dropped them on the floor. TJ slithered across the bed, rested her head on his chest, draped and arm around his waist and pushed her leg between his.

'You can give me a goodnight kiss, you know, it wouldn't kill you.'

'Goodnight,' he said kissing her on the top of her head.

TJ tutted and sighed. 'Is that it?' she asked. 'I think you can do better than that,' she replied and pulled Ed's head down and kissed him on the lips, forcing her tongue through his pursed lips. Ed felt himself becoming aroused and pulled away, his heart pounding.

Once again, his conscience telling him it was all wrong; strongly contradicting what his groin was telling him.

'You're boring,' she informed him sulkily 'I suppose that's goodnight, then.'

'Goodnight, TJ,' Ed replied.

# Chapter 9

By seven-thirty on Sunday morning, Ed was showered and drinking coffee, watching the news on TV. He had woken early, and further sleep had eluded him. TJ had been sleeping peacefully beside him so he had tip-toed out and left her there. After a second cup of coffee, he heard the kids next door shouting excitedly. That was his cue to go next door to collect Fat Boy. After some small talk with a hungover Mark, who looked none too pleased about the noise the kids were making, Ed made an excuse to leave. Ed took Fat Boy for a long walk down the river, stopping at the mini-market on the way back to pick up something for breakfast. He had no idea what TJ would want so picked up everything he needed for a hearty fry-up, plus some cornflakes and bread.

When he arrived back TJ was curled up in an armchair, nursing a coffee, watching the news. She stood up when he walked in and made a fuss of Fat Boy, who thrust his nose under the baggy T-shirt she was wearing and gave her crotch and enthusiastic sniff, wagging his tail even more enthusiastically.

'You're a randy little bugger aren't you?' she said, as she extracted Fat Boy's face out of her crotch. 'You've got a lot more sense of adventure than your lord and master has, that's for sure.'

Ed shook his head in despair, and studied her. Her hair was a complete mess and hadn't yet been brushed after a night's sleep. She had no make-up on, her eyes were still half-closed, giving her a tired appearance, and yet she still looked beautiful. He pushed those thoughts to the back of his mind.

'What can I get you for breakfast? I've got just about everything for a fry-up, or you can just have toast or cereal?'

'I'll have a fry-up, and I'll cook it.'

'You've obviously heard about my infamous fry-ups then? I'm certainly not going to turn you down.'

'You did last night.' Ed found something interesting on the ceiling to look at. 'What's the problem, Ed? Is it because of what I do for a living? Because I'd just like you to know, it doesn't make me a whore. I lap-dance and pole-dance, that's it. I've never slept with a punter or anyone connected to Johnny's or any of the other clubs I've worked at. OK.'

'TJ, it's got nothing to do with what you do for a living.'

'Oh, great. So you just don't find me attractive?'

'It's not that either. You're bloody gorgeous.'

'Really?' she said, pleased with the answer. 'So, what's the problem?'

'I'm the problem - or, more to the point, Laura's the problem,' he said, almost apologetically. TJ regarded him and smiled.

'OK, fair enough. But it's nothing to do with my work?'

'Absolutely not.'

'And you think I'm attractive?'

'Absolutely.'

'Good. And it's not because I'm too fat or too skinny?'

'Of course not, you've got a fantastic figure.'

'Thanks. Do you fancy me?'

'I think that's obvious. It's just my conscience, nothing personal.'

'Good. Why didn't you say all that last night?'

'I thought it might sound a bit lame.'

'It does, but it's quite sweet.'

With that she picked up the bag of shopping, making sure she gave him a flash of her backside, as her T-shirt rode up and walked, slowly and sensually to the kitchen. Ed breathed a sigh of relief or was it regret? He didn't quite know.

The cooked breakfast, when it arrived, looked fantastic and tasted better. Why was it, Ed wondered, that everyone he knew could prepare and present a cooked breakfast that looked and tasted perfect? The best he could ever manage was a nasty plateful of over and under-cooked blandness that tasted as disappointing as it looked. TJ seemed pleased that he tucked into it with relish and mopped the plate beyond clean, with a slice of bread and butter.

'They say the way to a man's heart is through his stomach,' Ed stated, rubbing his belly exaggeratedly.

'And there was silly old me thinking the way to a man's heart was to give him a blow job,' she replied happily, causing Ed to choke on his coffee.

'I'll just put this stuff in the dishwasher,' he replied. Not that he wanted to, but he wanted to avoid another conversation about sleeping with TJ.

'I'm going for a shower,' she called through from the dining room. That was more than fine with Ed, it got him off the hook. Why did he get himself in these situations? he asked himself, not for the first time in his life. On the positive side at least nobody had been hurt, well not yet anyway.

TJ entered the living room, freshly showered with perfect hair, perfect make-up, and looking great.

'Do you ever look anything but immaculate?' Ed stated more than asked as he put the newspaper down.

TJ considered the question and replied 'No,' making Ed laugh. 'Do you ever say anything but the right thing?'

'Oh yes. Believe me, on more times than I care to mention. I thought Johnny was going to lynch me when

I commented on his nose that Saturday. Sometimes I just can't help myself.'

'I think you took him so much by surprise, he didn't know what to say. Anyway, I didn't mean like that. I meant with me. Thank you.' Ed shrugged. 'Anyway,' she said as she moved towards him and sat down on his lap, 'you've got a very nice house but it's not what I expected. I thought you'd live in a mansion or a country estate, not on a housing estate.'

'Like I said, I'm more curry and lager than caviar and champagne. This is big enough for me. It's in an OK part of town. I've got nice neighbours and the rest of my life to retire to the country. Right now, this is fine.'

'But you're loaded. If I had your money, I'd have a big house in the country.'

'Would you? I thought that, once. You know, when you dream of winning the lottery but when I did have money, I realised I was happy - well, happy-ish - where I was. So what would you do, if you had a million pounds to spend?'

'I'd give up work, maybe buy a big house with lots of land or go to Spain or somewhere warm. I don't know, but I wouldn't work.'

'You'd get bored. I did, and that's why I started getting into property renovation. Remember, you've still got another 40 years or so to live yet. Doing nothing gets tedious when all your friends are at work.'

'Right now, you're about my only friend,' she said, giving him a sad look.

'That's really sad. I'm not sure what's sadder. That you have no friends or I'm your only one.'

'You've seen the hours I work, when do I get a chance to make friends? All my old friends have moved on and, as you know, I don't exactly get on with the girls at work.'

'So, why do you work there, if you don't get on with everyone or anyone it seems? There are other clubs that aren't complete dives, surely?'

She studied him for what seemed a long time, before finally answering. 'Can you keep a secret?' she said, almost childlike.

'Of course I can. My memory is absolutely crap. A few beers tonight and I'd have forgotten by morning.'

'Johnny's my father,' she said flatly. Ed stared back, completely wrong-footed.

'You're serious, aren't you?' TJ nodded. 'Fucking hell! So how come you don't get the royal treatment? I don't understand.' Ed was completely wrong-footed and utterly lost for words.

'He doesn't know who I am. When I told you my mother died when I was younger and I went to live with my grandmother - well, she didn't die. Johnny killed her.' By now, Ed's jaw was swinging like a lantern in a hurricane.

'Shit. This is a lot to take in, TJ. OK. So you were ten, right?' TJ nodded 'So, how do you know he killed her and how do you know that he's your father? I'm finding it hard taking all this in.'

'My mother, Helen Barnes, was Johnny's girlfriend and he got her pregnant with me. Things were OK for a while. My mother knew what he was like and turned a blind eye to his frequent affairs and the fact he was a criminal, even in those days. My mother gradually turned to drink and became an embarrassment to Johnny. One night after a blazing row, my mother, drunk again, threatened to shop him to the police. A few days later, she was found in an alley behind the Elephant and Castle, with her throat slit, and she had been raped. Johnny already had the police in his pocket by this time and the investigation was steered in the right direction, away from him, and it was put down to

68

a mugging gone wrong.' Tears were flowing down her cheeks as she stared blankly at Ed. Ed pulled her to his chest and stroked her hair in an attempt to comfort her.

'So, how do you know all this? Are you OK talking about this, by the way? I don't want to upset you any more.'

TJ wiped her eyes and nodded. 'Sorry about that. This is the first time I've ever told anyone about this. I've been bottling it up for years. I thought I would be OK talking about it.' She paused and took a deep breath before continuing. 'My grandmother told me all this before she died. Someone who used to work for Johnny told her. So, to answer your question, I'm working there so I can get revenge on my father.'

'Jesus. You gave up your job to become a lap-dancer, to work your way into his club so you could get revenge?'

'Yes,' she said, as if it was the most natural thing in the world to do.

'Respect! Surely you have enough by now? Some of the stuff you told me was pretty good, about the drugs and Blackthorn and Denton. Why not take that to the police and get out of there?'

'I've no proof. Until I get proof, it's just a rumour. Who's going to believe me, just one step up the evolutionary ladder from a whore? I've even thought about killing him.'

'Don't go there. That makes you as bad as him. Trust me on that. Look, I've only got a week to go but if there is any way I can help you, I will. Whether it's getting information or proof for you, I will. I might have to draw the line at killing him, unless he puts me in a position where there is no other option.'

'This is something I have to do. I need to get revenge, not you,' she said.

Ed blew out his cheeks. It was a lot to take in. 'Have you got anything on him yet?

TJ shook her head. 'I've been there a year and so far all I've got is rumours. It's so frustrating but I'll get something, eventually.'

Ed had trouble taking it all in. He felt so sorry for her, wasting her whole life to get revenge. There was a possibility that what her grandmother told her might just be the confused ramblings of an old woman. Unfortunately for Ed, he was a sucker for a sob story and decided he would do what he could to help, even if it meant staying on at Johnny's a little longer than planned. Get inside his inner circle and break it open.

'Fancy some fresh air, TJ?' She nodded and wiped her eyes. Ed looked up at her and pulled her toward him and kissed her on the lips. She sniffed and wiped her eyes again, and gave him a sad smile.

'I'll just go and sort myself out first. A girl needs to look her best.'

TJ went up stairs and Ed flopped back in the armchair and silently cursed himself. Once again, he was embarking on another crusade to help a damsel in distress, and he couldn't help himself. Same old Ed.

# Chapter 10

The sun was shining feebly through the grey sky, making little impact on the cold afternoon air that blew down the river. When the breeze abated and the sun broke through the clouds, albeit fleetingly, it was actually quite pleasant, ideal walking weather, as long as you kept moving. They walked in silence, both absorbed in their own private thoughts. Ed's mind was racing, thinking about Johnny, his sordid club, and how he could help TJ. Quite why he felt compelled to help, he didn't know. Well, he did. He was a bloody big softy and a sucker for a damsel in distress with a sob story to tell; always had been, and no doubt always would be.

He pondered over how he could help TJ so that she could get on with the rest of her life. Proving that Johnny really had murdered her mother was going to be impossible. The only evidence was hearsay and it was so long ago that, unless there was something concrete, it wouldn't be looked at. Even if there was proof, he was sure that Blackthorn and Denton would somehow make sure it didn't go anywhere. The only possible outcome from that would be a whole lot of grief from those two, and neither of them needed that. The only way for revenge would be to get some solid proof on his current nefarious activities. Either that, or kill the bastard.

Was he capable of killing someone? Probably not, he thought. Perhaps he could get someone else to do it - money wasn't an issue. It was just a matter of finding someone to do it. Would he be able to live with himself, knowing that he was a murderer by proxy? Again, probably not, but it was a nice thought.

The path led them to a bridge over the river, where TJ stopped and leaned on the railing to take in the view down the river. The water was still and peaceful and the clouds reflected on its glassy surface. Ed looked back down the bank they had just walked along to make sure Fat Boy was still with them. He was but about twenty yards behind them, concentrating on a small bush that obviously smelt appealing to him. Fat Boy urinated copiously over it and looked up to find his master. On seeing him on the bridge, he cocked his head to one side, before setting off at a trot to catch up.

Ed leaned back against the railing beside TJ and stared down the river in the opposite direction to watch Fat Boy make his way slowly towards them. TJ stood in front of Ed and moved towards him, putting her arms around his waist and leaning her head against his chest. Ed put his arms around her and hugged her, pulling her tightly against him. She looked up at him and smiled, and before he knew what was happening, they were kissing.

'There, that wasn't so difficult, was it?' she said, flashing him another smile.

Ed smiled back. 'Come on, let's get back before it starts getting dark. I want to be in that restaurant the minute it opens, I'm starving.'

'I don't think I've ever had an Indian on Sunday.'

'Personally I could eat it every day, but I don't think I'd have too many friends left.'

'Far too much information, Ed.'

'Probably. Look, I've been thinking about how I can help you. I really don't fancy taking on Johnny and his associates head on. So, maybe we should just give someone high up in the Met Police an anonymous tip and see if we can get him investigated. What do you think?'

After giving it some thought, she replied. 'To be honest, I want to make it more personal than that. An anonymous tip-off wouldn't give me a great deal of satisfaction. There is also the small matter of Blackthorn and Denton. Any investigation would probably get buried by those two crooks.'

'Possibly, but not if we put them in the frame as well. Surely, it would spark an internal enquiry?' TJ frowned. 'Look, I've got a friend who's a DCI in Cornwall. Bob's actually Laura's mother's partner now, which is a bit scary. One day he might be my father-in-law. Now, that would be weird, I've known him years. Anyway, some time ago he used to be in the Met, so might be able to give us a bit of advice. I bet he even knows Johnny. What about if I give him a call, when we get back?'

TJ shrugged again and they continued to walk in silence. Ed was optimistic that Bob would give them a good steer on whether they were wasting their time by speaking to a senior officer. He could even have some dirt on Johnny. By the time they arrived back, Ed was quite excited and felt that the ball had started rolling.

In the study, Ed put the phone onto speaker and dialled, hoping that Bob would answer.

'Brown,' was Bob's abrupt introduction on answering.

'Hi Bob, it's Ed. Is now a good time to talk?'

'Why don't I like that sound of this?' he replied suspiciously.

'Is it because you're a cynical old bugger or maybe you just know me too well? Look, I've got you on speakerphone as I've got my friend TJ with me and we need to pick your brains.'

'Hi,' TJ said.

'I might have bloody known it would involve a woman. Please, don't tell me, you're off on a bloody mission!'

Ed chuckled. 'Sort of. Look, here's the question. Hypothetically speaking, suppose I put in an anonymous tip off to your Superintendent or whoever is in charge, telling him that two of his officers were on the take and in league with a local villain. Would he take it seriously?' He could almost hear Bob thinking and could certainly hear him drumming his fingers on his desk.

'It would depend on whether the person you gave the information to had any balls. Therefore, it's likely it wouldn't go anywhere - if it was my boss anyway. Tell me, hypothetically speaking, do you have any proof?' he replied sarcastically.

'Absolutely bugger all! Does it make a difference?'

'Of course it bloody well does, you cretin!' he barked. 'Anyway, what the hell are you up to?'

'I've been doing a bit of bouncing in a club in Soho. Only for a couple of weeks, to relieve the boredom,' Ed told him sheepishly.

'Jesus Christ, Ed. For a reasonably intelligent bloke, you can be a right fuckwit at times.' Bob gave a huge sigh. Ed could almost see him shaking his head and grimacing. 'Anyway, you've got no proof, you say?' he added.

'Well, I've seen them doing a drug deal and it's pretty much common knowledge at the club but no physical proof. I don't suppose anyone at the club is likely to put their hand up and volunteer information, do you?'

'Well, without any proof you're a bit buggered, aren't you? It's just a bloody rumour. Who are we talking about here, anyway?'

'Bloke called Johnny Gold and the two coppers are DI Blackthorn and DS Denton, both with the Met. That's why I'm asking you.'

'I know Johnny. He's a fucking weasel, runs a string of strip clubs in Soho, or he used to. What the bloody hell are you doing in his company?'

'Bit of a long story, but like I said, I'm doing a bit of bouncing for him. TJ here works for him as well.'

'Well if you want my advice, get as far away from him as possible and don't go getting involved, just because of some stripper.'

'Bob, she's not a stripper,' Ed replied sharply. 'She lap-dances and pole dances and she's working there to get information on Johnny, because he killed her mother, so don't be so bloody judgemental.'

'Touchy bastard, you are. I don't suppose you have any proof of that either, do you?' He took the silence as a no, and continued. 'I remember Blackthorn, too. When I was there he was a DS in the drug squad so what you're saying ties in, but without proof, you're stuffed. He's a right bastard and bloody ruthless. Another one you want to stay well clear of. I mean it, Ed. These people are seriously bad news. I'll do some digging and see what I can find out. Maybe I'll even rattle a few cages and see what happens. Don't you go doing anything stupid. I know what you're like. If they find out it came from you, you'll end up propping up a flyover for the rest of your life.'

'Thanks for the advice, Bob, and don't worry. I don't intend to do anything stupid. Well, not if I can help it.'

'Make sure you don't. I don't want to be the one that has to explain to Laura and her mother - who, by the way, still thinks the sun shines out your arse - that you've got yourself a new pair of concrete boots, and you'll be round just as soon as we've fished you from the bottom of the Thames. OK?'

'I get the message. How's things with Raechael, do I need to buy a new suit yet?'

'Always the bloody comedian. She's fine and we're both doing our best to knock some sense into that pig-headed daughter of hers.'

'Do you know when the operation is?' Ed asked, knowing what the answer would be but asking anyway.

'Nope. Raechael knows but she's been sworn to secrecy, and she's as bloody stubborn as her daughter and won't tell me, because she knows I'll tell you.'

'Some copper you are, if you can't even get a simple bit of information out of your girlfriend. How the hell do you manage getting villains to cough up?'

'Funny bastard,' was his parting comment before hanging up.

Ed shrugged. 'He can be a bit of a prickly bastard at times but he'll do some digging. He's a good bloke. He can never resist a bit of intrigue.' He gave TJ a reassuring smile but it wasn't reciprocated; she clearly thought the call to Bob was a waste of time.

# Chapter 11

Lager and curry, the greatest partnership since stone-age man emerged from his cave and put copper and tin together to make bronze. If Ed had it his way, the man responsible for importing Cobra lager to the UK would be canonised. Having demolished the poppadoms and followed that with a lamb tikka, Ed was now tucking into his chicken jalfrezi with relish. TJ was a little more reserved and skipped the starter, and was now picking unenthusiastically at a chicken tikka bhuna.

The small restaurant was only half full, Sunday night not being a popular night for a curry. When Ed had commuted to London every day, he had abstained from curry if he was working the next day. He didn't want to risk getting caught short on the train journey in the morning. There weren't too many experiences in life worse than a train toilet in Ed's opinion, with the exception perhaps of having a gun shoved in your face, but even that was a close call. Not being busy suited Ed; it meant it was quiet with no need to shout over the conversations from other tables, and was a much more relaxing evening. TJ seemed pre-occupied and had a far away look in her eyes. It troubled Ed, as she had been so vibrant and talkative for the entire day, but was now quiet and reserved. She noticed him staring at her and gave him a weak smile.

'Tell me about the scar. You said it was a long story,' she asked, breaking the silence. Ed nodded and thought about where to start.

'I have a caravan in Cornwall and six months ago I got into a fight in the clubhouse on the site. One of the guys was a right nasty bugger and pulled a knife and threatened to stab me and the dog. To be honest, I forgot all about it.' TJ gave him a look that said how could you forget something like that? Ed gave her a shrug and continued. 'I went out for the day and left Fat Boy with Laura. While she was out taking him for a walk, he crept up on her, stabbed Fat Boy, and tipped Laura out of her wheelchair.'

'No way. The evil sod,' TJ interjected.

'Yep and a few days later he caught up with me, and we had a showdown on the beach. I was battering three shades of shit out of him, until he threw sand in my eyes and whacked me round the head with a lump of wood.'

'Is that how you got the scar over your eye?'

'Yep,' Ed replied, subconsciously rubbing at the scar. 'Anyway, he then pulled a knife and was about to fillet me. I got lucky and managed to deflect his lunge and ended up with it in my leg, but it stopped my internal organs becoming external organs.'

'I bet that hurt,' she said, pulling a face.

'It did sting a bit. I lost a lot of blood and spent a couple of days in hospital.'

'Christ. Did the police get him?'

'They didn't need to. I nearly killed the bastard. Bob was there watching anyway, so he wouldn't have gone far.'

'He was watching?'

Ed nodded. 'He was wanted for murder as well. He'd murdered a pensioner in an aggravated robbery. He also stole his old service revolver and he evaded the police at the hospital and came looking for me. A few nights later in the clubhouse, he jumped up on the stage and, to cut a long story short, shot Jacqui, a good friend of mine. The gun was old, bent and filthy and he missed me from a few yards and killed one of my oldest friends.' The memory still hurt Ed and he felt his eyes stinging.

'Shit, I'm sorry Ed. I didn't know I'd be dragging up such painful memories. I hope he's doing a long stretch now.'

'He's dead. There were problems with the electrics in the clubhouse and Bob fused the lights. He ran across the stage and shot the bastard and made it look like suicide.' TJ gave him a look of sheer disbelief. 'Bob's not a malicious bastard. He did it because if he didn't do it, he knew I would have, so he did it to save me. Because of what happened between us, no jury in the world would have given me the benefit of the doubt and I'd have been the one in prison. He's a good bloke, don't judge him on that.'

'Is that what he meant by being on another mission?' Ed nodded. 'What about his comments about involving another woman?' she asked.

'Remember that Saturday, when Matt and I came to Johnny's?' TJ nodded 'Matt said that I put women on a pedestal - well, I do, and I've had more than a few punch-ups because of it. It's just my nature. It's why I gave that bloke a slap at Johnny's. It's why I ended up being stabbed on the beach. It started because one of the guys in the clubhouse grabbed Laura's breast. You'd think I'd learn, eh? I just hope what happened on Saturday doesn't end the same way. Not sure I could cope with that.'

'I can't work out, if you're completely fearless or just completely stupid,' TJ replied, her face etched with concern.

Ed shrugged, got the waiter's attention, and asked for the bill, which TJ insisted on paying.

The taxi journey home was completed in silence. Ed was still brooding over the memories of that night in Cornwall, for which he still held himself responsible. If he had tried harder to avoid the initial altercation in the clubhouse, which was the catalyst for the chain of events that culminated in the death of Jacqui, she might well still be alive today. No matter how many times friends tried to reassure him it wasn't his fault, deep down Ed knew that it was. For the last six months, the memory had been pushed into a deep dark corner of his mind and filed with all his other disasters, personal tragedies and general fuck-ups; and dragging it out of its hiding place hurt.

When they arrived back, Ed headed to the kitchen, and after letting Fat Boy into the garden grabbed a couple of beers from the fridge. He handed one to TJ and let out a long sigh. TJ walked towards him, put her arms around him and hugged him.

'Sorry to have dragged up your past. I didn't think it was going to be a pleasant story, but I didn't realise it was going to be so tragic. Were you and Jacqui close?'

Ed nodded. 'I'd known her since I was twelve years old. It was one of the worst days of my life. The only good thing to come out of that holiday was meeting Laura, but that's all gone to rat shit, too. In case you haven't realised, I'm a bit of a walking disaster.' TJ didn't respond but hugged him harder

They stood there in the kitchen, neither saying that much, and finished their drinks. Ed said he was taking Fat Boy for a quick walk and left TJ standing in the kitchen. When he returned, TJ was nowhere to be seen. Ed assumed she had gone to bed and trudged up the stairs himself. His bedside light was on in his bedroom, when he entered, and TJ was lying there waiting for him.

'You're brave. Most people wouldn't want to be in the same house as me after a curry, let alone the same bed.'

'Oh, shut up and show me your scar,' she replied seductively. Ed gave a half hearted smile, stripped and got into bed.

'Ed, do you trust me?' TJ asked, which threw Ed completely. It wasn't a question he had expected.

'I suppose so. You've not given me any reason not to,' he replied, thinking it was a strange question.

'Good, then close your eyes.'

Ed eyed her suspiciously, and did as he was asked when she gave him an impatient look. She then slipped a blindfold over his eyes and tied it tightly. Ed was about to protest but she put a finger gently against his lips and said 'Trust me.' She tied two of Ed's silk ties to the headboard and told him to lift his hands up. Ed complied, not having a clue what was going on. She slipped his hands through the loops she had made earlier and pulled the slipknots, tight over his wrists and removed the blindfold. Ed looked at his hands and began to panic.

'TJ, what the hell are you playing at?'

She smiled back at him and straddled him. 'Well, I know you have a problem with your conscience, but I know you want me and I want you. This way, you're powerless to do anything to stop me, and you can have a clear conscience.'

'Jesus Christ, you're bloody devious,' he replied, still more than a little nervous. TJ giggled and leaned across to pick up a bottle of baby oil from the bedside unit. Next, she began drizzling the oil down her chest. Ed watched, fascinated, as the rivulets of oil snaked over her breasts and down her cleavage, pooling in her belly button, before spilling over and making their way between her legs, dripping onto his stomach, making him gasp. TJ then squirted oil over his own chest and over her thighs. She leaned forward and tenderly massaged the oil into his chest. Her touch was electric and Ed felt himself becoming aroused, easily overcoming his initial apprehension. TJ smiled at him and began to work the oil into her own body, kneading her breasts and pinching her nipples. Her hands travelled over her taut belly and slid down her thighs and finally between her legs, where they lingered, before moving back up her body.

Ed's heart was racing, each beat making his temple throb, as his excitement mounted. TJ began slowly sliding back and forth across his stomach, her hands still sliding across her breasts, her eyes never leaving Ed's. She leaned forward and brushed her lips against his. Ed lunged forward to kiss her but she moved her head back and smiled at him, teasing him. It was as erotic as it was frustrating and TJ, sensing this, pouted and gave him a look of mock pity. She stretched languidly and slid up his body, her breasts just inches from his face. Ed slowly pushed his head forward and sucked greedily at her nipple, ignoring the bitter taste of the baby oil. TJ slid down the entire length of his body and sat between his legs, staring up at him over the length of his body.

She ran her hands up his calves and across his thighs, sending waves of sensations through his body, making him shudder. Her hands continued up his legs and lingered on his hips, before journeying down to his groin and massaging his testicles, which tightened in anticipation as her head came forward and engulfed him. Just as Ed was about to reach his climax, she stopped and slid back up his body. Still smiling, she slid over his penis and gasped when he entered her. She began slowly rocking backwards and forwards, increasing her rhythm as her own climax approached. When it did, she collapsed across his torso and lay, exhausted, with her head on his chest.

She looked up at him and smiled and kissed him. Ed responded and kissed her passionately.

'You're not mad at me, then?' she asked mischievously.

'No, of course not, that was probably the most erotic experience in my entire life. Do me a favour though and get these things off my wrists.'

'Don't you want to do it again?'

'I do, but this time I'd like to be a bit more involved, if you know what I mean. Not being able to touch you has been driving me bloody mad.' TJ giggled and began to pull at the knots around his wrists, the baby oil making the task difficult. Ed urged her on and as soon as one hand was free he was caressing her lithe, oily body. When the second hand was freed he pushed her down on the bed and they made love a second time, this time on equal terms. Afterwards they lay utterly exhausted, still entwined together, and slept.

That morning they had made love again, this time without the aid of bondage and baby oil, which Ed thought was a combination that could well rival beer and curry.

'It doesn't change anything,' TJ said to him afterwards. Ed wasn't sure what that meant or what the response was, and gave her a confused look. TJ gave him a shake of the head and sighed exasperatedly, as if the statement was obvious. 'What I mean is, I don't love you or anything and I'm not trying to prise you away from Laura, OK.'

'Right,' Ed said, now he understood what she meant. 'Tell me, was that completely premeditated, or was it a spur of the moment thing?'

TJ gave him a sly look. 'A bit of both, really. The idea just came to me, that if you were tied up, you'd have a clear conscience when you see Laura next.'

'What about the baby oil?'

'I use it in the shower. I didn't buy it especially, if that's what you think.'

'No, but it was a nice touch. Like I said last night, it was the most erotic experience of my life,' he said, smiling broadly. TJ seemed pleased

'Really? You need to be a bit more adventurous, you're really missing out. I'm glad you enjoyed it, though. I'm not normally that forward.'

'So, what made last night the exception?' Ed asked, intrigued.

'I like you and you're the first bloke I've spent any time with for a long time. I guess I was gagging for it, as you'd say to your mates.' Ed laughed and got a punch on the arm for his troubles.

'It was nice. You're nice - and thank you.'

'Can I ask you something? You don't have to answer if you don't want to but if you do, just answer honestly. OK?'

'Ask away.'

'If things were different and you weren't with Laura, do you think you and I could have a relationship?'

'Definitely,' Ed replied without hesitation. 'I don't care what you do for a living, although with the hours you work, it wouldn't be much of a relationship. You're beautiful, you've got a great figure and you're fun to be with, and you've got lots of baby oil. What more could a man want? The only down side is you're a bit old for me, I've never been a toy-boy before.' That earned him another punch on the arm.

'Was that an honest answer?' she said, scrutinising him.

'Of course, it was. You're far too old for me,' he said, grinning and grabbing her hands to ensure he wasn't punched again. 'Joking aside, yes it was an honest answer.' TJ nodded and smiled broadly.

'Thanks. Right I'm off for a shower,' she replied and jumped out of bed and headed to the bathroom. Ed called after her and threw the bottle of baby oil at her, which she caught, gave him one of her seductive smiles, and beckoned him with her finger. Ed didn't need to be asked twice.

# Chapter 12

The next two days at Johnny's were no different from any other day, and Ed was once again wondering why Johnny seemed insistent that he was a necessary requirement. Ed only saw himself as surplus to requirements. The only difference that Ed had noticed from last week was that TJ was putting in a lot more effort up on the stage, while she was pole-dancing. Whenever she thought that none of the other bouncers were watching her and their eyes met, she gave him one of her seductive smiles. Ed found it difficult to do his job as he was too busy watching TJ. Not that it was a particular problem, as the clientele was for the most part well behaved.

He had arranged to go to TJ's flat after work on Wednesday with the promise of home cooking, if she could stop herself from ripping his clothes off, as soon as he walked through the door. Unfortunately, Johnny had other ideas. Ed was summoned to his office mid-afternoon and was asked to work a full day, due to staffing problems. Ed couldn't work out exactly what staffing problems Johnny was referring to but saying no didn't seem to be an option, and Johnny made that perfectly clear.

He phoned TJ when he was alone in the canteen and told her he would be unable to make it round, due to having to put in a full shift. She too queried the need for him to work and seemed genuinely disappointed, although she also added that no food had been ruined, as she had decided to seduce him as soon as he walked through the door, and phone for a pizza only if his energy levels started to flag. Ed laughed, apologised, and promised to make it up to her another time. Quite when that would be, he didn't know, but it seemed the right thing to say.

Ed was a bag of mixed emotions. Since TJ had opened up to him and told him of her reasons for working at Johnny's, he had been permanently on edge. Johnny asking him to work a full shift concerned him. When Johnny had asked him, there was something in his demeanour that Ed didn't like. When Ed had stared back at him, scrutinising his face for signs of a lie, he was sure Johnny appeared nervous, albeit fleetingly, before he dismissed him.

Then there was TJ. Since the weekend he had been struggling with his guilty conscience for cheating on Laura. He could excuse himself for the first time, just about, as he was tied to the bed and he was, after all, only human. The subsequent times however, there were no mitigating circumstances that he could use to justify his actions. It was pure lust. The ease with which he had pushed all thoughts of Laura to the back of his mind for the entire weekend did nothing to ease this guilt. Neither did the fact that his feelings for TJ were growing to something beyond friendship. She had been right in her assumption on Sunday night; he did want her. The question he had to ask himself was did he want her more than Laura?

Later that afternoon, his Asian friends returned and took up position in front of the stage, where they had sat the last time they had been in. Mo looked over at him, patted his jacket pocket, letting him know he was carrying a gun. Whether he was or not was something Ed didn't want to find out. Once again, Mo made a gun of his hand, pointed it at Ed and pretended to fire it. Just for maximum effect, he made a point of lifting his fingers and pretending to blow the smoke from the barrel. It was all very melodramatic and childish but it made Ed shudder all the same. Perhaps in his last three days of working, he would have the opportunity to wipe that smug smile off his face.

It was just before closing time with only two punters remaining, when Ed was once again summoned to Johnny's office by Spike. He knew better than to ask what for, knowing the curt answer he would receive in return, and just made his way to the office. He knocked and walked in. Johnny was sitting behind his desk, unsmiling as usual. Ed finally worked out who he reminded him of - Ray Winston - only with a much bigger nose. The thought made him smile to himself. Also in the office were Barry and Jim. Ed stood in front of the desk and raised his eyebrows in a You wanted to see me? look.

'Ed,' Johnny began. 'We had a little chat last week, if you remember? I mentioned that the bar takings were down, right?'

He wasn't sure if it was a question to be answered or a rhetorical question. Either way, he didn't like the implication. 'I hope you don't think that's got anything to do with me? I'm not a thief and, to be frank, I don't need the money,' he said defiantly. Johnny gave a chuckle that was more menacing than friendly.

'I think you might be a lot of things, Ed, but I don't have you down as a thief, so don't worry on that score.' Ed was relieved.

'So, what's all this about, then?' He was confused now.

'Barry. He's been taking me for a fucking mug!' he said with venom, looking at Barry. Barry started to protest but Jim slammed his fist into his stomach, making him double over and gasp for breath. 'I don't like being taken for a mug. I pay well and I expect a bit of loyalty for that. Barry needs to be taught a lesson in respect.'

88

'So, what's that got to do with me?' Ed asked, becoming concerned with the way the conversation was going.

'I want you to teach him a fucking lesson,' he said, glaring at him.

'Sorry Johnny, that's not what I do. You pay me to make sure the punters stick to the rules and if they don't, I throw them out and if necessary give them a bit of a slap. I'm not roughing Barry up just because you caught him with his fingers in the till. Sack him or report him to the police, but don't bring me into this. No way. I'm not up for that.'

Johnny put his hands on his desk and leaned forward. 'You'll do whatever I fucking tell you to do!' he snarled.

Ed waved his hand dismissively. 'Will I bollocks - I'm out of here.'

He turned to leave and Jim pulled a gun on him, stopping him in his tracks. His mind was racing, his pulse was going into overdrive, and he felt physically sick. He knew working here was probably not the best decision he had ever made, but he wasn't expecting this. 'What do you want, Johnny?' he finally asked.

'I want you to shoot Barry,' he said, as if it was the most natural thing in the world. 'And if you don't, I'll get Jim to shoot you.'

'Why me? Why not get Jim to do it - or anyone else, come to that?'

Johnny gave another of his sinister chuckles. 'I told you, before. I need people like you on the team. You could be useful to me. You've also seen too much working here. I know you were watching me and Blackthorn on the CCTV last week. How do I know you're not going to go to the police with that? If you shoot Barry, you'll need my protection and I'll know you'll be with me, not against me. If you don't, I'll just get Jim to shoot you both. It's your choice, Ed. Are you with me or not?'

Ed wanted to ask if he could get back to him tomorrow on this but that wasn't an option. Right now, he didn't see that he had many options open to him.

'I'll do it, on account of not having a great deal of choice,' he replied angrily.

'Good lad, you know it makes sense. Welcome to the team.'

Barry began to protest but was abruptly stopped by Jim smashing his fist into his stomach once more. Barry doubled over and struggled to catch his breath. Ed was tempted to do exactly the same to Jim, but the look Jim gave him and the fact he was still pointing the gun at him made Ed think twice.

They exited via the back door. Jim was driving one car, with Ed a reluctant passenger, and Spike took Barry separately in a second car, although Barry had been knocked unconscious by Jim with the butt of his gun, and dumped unceremoniously into the boot. Jim kept his gun wedged firmly between his legs, in case Ed gave him any trouble - not that he would. Ed was desperately thinking of a way out of this. Killing Barry was not an option. He had never warmed to the bloke, but there was absolutely no way he could kill him. At some point he would be given a gun - he knew that much. Would he be able to turn that on Jim or Spike and shoot them? He didn't think so. That was no easier than killing Barry. Granted, he could justify it to himself more than killing Barry, but it would still make him a murderer and that was something he hoped he would never become; not even to save his own arse. He was still mulling over his choices when they pulled up onto a deserted piece of wasteland. Where they were, Ed didn't know. The journey could have been a couple of miles or a hundred miles. He had spent the entire journey going over all the options and lost all sense of time and distance. All he knew was that they had arrived at their destination and it was make your mind up time. Ed was beside himself with worry. What happened in the next short period of time would be a life-changing event. He tried to think logically, but struggled. All that he could think of was that he was in the shit and his options were limited. Bob would know what he should do, but somehow he couldn't see Jim letting him phone a friend.

'Ever fired a handgun?' Jim asked him, when they exited the car.

'What do you think?' Ed replied nervously, still thinking of a way out of this. Jim gave him a malicious smile and pulled out a second gun from his inside jacket pocket. He put his own handgun into the waistband of his trousers. Ed prayed that the safety catch was off and he would blow his bollocks off, but something told Ed that Jim had done this before and that was an unlikely event.

'It's a piece of piss. You pull the slide back like this. Take the safety catch off here, point at the target and pull the trigger. Bang! Barry falls to the floor and he doesn't get up again. Hold it with both hands like this.' He held the gun in his right hand and put his left hand over the top, locking his wrist. Ed nodded but wasn't really taking it in. 'Don't think it's fucking easy, because it ain't. It's not like in Dirty Harry. A Colt 45 has a kick like a mule and so does this baby. Hold it steady and aim low, otherwise the kick will send the bullet over his head and God knows where it will end up. The range of these things is something else. Got it?' With that, he handed Ed the weapon. It was heavier than he had expected and he weighed it in his hand, not liking the feel of it.

Ed thought about turning the gun on Jim and making an escape. He knew he couldn't shoot Jim, but did Jim know that? It might work but he would then spend the rest of his life looking over his shoulder, sure in the knowledge that Johnny wouldn't leave it at that. Jim seemed to sense that Ed was planning on making a run for it and pulled his gun from his waistband. He nudged Ed in the arm with it and told him to get on with it. Ed complied, holding the gun carefully at his side, knowing that he was just a flick of the safety catch away from being a murderer.

Spike exited the second car and sprung the boot. He hauled Barry up and helped him out, pushing him roughly towards the centre of the waste ground after removing his blindfold. The clock was ticking and Ed was more nervous than he had been at any other time in his entire life, because he still didn't have a plan. He couldn't kill Barry - he knew that much - but how he could get out of this alive was a question he didn't yet have an answer to.

'Go on then you dozy cunt, follow that useless, thieving bastard and shoot the fucker,' Jim said coldly, as if it was as easy as going down the shops for a pint of milk. Ed followed Barry reluctantly to the centre of the waste ground, on shaky legs.

'That'll do, Barry. I've still got to run back after this,' Ed said, his voice quavering. Barry turned round and looked at him pleadingly, tears coursing down his cheeks. Ed had never felt like such a bastard in his entire life. He had been in more fights than he cared to remember, but each time the person on the receiving end had been fully deserving of a good kicking. This was an entirely different matter.

'Just get it over with, Ed,' he said, and closed his eyes. Ed looked behind him and saw Jim and Spike thirty or so yards back, well out of earshot. Ed pointed the weapon at him. Jim's comment about Dirty Harry was bouncing around Ed's mind, and he was humming the Lurkers song "Dirty Harry" subconsciously.

'Go ahead, punk, and make my day - that's what Dirty Harry used to say,' Ed said out loud, and laughed nervously. Barry opened his eyes and stared back, wide-eyed. 'Barry, listen. I'm going to fire the gun and you're gonna fall over. Got it?' Barry hadn't, and shook his head in bewilderment. 'Look, it's simple, Barry. I don't want to kill you and I've no intention of doing so. I don't particularly like you but I can't shoot you. I'm going to fire the gun and I'm going to miss. When I do, you fall over and pretend to be dead. I then bugger off back to the car and after we've driven off, you can get up again. When you do, piss off out of London and make sure you don't cross Johnny's path again. I don't want to be standing here with Jim pointing a gun at my head. Somehow, I don't think he'll give me a second chance. So make it fucking realistic or you'll be signing my death warrant. You got that?' Barry nodded quickly and almost gave Ed a smile. Ed looked behind him and tried to move to a position where he was shielding Jim and Spike's view of Barry, just in case he was too theatrical. Ed had only seen people being shot in movies and it seemed to vary enormously. Some would be propelled back across the room and others would clutch at the entry wound and drop to their knees. How it was supposed to happen in real life was anyone's guess. Jim probably knew, hence shielding his view of Barry.

'On the count of three, Barry. One. Two. Three.' Ed pulled trigger, the loudness of the rapport startling him. It was far louder than expected. Barry fell to his knees, clutching his stomach, and dropped onto his front, landing on his face. Fair play to the bloke, Ed thought, he probably broke his nose doing that. Still, it was better than being dead. Ed panicked and threw the handgun to the ground and ran back to the car, wanting to get as far away as possible, as quickly as possible.

He jumped into the passenger seat and waited, while Jim sauntered to the driver's side and got in beside him.

'What did you do with the piece?' Jim asked, as soon as he pulled the door shut.

'Shit! I panicked and dropped it on the ground. Hang on, I'll go get it.'

'It's too fucking late now. Some do-gooder will have heard the shot and called the old bill. You shouldn't have been so fucking stupid. I don't give a shit if they find it. It's your prints all over it, not mine.'

'You're all heart, Jim, I'll give you that,' Ed replied, now even more concerned - but what the hell, he hadn't shot him. The only problem was if the gun had been used before and the police found it and made a connection.

'Feels fucking fantastic though, doesn't it? Better than losing your virginity, eh?' he said, genuinely pleased for Ed.

'Just drive me back to my car. If you must know, I feel sick to my boots and I can't believe I've sunk to this level; it makes me no better than you.'

'You know, one day I'm going to drive you out to this waste ground and do what you just done to Barry, to you.'

Ed had a feeling he meant it but right now he didn't give a toss, and just wanted to go home and sleep. Maybe when he woke up the last two weeks would turn out to be a bad dream. Fat chance of that; welcome to the real world, Ed.

How he had driven home in the state he was in, he had no idea. It was almost as if he had forgotten how to. He had stalled three times at traffic lights and crunched the

94

gears more times than he could remember. He was a bag of nerves and cursed himself the entire journey home for being such an idiot. On the bright side, he was still alive. Barry was still alive and he wasn't a murderer. Not much consolation, but he was clutching at straws.

When he arrived home, he contemplated phoning Bob - he'd know what to do. Tempted as he was he decided not to, thinking that there was a chance he'd got away with it. He ascended the stairs on legs like jelly and flopped onto his bed, not even bothering to switch on the light. He curled up in a ball and willed sleep to overcome him. It never came.

# Chapter 13

In the morning he showered, but couldn't be bothered shaving. After a quick cup of coffee, he went next door to collect Fat Boy and took him for a long walk across the fields and down by the river. He felt like shit, and according to Julie next door, he looked like shit. Ed made an excuse about the long hours taking their toll and left hastily, not feeling very sociable. The fresh October morning air perked him up a bit and cleared his head but did nothing to lift his sombre mood.

The question was what to do next. Should he turn up for work as was expected, or not bother and just make himself scarce? Assuming Barry had done as he was told, nobody would be any the wiser that he was still alive, so there was no reason not to go into work. If he didn't return to work, Johnny knew where he lived and would no doubt send the boys round. Where that would lead to was anyone's guess. There was still the fact that Johnny had made it clear leaving was not an option. In addition to that, he had effectively promised TJ he would stay on and try to bring about Johnny's demise. He certainly knew how to dig himself into a corner. In the end, and for no real reason, he elected to turn up today and play it by ear. He'd deal with what to do in the long run later. Why do today, what can be put off until another day? Whoever said that was a wise man or an utter coward - either way, it worked for Ed.

Jim and Spike were both behaving very strangely towards him. Ed had a nasty feeling that they knew Barry was still alive. However, as neither of them ever gave him the time of day anyway, he wasn't sure. Generally, the two of them were pretty much uncommunicative so perhaps he was just being paranoid; but he didn't think so.

A new face was behind the bar and Ed introduced himself, as it was clear Jim, Spike or Dave weren't going to. Adam shook his hand and stared at him coldly. Conversation was definitely not one of his strong points and it was an effort to get a name out of him. Ed had a lot more on his mind to worry about than that, and shrugged it off.

While Ed was taking a break around lunchtime, Pandora walked by the open door to the canteen area and blew him a kiss, following it up with the middle finger, but at least she did it with a smile now. TJ walked in, pulling the door shut behind her, before running up to him and launching herself at him. She threw her arms around his neck and wrapped her legs around his waist and kissed him passionately on the lips.

'I missed you yesterday,' she said, almost childlike. 'What was so important you couldn't make it?' she said pouting.

Ed let out a long weary breath and smiled. 'Not here. I'll tell you later, OK. Let's just say, I've put myself in a bit of a tight spot and to be honest, I don't know how I'm going to get out of it.'

'That sounds serious,' she said, with a smile that faded when she saw that Ed was genuinely worried.

'TJ, I'm not kidding but I don't want to talk about it, at least not here anyway. I'll come round after work and tell you all about it, OK?'

'Want to share a cab home?'

'No, I've got the car, haven't I. You go and I'll drive round after.' He bent down and kissed her and gave her what he hoped was an I'm OK smile, but it didn't seem to work. TJ frowned at him, kissed him quickly on the lips and gave him a hard stare, before leaving.

Blackthorn and Denton came into the club in the early evening and paused to give Ed a long, hard, menacing stare, before going through the door to get to Johnny's office. Was he being completely paranoid or was everyone either giving him a wide birth today, or glaring at him like he had just pissed in the font at a christening? He had expected to be summoned to Johnny's office first thing, but that never happened. He thought after what he'd done or was supposed to have done last night, he would want to congratulate him or kill him. That in itself seemed suspicious and Ed became more suspicious as the day progressed. By early evening he was a complete bag of nerves and had worked himself up into such a state of panic that he could feel his legs trembling, and he constantly felt the need to piss.

He knew why he was so nervous but it never ceased to amaze him that the thought of getting into trouble made him like this. When he was actually talking or fighting his way out of trouble, he was self-assured and never concerned with the consequences, trusting his instincts to do the right thing. It was easy, there were only three choices: fight, talk or run like hell! Ed had a feeling that by the end of the week, he would be doing at least one of the above, if not all three. His bladder tightened at the prospect.

The moment Ed had been waiting for came towards closing time, just as Ed had expected. Adam, the new guy, drew the short straw and gave him his summons to the office. Ed followed behind Adam, towards the door at the other end of the bar, and caught TJ's eye. She gave him a worried look and stared after him. Ed gave a quick smile and stopped off in the gents, once again feeling the need to piss. No more than a few drops later, he was knocking on Johnny's office door.

He walked in and faced Johnny, in his now customary position behind his desk. His face as usual was expressionless, apart from his eyes, which were hard as flints and piercing. To his right was Jim, leaning nonchalantly against the wall. Ed gave him a fleeting glance and was sure he detected a hint of a smirk on his face. Ed was unfazed.

'You wanted to see me?' he said calmly. Johnny said nothing for a while and stared at Ed with his poker face.

'How do you feel after last night?' he finally said.

Ed scoffed. 'I can't say it was my finest hour,' he said noncommittally. Johnny again regarded him silently, nodding slowly.

'I must say Ed, you're full of surprises. You know, I said to Jim yesterday that you'd lose your bottle and wouldn't go through with it. You agreed, didn't you Jim?'

'Certainly did, boss. He had me fooled for a minute. I thought he was shitting himself, obviously a dark horse. I think we'll have to keep a close eye on him.'

Ed looked at Jim and saw a smile playing on the edge of his mouth, and he didn't like the furtive glance he gave Johnny.

'You know, Ed, when I said shoot that thieving bastard, I thought you'd bottle it or if you did go through with it, it would be a body shot. Shooting him in the back of the head like that, takes some fucking nerve. A nice touch, though. I keep underestimating you.' Ed felt the colour drain from his face and the room suddenly became hot. He looked anxiously between Johnny and Jim, desperately trying to think straight.

'I didn't shoot the dopey bastard. I fired into the ground and told him to fake it. I'm not a bloody murderer. You bastards have set me up,' Ed shouted, the anger inside him rising.

'No need to be so modest, Ed,' Johnny said calmly. 'It says so in the paper,' he continued, turning to the right page of the Evening Standard.

There in black and white was the headline Gangland Execution. Ed didn't need to read further. Panic began to set in, and the blood drained from his face.

'The bottom line is, it's your prints on the gun and that can be matched to the bullet, embedded in Barry's head. Of course, with my contacts I can protect you. I'm sure DI Blackthorn could make the murder weapon vanish and you can work for me. On the other hand, you could try walking away, but I wouldn't fancy your chances. Would you, Jim?' Johnny's tone was flat and unemotional but still managed to chill Ed to the bone.

Ed turned and looked at Jim, who gave him an evil smile, pulled out his gun and pointed it at Ed.

'I don't rate his chances at all, boss,' Jim said laughing.

'So are you part of the team, or does Jim have to shoot you? I hope you make the right choice. It'd be a shame to get blood all over my new carpet. And besides, I really think you'd be useful, especially now as you've nothing to lose. I could make you one of the most feared hired hands in London. The sky's the limit.' Johnny smiled triumphantly and held his hands out in front of him. Ed was on the verge of erupting, he was so angry with Johnny - and with himself, for being so utterly stupid by getting involved in this.

He looked at Johnny and sneered. 'I'm going to turn around and walk out of here. I'm sick of all this bullshit and I'm sick of you!' he said, jabbing a finger at Johnny. Ed turned around and Jim stepped away from the wall and blocked his path, his gun aimed at his head.

'Just waste the bastard, Jim,' Johnny spat. Jim shrugged and looked coldly at Ed.

'Anything you say, Boss. In fact, it'll be a pleasure to waste this cocky bastard,' he said, smiling broadly. Ed was thinking on his feet and desperately searching for an idea, anything to stall for a few more precious seconds. An idea came to him and he smiled at Jim. Ed was sure that he detected a look of uncertainty in Jim's eyes, albeit momentarily.

'You need to take the safety catch off, if you want to shoot me, you daft twat,' Ed said calmly. Jim took his eyes off Ed and half-turned the gun in his hand, to look at the safety catch. That was all Ed needed. He launched a right-handed blow to Jim's jaw, putting everything he had into it. Jim slammed into the wall, stunned but still holding onto the gun. Ed wasted no time and followed up with a ferocious blow to the stomach, doubling him over. He grabbed his arm that was holding the gun and smashed it repeatedly on the corner of the desk. Eventually, the gun flew from his hand and bounced across the floor. Ed pulled Jim's head down and drove his knee into his face, hearing a satisfying crunch as his nose flattened under the force.

He looked at Johnny out of the corner of his eye and saw a look of panic drift across his usually stony face. Johnny rose from behind the desk and darted towards the gun, where it lay on the floor to his right. Ed hurled Jim into the corner, where he slumped, barely conscious. He leapt the short distance to Johnny, who was bending down to retrieve the gun, which lay inches from his grasp. Ed picked up a silver attaché case at the side of Johnny's desk and swung it left handed, with all his might, catching Johnny on the temple. His head snapped back and he fell backwards into the filing cabinet behind, dazed. Ed kicked the gun to the far side of the office and took a quick look at Johnny. Blood was streaming from a cut above his left eye and he glared back at Ed, but was too dazed to speak. Ed turned and saw Jim attempting to get up. He calmly walked over and kicked him hard in the ribs, sending him back to the floor, where he rolled, clutching his side, hissing in pain.

Ed pulled open the door to the office and ran down the stairs. He was two-thirds of the way down when Spike came running through the doors at the bottom, heading towards him. He froze when he saw Ed and Ed instinctively launched himself down the remaining flight and landed a drop-kick to Spike's chest, sending him crashing backwards into the door. His head hit the door with a sickening thump and he lay there, unmoving. Ed didn't stop to check if he was conscious or not. He was running on pure adrenaline, and now just wanting to be out of the club for the last time.

Ed burst through into the main bar area and headed right towards the steps, to the main entrance and street level. Dave stared back at him but made no attempt to stop him, as he flew by him and smashed into the main door and out into the street. Lady luck was on his side, tonight. Directly in front of him, a black taxi was parked at the kerb. Without thinking, Ed pulled the door open and threw himself in, pulling the door to behind him, in one fluid movement

'Just fucking drive, now!' he shouted at the driver from the floor. He turned to his right and noticed the cab already had a passenger. He looked up into the welcoming and slightly alarmed face of TJ.

'Do as he says and drive,' she screamed at the driver. 'And put your bloody foot down!' The driver didn't need to be told again and pulled out as fast as the cab could muster and headed away from the club. Ed pulled himself onto the seat and gave TJ a quick smile.

'I thought you didn't want to share a cab with me?' she said shakily, making light of it.

Ed shrugged. 'Missing you, already,' he said breathlessly, pulling in deep a deep lungful of air.

'Care to tell me what's going on?'

Ed shook his head. 'Let me get my breath back.' He took a few more deep breaths and nodded. 'Well, I think I've just made about the biggest bloody mistake of my entire life.' He leaned back, closed his eyes, and blew out a long breath.

# Chapter 14

Once inside TJ's flat, Ed slumped down onto the sofa, dropping the attaché case onto the floor. He hadn't actually meant to steal it. It was just a heat of the moment thing. Had he picked up a wastepaper basket to hit Johnny over the head with, he would probably be placing that down by the side of the sofa. As it was, he had Johnny's briefcase and whatever its contents were. Perhaps running off with it might have been a good thing. If there was something inside of importance, it might give him a good bargaining position. On the other hand, it might give Johnny reason to send out a search party; not that he wasn't expecting that to happen anyway. People like Johnny didn't let anyone get one over on them as easily as Ed had done, without looking for revenge.

'So, care to tell me what this is all about?' TJ asked, handing him a tumbler half-full of something. Ed took a healthy sip, and coughed.

'Jesus, what is that?'

'Cooking brandy, it's the only spirit I've got in the place. I thought it might help with your uncontrollable shaking.' Ed hadn't realised he had been but now she mentioned it, his hand was trembling. He took another large gulp and held his arm out in front of him. His hand was still trembling, the ice cubes rattling against each other in the tumbler. He placed it on the coffee table in front of him.

'Doesn't appear to be working,' he said with a smile. TJ sat down next to him on the sofa and took hold of his hand, and gave it a squeeze.

'Are you going to tell me what the hell's going on, or not?' she asked impatiently.

Ed nodded and told her about the events of the last two days. He started with being asked to shoot Barry

104

and trying to bluff his way out of it, and ended with the fight and his panic-stricken flight out of the club, not twenty minutes ago. TJ stared back at him open mouthed but didn't interrupt.

'Bet you're glad you're not in my shoes, eh?' Ed said dryly.

'Why the bloody hell didn't you just walk away yesterday, when he asked you to kill Barry? You could have saved yourself a whole load of bother!'

'Because Johnny said if I didn't, Jim would pop the both of us. If I'd had the choice, I would have done. I thought about not turning up for work today but I was hoping that my bluff would work. How was I to know Spike - at least I assume it was Spike, as he was in the second car with Barry - would finish the job? If I hadn't turned up today, they would have come looking for me either way. For some reason, Johnny wants me on his team. He seems to think he can turn me into some sort of "super thug" that will give him the edge over everyone else.' He gave TJ a worried look and shrugged. 'Looks like I've screwed up, big time.'

TJ put her glass down and leaned over and gave him a hug. 'So, what's the plan now, then?' she asked softly.

'I have absolutely no bloody idea. I need to get my car back at some point but not tonight. Then I think I'll disappear for a while and try and work out what to do. To be honest, I haven't really got a clue. I can't go home as he knows where I live, and I can't stay here and put you in danger. Maybe I'll take a holiday or something.'

'You can stay here as long as you like. I'll be OK,' she said, but not really believing it.

'No. I don't want to put you or anyone else in any danger.'

'Why don't you go to the police, tell them everything that's happened?'

'That's the other problem. I'm now on the police most-wanted list. Blackthorn and Denton will make sure the gun with my prints on it turns up, and I'm going to be framed for Barry's murder. To be honest, I don't know how I can get out of that one. I certainly can't go to the police. They'll just think Christmas has come early.'

'So, where will you go?'

'I don't know. I'll think of somewhere. I don't want to sound melodramatic but I can't risk going abroad, just in case I really am in the frame for murder. Trying to leave the country is as good as admitting you're guilty. It'll have to be somewhere in the UK. Certainly not Cornwall, though, not after the misery I brought everyone the last time I was there. I don't know. I just can't think at the moment.'

'What you need is a good night's sleep.'

'What I need is a bloody time machine so I can turn the clock back two weeks,' Ed said, giving TJ a brief smile.

TJ stood and pulled Ed up by the hand and led him into the bedroom. It was small and very pink but had a comfortable-looking double bed. Ed stripped and climbed in, feeling completely shattered but knowing that he would be lucky to sleep a wink the way his mind was racing. TJ came back from the bathroom and Ed watched her undress, but even that couldn't lift his spirits.

She slid into the bed beside him and looked at him and tried to give him a reassuring smile, but it came out as more of a frown. Ed pulled her across to him and crushed her to his chest, and wondered where and when, this was all going to end. He had a bad feeling things were going to get very messy. He closed his eyes and prayed that sleep would overcome him. Tomorrow he would need to start thinking with a clear head.

# Chapter 15

The sleep Ed craved so much never came. He lay there and listened to TJ, breathing softly and peacefully, and envied her. Restless and not wanting to wake her, Ed slipped out of bed and made for the kitchen to see what there was for breakfast. The fridge contained half a loaf of bread, a carton of milk, and not a lot else. In the living room he found TJ's handbag and after finding her keys, headed out to find a mini-market. Despite not yet being seven in the morning, he knew his chances of finding somewhere open were good. Sure enough, on Borough High Street, he found what he was looking for and headed back.

By the time he got back to TJ's flat he was freezing, as he was only wearing the Johnny's T-shirt he had been wearing when he fled the club last night. He needed to do something about that, because he stuck out like a sore thumb and what he really needed now was to blend in.

While waiting for the kettle to boil, TJ walked in, looking tired with her hair sticking out in every direction but somehow still managing to look great, as she always seemed to. She stretched and yawned and gave him an apologetic smile, her eyes barely open. Ed smiled back weakly, as she put her arms around him and yawned into his chest.

'Want a fry-up?' he asked.

'Can you cook one properly?' she asked, looking up at him, smiling in anticipation of the answer.

'I can but it's usually not that good to look at and is just about edible, as long as you like extremely crispy bacon.' He gave her his best I'm a bloke - what do you expect? look, which seemed to do the trick.

TJ shook her head. 'Are you asking me to cook it?' Ed nodded and gave her a little-boy-lost look. 'Go and have a shower or something and do something about your breath. Use my toothbrush if you like.' Ed went to kiss her and she moved her face to one side. 'Not until you've brushed your teeth, dog breath.'

Showered, feeling and smelling a little more human, he entered the kitchen just as TJ was dishing up breakfast. It looked and smelt as appetising as it had on Sunday, when she had cooked at Ed's house. She turned to look at him and frowned.

'I thought you hated beards?' she said, teasing him. 'You could've used my razor, you know.'

Ed ran his hand over TJ's chin and nodded appreciatively 'I should've done, it's obviously got a fresh blade in it.'

'Do you want to eat this breakfast or wear it?' she asked, and slapped him playfully on the arm.

After breakfast, TJ showered, and walked back into the living room looking immaculate. Ed pulled his mobile phone out, told her to smile, and took her photo.

'Why is it I have a horrible feeling this is the last time I'll ever see you again?' she asked sadly.

'Because you're a pessimist? Of course you'll see me again. It says in my will I want an open casket funeral,' he said, trying to make a joke of it.

'That just isn't funny, you stupid bastard!' she said angrily. The smile dropped off Ed's face and he looked at TJ. Her lips trembled and tears spilled down her cheeks. Ed felt guilty and apologised, and hugged her. TJ clung to him like her life depended on it, and sniffed back her tears.

When her sniffing abated, Ed held her by her shoulders and looked straight into her eyes. 'TJ, I promise you, I will see you again. It'll take more than that big-nosed bastard and his dumb gorillas to see me off. You could always come with me.' He hoped he sounded confident, because inside he was less than convinced. TJ leaned forward and kissed him passionately.

TJ shook her head and gave him a weak smile. 'I can't come with you.'

Ed shrugged and just said 'OK,' not wanting to push her, knowing she must have her reasons.

'Ed, be careful and don't do anything stupid, OK?'

'I'll be careful, but I can't promise not to do anything stupid.'

TJ sighed. 'Just make sure you keep safe.'

'Don't worry. I'm like a cat. I've got nine lives,' Ed replied grinning.

TJ frowned. 'You're forgetting, I've seen the scar on your leg and you've had a gun pulled on you three times since being at Johnny's. By my reckoning you're down to five.'

Ed shrugged. 'That's still pretty good odds,' he replied, as convincingly as he could.

'Ed, just look after yourself, OK.'

'TJ, you've got my number, give me a call if you hear anything or anything happens. I'll give you a call and let you know I'm OK and not doing anything stupid - or too stupid, anyway.'

TJ nodded, but didn't speak. She walked over to a sideboard, opened the top drawer and handed him a spare key to the front door. 'Just in case you need it through the day, or any other time, come to that.' She looked at her watch and frowned.

'I'll walk you down the road and wait while you get a cab,' Ed offered.

TJ shook her head 'No. I don't want to cry in the street.'

'Are you gonna be OK?' he asked, genuinely concerned.

TJ smiled and nodded. 'Sure. The question is, are you?'

This time Ed smiled and nodded, as TJ turned around and walked through the door.

Ed made a mental list of what he needed to do. First on his list was to phone Julie next door and apologise for not picking up Fat Boy. He apologised profusely and said he would be round early tomorrow. Julie obviously detected that something was wrong and saw through Ed's clumsy attempt to sound normal. He brushed it off and told her something came up and he couldn't make it home. He further embellished it with a few more white lies, about being so busy. This aroused her suspicions further, and prompted more questions on how a club could be busy after hours. Thinking on his feet, which seemed to be the norm lately, he decided another white lie was in order and mumbled something about stock-taking. There was silence on the line for what seemed a long time, before she asked if Ed was in trouble. He cracked and said yes, which was met with further silence. With a promise to fill her in with the details in the morning, he was off the hook. Julie never could resist a bit of gossip.

Next, he needed to do something about his clothes - or rather, lack of them. He headed up Webber road and turned onto Borough High Street, in the direction of London Bridge market, where he was sure he could get a new T-shirt and a jacket of some description. Even though the sun was out it was still cold, and his arms were covered in goosebumps. During the brisk walk to the market he kept a keen eye on his surroundings, not confident that Johnny hadn't sent out a posse to round him up. He reasoned it was unlikely and that the chances of them knowing he was in Southwark were slim but he wasn't taking any chances. In his own mind he felt conspicuous, as he was clad in the distinctive Day-Glo Johnny's T-shirt and everyone else around him wore coats or thick jumpers.

He located a likely-looking clothes stall in the labyrinth of the market and purchased a Nike T-shirt. He had no doubts it was a replica, but right then wasn't really concerned with the ethics of children being made to work long hours for little pay to satisfy the demand for fake branded goods. He pulled off his Johnny's T-shirt and put on his new one, much to the delight of the woman running the stall. He selected a fleece and put that on, paid, and hurried out onto Borough High Street. After stopping at the cash point in the post office he headed down to Waterloo station, slightly warmer and slightly happier at actually doing something, other than sitting on his arse and feeling sorry for himself.

At Waterloo station he purchased a huge bouquet of flowers and a cute card too, and headed back to TJ's flat, hoping that she would be pleased with them. By the envious looks he received from some of the women he passed, he thought she would be. He didn't want to go hunting through TJ's cupboards for a vase so filled up the sink with water and placed the flowers in the sink. He found a pen and wrote a message in the card and left it on the work surface next to the sink. He contemplated sitting down and having a coffee but decided that he would be better off keeping on the move. If he sat down too long, he would start thinking too much, and then start to worry.

After grabbing some lunch at a greasy spoon he headed off once again in the direction of Waterloo Bridge. He had intended to drop down onto the embankment and walk to Westminster and up around St. James's park. When he arrived at Waterloo Bridge, he carried on walking and found himself heading back to Soho.

# Chapter 16

The atmosphere at Johnny's was unlike anything TJ had experienced before. When she walked in she smiled at Spike, who glowered back moodily. TJ shrugged, barely able to suppress a laugh, knowing his head and chest must be hurting like hell from the drop-kick to the chest he received the previous night. She hadn't seen Jim yet, but she couldn't wait. From the account Ed had given her, he wouldn't be a pretty sight. Not that he was, even before Ed had rearranged his face. Johnny would be sporting a few bruises too. Not that she cared about that murdering bastard. Even cancer would be too good for him.

TJ was the last of the girls to arrive and was greeted by a room full of stares and complete silence. The type of silence reserved for when the villain in a cowboy movie throws back the saloon doors and saunters up to the bar. If there was a piano in the dressing room, it would have stopped playing. Pandora was the first to break the silence.

'Did you hear what lover boy got up to last night?' she asked, in a hushed excited tone.

'Very funny. I assume you mean, Ed? And the answer is no,' she lied, trying to sound indignant.

'Apparently on Wednesday night, he shot Barry. Spike said that Barry and Ed were on the fiddle and had a row about splitting the money. Last night, Johnny confronted him and he totally lost it. He broke Jim's nose and a couple of ribs and then turned on Johnny. Smashed him over the head with a chair and run off with the night's takings,' she said excitedly.

TJ was horrified at the lies she was telling her, which was to her advantage as she was able to look genuinely shocked. 'No way! He was a bit handy in a fight but he was straight as they come. I can't believe

113

he would kill anyone - and he's a millionaire as well, so he didn't need the money. I can't believe it.'

'Bullshit. If he was a millionaire, he wouldn't have been working here, would he?'

TJ felt compelled to stick up for Ed. If she was honest with herself, she was a little bit in love with him. 'Well that's what he told me and to be honest, I believe him. He was a nice bloke.'

'Well, if you ask me, I think he was a bloody con artist and we've all been taken in by him,' Pandora said triumphantly.

TJ had never thought about that. Had she been taken in? His house was nice but didn't strike her as the type of house a millionaire would live in and his car was a Mondeo, which was a far cry from a Rolls Royce. She pushed the thoughts to the back of her mind, not wanting to believe it. Could she have been that naive and fallen for his lies?

'I don't think so. I spoke to him quite a lot and I think he was genuine. Do you really think he was a con artist?' TJ replied softly.

Pandora gave it some thought, and smiled. 'I don't know. I know I gave him a hard time, but I think he was straight. I actually quite liked him, if you must know. At least you didn't have to give him a blow job or let him fuck you just so that he would pull a punter off you when they got a bit fresh. I think I might actually miss not having him around,' she said, smiling at TJ.

That surprised TJ but she was secretly quite pleased and smiled broadly. 'Me too,' she replied happily. 'I can't say I'm too upset about Jim getting his nose broken. I wouldn't like to be in Ed's shoes though. Johnny must be pretty pissed off.'

'Spike was telling me that Blackthorn and Denton are on the case. They've got the murder weapon and it's got his prints all over it. Not that I trust those two bent bastards one little bit. They probably fabricated the evidence because Johnny told them to.'

TJ nodded and gave her a worried smile. She would give Ed a call at some point and let him know about Blackthorn and Denton. Whether he was a con artist or not, he'd been nice to her and it had been a long time since any man had treated her like that, and he deserved the benefit of the doubt. Not that there was really any doubt in her mind.

# Chapter 17

Once over Waterloo Bridge, Ed headed up Wellington Street and turned left down Long Acre, heading in the general direction of Soho. It wasn't the most direct route but they were main roads, busy with both people and cars. Still a little paranoid, he wanted to avoid quiet back-streets, just in case he was being followed. Periodically he would check, and although no expert in the matter, was fairly confident he wasn't. He became more vigilant as he reached Soho, just on the off chance someone from the club was out getting coffee or was out on an errand.

Ed didn't know why he had crossed the river, rather than walking along the embankment. However, now he was in Soho he thought he would chance a look round the back of the club to see if his car was still there. He walked slowly and cautiously and, to any passerby, probably very suspiciously. Not that he cared, unless that passerby was someone from the club or Blackthorn or his trusty sidekick, Denton. On the opposite side of the road to the yard he crept by, looking in all the doorways and shadows for any signs of movement. He detected none and was tempted to stroll up to his car and drive away. He thought better of it as the traffic was heavy and if he needed to get away in a hurry, he had no chance. Better to come back later and do it under cover of darkness, when the roads would be empty. That way he could put his foot down if he was seen.

Having seen enough, he headed off in the direction of Piccadilly Circus, turned down Regents Street and headed for St. James's park, as he had originally intended to do. The wind had picked up and the sun was now a dusty glow, behind a gradually thickening, grey blanket. The cheap fleece Ed had bought earlier was barely adequate to stave of the chill so he quickened his pace in an effort to keep warm. St. James's park was peaceful, with only a handful of tourists braving the now inclement weather. He wished it was a little less breezy so he could sit one of the may empty benches and watch the world go by and think of what to do next. So far, apart from getting his car back and relieving Julie of Fat Boy, he hadn't a clue what came next. He turned up the collar of his fleece and headed towards the park exit. Westminster Bridge was busy with office workers, making their way home or, as it was Friday, to the pubs and clubs in the city. How many would be heading to Johnny's tonight? Ed wondered. He pushed all thoughts of Johnny's from his mind, put his head down and made his way along the embankment, back towards Waterloo.

During the course of the day the girls were called to Johnny's office. TJ was getting apprehensive as she was the last to be invited. Because it was a Friday the club was busy with the after-work crowd, so she didn't get the opportunity to find out what it was all about from the other girls. She knocked, walked in, and faced Johnny who sat behind his desk, looking moody and sporting a black eye with a large cut, just above the brow. Jim was standing in the same position by the wall, as he had been when Ed had walked in less than 24 hours previously. He looked pissed off and his face was a mass of bruises. His eyes were puffy and yellow and there was a scab on the bridge of his nose where Ed had broken it. Despite his wiry frame, easy smile and good nature, he was lethal with his fists. Both of them deserved what they got and more, and she just wished Ed had inflicted more damage than he had.

'TJ, I'm sure you've heard the rumours?' Johnny stated.

'I have and I have to admit, it came as a bit of a shock. I didn't have him down as a murderer or a thief. Looks like he played us all for mugs,' she said, hoping that it sounded matter-of-fact and convincing.

'Seems that way,' he said, staring back unblinking, studying her. 'From what I hear, you and him were pretty tight?'

'Not really. He seemed a nice enough bloke. He used to flirt with me but only because I was the only person who really spoke to him. I suppose I felt a bit sorry for him, really.' She gave Johnny another shrug.

'So, you two didn't have anything going on, outside work then?' he said with a sneer.

'No!' she said defensively and perhaps a little too quickly. 'On his first night here, he couldn't get home as Barry drove him here and there were no trains. I said he could stay at my place and he spent a few hours on my couch and left to catch the first train home. Like I said, I felt sorry for him, but that was it.'

Johnny continued to stare, weighing up her answers, almost daring her to slip up. TJ stared back defiantly, full of loathing for the man who killed her mother.

'Fair enough. So, you've no idea where he is now?'

'No. Why should I? At home, I suppose.'

'He's not there. I sent Jim round to check. Did he mention any friends or somewhere he might be? Only, he stole a great deal of money from me, which has put me in an awkward situation with some of my associates. I want it back and I want him, and God help anyone that gets in my way.' His voice remained steady but the hatred he exuded was palpable. TJ shuddered involuntary.

'In the unlikely event he gets in touch or I hear anything, I'll let you know,' she said shakily.

'Be sure you do. If I find out you've been lying, I'll make sure you never work round here again. I don't mean putting the word out that you're bad news. I mean making sure that nobody would pay to have someone looking like you dancing for them. Do you hear what I'm saying, TJ?'

TJ nodded quickly. She felt dizzy and nauseous and needed to get out of this office. She took a deep breath and composed herself. 'Johnny, I need this job. I'm not going to let that murdering bastard ruin it for me. Am I?' she lied convincingly.

Johnny nodded. 'Right then, get back to work and earn me some bloody money.' He stared past her, looking at the door, which she took as the signal to leave. She turned to leave but was stopped by Jim, who threw his arm out across her chest. He moved his hand slowly up and grabbed her jaw, squeezing it painfully. God she hated him, almost as much as she did Johnny, and stared back at him in an act of defiance.

'You better not be lying, or I'll take great pleasure in rearranging that pretty little face of yours.' He gave her a cold smile and pulled his hand away. TJ pulled the door open with a trembling hand and headed down the stairs, gripping the handrail tightly, her legs like jelly and regretting not having taken Ed up on his offer of going with him. However, now she knew that Ed had stolen a great deal of money, she could make herself useful and stir up a hornets nest with Mo. She assumed that the silver attaché case he'd stolen could only have contained one of two things - drugs, or payment for drugs. TJ assumed it was the latter and thought that a quick call to one of Mo's clubs would be a good idea, just to add to Johnny's misery.

'What do you think, Jim? Is she telling the truth?' Johnny asked

'Dunno boss. I've never been able to work her out. Want me to apply a bit of pressure?'

'Leave it for now, but keep an eye on her. If there is anything going on between them, it might be useful and lead us to him. I need that briefcase back. It's not just the money. There are other things in that case, which in the wrong hands could ruin everything, and I don't want to think about the consequences of that.' Johnny slammed his fist down on his desk. 'Where the fuck is that little shit?' he roared.

'Well, he didn't go home last night. Me and Spike paid him a home visit and he wasn't there. Had a good look around and couldn't find anything. It's not exactly a millionaire's mansion, though. I think he's full of shit on that score. My guess is he's still in London.'

Johnny nodded and rubbed a hand across his chin. 'I'll get Blackthorn in. I'm sure when he finds out what else was in that briefcase, he'll be more than happy to pull a few strings to get the bastard.' He picked up the phone, and dialled.

# Chapter 18

Ed was killing time back at TJ's flat, drinking coffee and watching crap on TV. Once it became dark, he ventured out for what he hoped would be the penultimate time. He grabbed a quick burger and chips at Waterloo station and ate it standing, watching the crowds for any familiar faces on the station concourse. He cursed himself, not for the first time that day, for being paranoid. Having to be vigilant whenever he stepped out into the street was not a nice feeling. He didn't like being on edge all the time - it was tiring. Nonetheless, he reasoned it was necessary, at least until he got his car back and got out of this dirty, corrupt and sleazy city. Completely unsatisfied by the greasy, tasteless burger, over-salted chips and flat Coca-Cola, he headed out of the station and made his way north of the river.

Earlier in the day he had blended in with the crowds, made up mostly of tourists, too early for the after-work drinkers and those travelling into London for a night out. Tonight however, still dressed in his T-shirt and fleece, he was conspicuous. The later it got, the more conspicuous he would become as the tourists went back to their hotels and changed into eveningwear and mingled with the after work office crowd in their business suits. Concerned about standing out in the crowd and still paranoid that Johnny had a search party out looking for him, not to mention the police on a murder charge, he took back streets whenever it was practical to do so. He wasn't overly familiar with his surroundings but guessed he was heading in the right direction.

Once he reached Long Acre, he turned left and walked down Neal Street. When he reached the Crown pub, he paused and decided to delay retrieving his car, on the basis it was perhaps still too early and a little Dutch courage was in order. Ed bought a pint of London Pride and found a space at the back of the narrow bar, facing the street. He chose this pub for two reasons. The clientele was not the usual city crowd, so he wouldn't stand out in his fleece. Additionally, he knew they did a decent pint or at least they had done, nearly four years ago, when he had last drunk there.

While sipping his pint to make it last, not wanting to risk another one in case he got pulled over by the police when he got his car back, he made a decision to stall getting his car until around half past eleven. This, he recalled, was about the busiest time of the night at Johnny's. About this time it would be filling up, keeping the thugs that passed as bouncers fully occupied and not having time to nip out the back for a crafty smoke. Deciding it was now or never, Ed downed the last few warm dregs of his pint and walked out the door, taking a good look in either direction, before continuing down Neal Street.

Approaching the yard behind Johnny's, he noticed two youths down a small side turning. They were eyeing up a couple of parked cars, either to take or steal from, he assumed and immediately felt guilty for assuming the worst of them. It turned out he was right. While one kept watch, the other smashed the window, reached in and took whatever it was he had liked the look of. They walked casually up the street towards Ed, one carrying a small rucksack, which by the look of it contained a laptop; some people were so dumb.

On noticing Ed, the two youths looked furtively at each other, whispered something and continued. Ed tried to look casual as if he hadn't noticed what they had done, hoping that he wasn't making them nervous. He obviously wasn't as they strolled confidently towards him.

'Fancy earning a bit of cash?' Ed asked when they were a couple of paces in front of him.

'Are you some kind of faggot or what?' The youth nearest asked him.

Ed laughed, not having considered the reaction his question would have. 'Am I bollocks!' he said defensively. 'I was thinking something more along the lines of stealing a car for me.'

'We don't do that sort of stuff, mate,' the other youth said, trying to act innocent and failing badly.

'So, that wasn't you two I just saw, smashing the window of that car and taking that laptop. It's a real bugger getting old, you know. The old eyesight plays a lot of tricks on you. Let's not fuck around, eh? I need a car stolen. I'll even make it easy for you, I've got the key.' Ed said, waving his car key in front of them.

'It'll cost,' the first one said. Ed nodded. 'A ton. OK?' Ed nodded again. The youth smiled and said 'Each.' Ed nodded again 'And half up front.'

This time Ed laughed at their sheer cheek. 'Tell you what. If you don't smash the window and nick the radio, I'll give you two each. How does that sound?'

They eyed him suspiciously and turned to each other and shrugged, both thinking that Ed was a little bit touched.

'OK, you get half up front and the other half, when you hand me back the car. It's the Mondeo, parked in the yard at the back of Johnny's. You know where that is?'

The first youth nodded and laughed 'You want me to steal a fucking Mondeo. What the fuck for? They're a pile of shit!'

'Yeah, but this is my pile of shit and I want it back. OK?' Ed said defensively

'Why don't you just walk into the yard and drive off with it?' he asked, as if Ed really was stupid.

'Because I had a bit of a set-to and got kicked out. If any of the bouncers see me, I'll get a kicking. If they see you, they probably wouldn't give a toss that you're nicking my car. What is it with you? Don't you want four hundred quid for driving a couple of yards? I'll find someone else if you like. There are plenty of other mugs out here,' Ed said, trying to call their bluff. It worked.

'Alright mate, keep your hair on. I didn't say we wouldn't do it. Just curious, that's all.'

'Right. Here's the keys. Off you go, I'll see you back here and try not to smash anything or scratch it.'

'Half up front, you said.'

Ed pulled out his wallet and handed over a hundred pounds.

'That's not half. That's... half of half.'

Ed laughed. 'That'll be a quarter then, and it's half of what you asked for. I said I'd make it two a piece. Look, I'm making this bloody easy for you.' He pulled out the remaining notes from his wallet and wafted them in front of the youths' faces. 'Look, I'm good for it, OK, and make sure you leave the engine running.'

The two youths looked at each other again. The second youth took the keys Ed was holding and turned and headed in the direction of Johnny's.

Ed felt a bit stupid waiting on the corner, freezing his tits off, waiting for two minors to steal his car and park up in front of him. Money well spent if they pulled it off and didn't sod off with his cash to score some crack or whatever they liked to do with their money.

After what seemed a very long wait, Ed's Mondeo came screaming round the corner and skidded to a halt in front of him. The two youths jumped out with big grins on their faces.

'No bother?' Ed asked, thinking something must have gone wrong, the speed they were driving.

'Nah none at all, mate. Cough up,' the second one, who had been driving said, holding his hand out.

Ed smiled and handed over the three hundred he'd promised them. The youth made a point of counting it before saying 'Cheers, easy,' and jogging off down the street with his accomplice. Ed got behind the wheel and headed towards Shaftesbury Avenue. At the first opportunity he opened the dash to retrieve his Sat-Nav, which wasn't there. It wasn't there, because it was safely ensconced in a laptop bag, on the other side of the West End, on the back of a toe-rag car thief. Ed gave a wry smile and made a mental note to buy a new one.

After getting tied up in one way streets and without the benefit of Sat-Nav, he finally made it over Waterloo bridge and headed back to TJ's flat. Once there, he climbed the stairs to her flat, opened the door and picked up the attaché case, he had left in the hallway. The fact that it was still there was a good sign and meant that Johnny hadn't worked out he had stayed with TJ last night and hopefully, that meant she was in no danger. He was still worried about her and wished she had taken him up on his offer of coming with him. He contemplated waiting for her in the flat to ask again, but decided against it. If she wasn't currently in any danger, coming with Ed might put her in danger. Ed switched on the ignition and pulled out into the dark night, wondering what his next move was.

# Chapter 19

Johnny was on his back foot. Blackthorn and Denton were with him in one of the private rooms, along with Jim. Jim remained standing at the back of the room, the bruising on his face spreading and becoming darker. The painkillers he'd taken had done little to alleviate the agony of either his nose or his ribs. At least one was broken, and made breathing a painful experience. The thought of catching up with Ed and killing him slowly was ever-present.

'So, basically what you're saying Johnny, is you've fucked up and put the whole operation in jeopardy. I told you that skinny prick was bad news but oh no, you thought you knew better! Jesus Christ, Johnny, how could you have been such an arsehole?'

'Look, I've made a mistake. I know! Reminding me isn't going to get our money back, is it?'

'My fucking money, Johnny. Mine, not just yours. Let's get that straight,' Blackthorn spat back.

'It wasn't just your money. It was Mo and his outfit's money, too,' Johnny came back with angrily, getting frustrated with Blackthorn's attitude. 'The last thing we need is that lot breathing down our necks. You know what they can be like.'

'I told you, I don't give a fuck about their money. Those three lunatics are your problem, not mine,' Blackthorn replied with a sadistic grin.

'You just don't get it, do you? It wasn't just the money in that briefcase. There were other things. Things that if they got into the wrong hands, could see us all going to prison,' Johnny said, playing his trump card and praying it would work.

Denton shot Blackthorn a worried look. 'What other stuff is that, Johnny?' he asked nervously.

'I keep records of everything. My memory isn't that good sometimes so I've got records of every payment and every transaction, going back years. Names, dates, times, amounts - you name it, it's in there. My two ledgers were inside the case.'

'You stupid bastard! I don't fucking believe this. What the bloody hell were they doing in the briefcase?'

'I thought they were safe in there. I've got a safe in the office but I don't like leaving them here overnight. Every night I put them in my briefcase and take them home. Anyway, don't just sit there blowing smoke out your arse. What are you gonna do about it? You're the bloody copper with all the resources. Pull a few strings and find the little prick. Don't just sit there with your thumb up your arse, bleating about losing a few quid,' Johnny said, happy that the tables had turned and Blackthorn was now feeling the heat.

Denton rose in his chair, his hands gripped the edge of the table and took a deep breath, ready to attack Johnny with a verbal onslaught. The door opening, and Mo, Asif and Abdul walking in, stopped him in his tracks and he sat down meekly. Johnny turned round, his heart sinking; this was all he needed.

'I hear you've got a bit of a cash-flow problem, Johnny,' Mo said coldly, his eyes dark and foreboding.

'Word gets round quickly. Who told you?' Johnny said calmly.

'You know what the jungle drums are like round here. You can't fart without it making the headlines in the Evening Standard. It's not important. What's important, is whether or not it's true.' He stared hard at Johnny to infer it was a question, not a statement. Johnny nodded.

'Your mate Case, the bouncer I had on the books for a couple of weeks. I misjudged him and he flew off the handle and ran off with our money.'

Asif grinned. 'I hear he shot Barry as well,' he said, through a half-smile. 'He didn't strike me as the murdering type. Seemed far too straight for something like that.' Johnny cringed.

'Like I said, I fucked up. Right now, getting our money back is what matters,' he said, wanting to move on quickly to avoid further awkward questions. 'As far as the police are concerned,' he said, glaring at Blackthorn and Denton, 'he's wanted for murder, so they're going to try and find him. Of course, I'm sending a few of my boys out to get him. That way, I get the money back and the taxpayer is saved a whole load of money as it won't go to trial - if you see where I'm coming from.'

Mo stared down at Johnny from his standing position opposite, sizing him up. He knew he had lied during his explanation and didn't trust him. He never had trusted him but, to date, he had always been good for the money. The current situation gave him a good position from which to bargain from.

'This is an unexpected inconvenience, as I'm sure you'll agree, Johnny. We'll help you with your search, personally. I'm sure Asif would like to even the score, for their encounter last week, as would I. In return, I expect ten percent interest on the money owed.' Mo extended his hand toward Johnny. He grimaced, but knew he had no choice. The last thing he needed was a falling out with Mo; he was too well connected. Johnny extended his hand and shook. Mo smiled, knowing he had got one over on Johnny and wanting him to know. Johnny, Denton and Blackthorn all stood as one as Mo, Asif and Abdul filed out of the room.

TJ had seen them arrive and was glad that her tipoff had reached its intended target. Asif gave Mo a hearty pat on the back as they emerged back into the bar area, which didn't go unnoticed by TJ or Dave, standing by the entrance. It seemed that everything went well and Johnny was now up to his neck in it. She only hoped that it hadn't put Ed in any further danger.

Blackthorn and Denton left shortly after, both looking extremely unhappy, which cheered TJ up even more. Dave nodded as they departed and was left wondering what had transpired upstairs. He'd ask Jim when he came back down - not that he'd been very talkative today, and who could blame him? If someone four inches shorter and half his weight had beaten Dave up, he'd be pissed off. The fact that, when Ed had rushed past him last night he didn't appear to have a scratch on him, meant he was either very lucky or very good. If it was luck, then he needed to be careful; luck never lasted.

TJ arrived home from work in a state of mixed emotions. She was nervous, due to the conversation with Johnny. She couldn't work out if he was just fishing or if he knew that she and Ed were much closer than she had let on. The look Jim had given her had chilled her to the core. It was almost as if he could see inside her mind and knew she had been telling lies. She was pleased that Mo and his friends had put in an appearance. Judging by their mood when they left it had obviously gone well, which could only spell trouble for Johnny. She was also worried for Ed, and was missing him already. The atmosphere at work had been oppressive today and she had missed not having Ed keeping a reassuring protective eye on her. Fortunately work had been busy, but she was just going through the motions. Not that the punters either noticed or cared. Most of them were either too drunk or too horny to. She was just glad the day was over.

She opened the front door and was greeted by the lingering smell of that morning's breakfast; another reminder of Ed's absence. She walked through to the living room and opened the window to let in some fresh air, before heading to the kitchen to make a coffee. When she turned on the kitchen light, the first thing she saw was the biggest bouquet of flowers she had ever received in her life. Not that she had received that many; suitors in her profession had been very few and far between. She picked them up and pushed her face into the petals, and inhaled deeply. They smelt as good as they looked and the aroma made her heady. She put them back in the sink and opened the card on the work surface. The picture was a cute puppy, with large, dark doleful eyes. Even before she started to read the card, tears were prickling the corners of her eyes.

# Chapter 20

Ed awoke, cold, stiff and miserable, having spent the night in the passenger seat of his car with the seat as horizontal as he could get it. Sleep had been a long time coming, and interrupted. He looked at the clock on the dashboard and was surprised to see it was nearly seven o'clock. He stepped from the car and stretched, feeling his joints crack and pop as he did. He took a few deep breaths of the fresh morning air and walked the short distance to the services. He was only two miles from home but, being cautious, he didn't want to go there until it was light and he could assess the situation. In his tired and emotional state, the last thing he needed was to walk into his house and find he had unwanted guests. After using the toilets to freshen up, even buying a chewable toothbrush from the vending machine, which tasted like chewing gum but did lift the fur from his teeth, he went in search of breakfast. He wasn't particularly hungry but he didn't know when his next meal would be, so thought he would eat while he could.

The fry-up looked good but the eggs were cold, the yolks rock-hard, and the white was rubbery. The sausages were warm and tasteless as was the bacon, and the baked beans were like mini bullets. Overall, it was all very unsatisfactory as well as being overpriced. It wasn't a patch on the two fry-ups TJ had made for him. The one redeeming factor was the coffee, which was strong and hot and managed to flush away the taste of the greasy fry-up.

He completed the short journey home in a few minutes. As he drove up the road to his house, he noticed a dark-blue Mercedes, parked in front of his drive. He didn't notice anyone in the car but, rather than arouse suspicion, he carried on and pulled up onto

Julie and Mark's drive next door. He exited the car, shielded by the shrubs separating the two drives, and entered the gate to the rear garden. Edging along the side of the house, he peered round the corner, his heart pounding loudly. He looked into the conservatory, which was empty, then crept slowly along the wall and looked into the kitchen, where Julie was making coffee. Ed noticed four mugs and his heart raced. Julie looked up, saw him and froze. She shook her head quickly and motioned with her eyes that they had company, which Ed assumed was the police. Either the police, or Jim and Spike were chancing their luck. He nodded and returned back to the side of the house, where he slumped to the floor, hugging his knees to keep warm. It seemed a long time before Mark came out and gave him the all clear.

'Bloody hell, mate, you look like shit,' Mark said cheerily. 'They've gone now. You can come in and warm up. You look frozen.'

Ed got slowly to his feet and blew out a long breath. 'Thanks, Mark. I think I owe you an explanation,' he said feebly. Mark nodded and put an arm on his back and pushed him towards the kitchen door.

Fat Boy was more than a little pleased to see him, whining, wagging his tail and spinning round, before collapsing on the floor to receive a belly rub. Julie came in and gave him a steaming mug of black coffee and sat down next to Mark on the couch. Both were looking at him expectantly.

'I take it that was the police?' he asked. They both nodded in unison. 'Was it a DI Blackthorn and DS Denton by any chance?' They both nodded again. 'Can I ask you what they told you?'

'They want to question you about a murder. Not that I believed them, pair of shifty buggers they were,' Julie

132

said, her voice shaky and nervous. Ed hoped it was a result of Blackthorn's visit and not because of him.

'OK. The club I've been working in is a lap-dancing club.' Mark was impressed but Julie wrinkled her nose up. 'Long story, but it was only supposed to be for two weeks. The club is actually quite respectable - or as respectable as that sort of thing goes. Those two coppers who just paid you a visit are bent and are supplying drugs to the owner. The owner wanted me on the books full time, for one reason or another. To trap me, he tells me to shoot the barman, as he was on the fiddle. If I didn't, he'd shoot me. I had no choice really so I sort of went through with it. What I mean is, I pretended to,' Ed added hastily, when Julie recoiled in horror. 'They took us out to some waste ground and I fired a bullet into the ground and got the guy to fake it. I threw the gun down in disgust and walked off. One of the others obviously came back and finished him off with a bullet to the back of the head. The owner tried to blackmail me so I gave a couple of them a slap, including the owner, and did a runner. And here I am.'

Mark and Julie looked at him, stunned. Ed looked back at them, urging them to say something to break the silence.

'Do you know how hard that is to take in?' Julie said eventually. Ed nodded 'I find it even harder to believe you'd kill anyone, though,' she said, giving him a reassuring smile.

'So, if they're bent and know you didn't kill him, why are they bothering you? What's the point?' Mark asked.

'Well, for one, the owner's pissed off with me, so it's vindictive. I either join his band of brothers in a life of crime or I go behind bars. I think he also might be a bit pissed off that I stole his briefcase - accidentally. I smacked him round the head with it and ran. I was so fired up, I didn't even realise I had it. So that could be another reason, but mostly it's just to get even. Somehow, I need to prove my innocence and I haven't got a clue how to go about doing that. I'm a bit fucked. Excuse the French. So, what were those two after, then?' he asked, putting his head in his hands and raking his fingers through his hair.

'They asked when was the last time we saw you? I had to let him into your house. He said it would save breaking the door down. Sorry, Ed,' Julie said apologetically.

'Do you know if they took anything?'

'I don't think so. I was looking out the window of course, like you do, and didn't notice anything being taken.'

'What are you going to do next?' Mark asked.

Ed shrugged. 'Nip next door and have a nice shower. Then I'm going to pack a few bits and make myself scarce and try and think of something useful to do. To be honest, I don't know. Can I ask you something? Do you believe me?'

'Of course we do! It's a lot to take in and you have to admit it's a bit like a film plot, but we've known you a long time and know you're not a liar - and you're certainly not a killer,' Julie told him.

Ed smiled weakly. 'Thanks. That means a lot to me. Look, thanks for looking after the dog. Once I've sorted this bloody mess out, I'll take you out for dinner or something, to say thanks properly. Right now, I need to get a shift on and go and lose myself.'

'Ed, be careful and don't do anything stupid,' Julie said earnestly.

Ed laughed out loud 'You're the second person to say that to me in as many days. I'll give you the same answer. I'll be careful, but I can't promise not to do anything stupid.' He smiled broadly but neither Julie nor Mark seemed particularly convinced.

Ed only had a quick shower, wanting to get on the road as quickly as possible, and still felt dirty, despite smelling a whole lot better. The three days' stubble on his face did little to help, but that would come off as soon as he had more time. During his short shower, he had made up his mind to go to the Lake District. He wanted to be as far away from London as possible but also be somewhere he was familiar with. The Lake District ticked both those boxes. He grabbed his rucksack and walking clothes and a few other essentials and threw them in a holdall. Next he packed up bedding, bowls and food for Fat Boy and headed out to the car, still parked on next doors' drive. First stop, St Albans.

# Chapter 22

Just pulling up outside Laura's house and looking at the front door made him nervous. He hadn't seen her for a month and had no idea what her reaction would be. She hadn't returned his calls, replied to his texts or emails; so would she even open the front door? Ed hoped so, but was less than confident. No time like the present, he said to himself, and stepped out of the car, releasing Fat Boy from the boot. He jumped out clumsily and sniffed around the borders, urinating on his chosen bush before trotting up to the front door, wagging his tail excitedly next to Ed.

The front door opened and Ed looked down at Laura, sitting in her wheelchair. She stared open-mouthed at Ed, who smiled back nervously. Fat Boy showed no such reservations and put his paws in Laura's lap and began licking her face. He received a warm welcome in return, which seemed to be more than Ed was getting.

'You'd better come in,' she said flatly, turning her wheelchair round and heading down the hallway. Ed closed the door and followed. In the living room, Ed bent down and kissed her on the cheek, which seemed strange having been so intimate with her only a few weeks ago.

'I know I promised not to come round, but I need a really big favour, Laura. I know we agreed I wouldn't come round until after the operation, whenever that is, but this really is an emergency. I wouldn't have come otherwise.'

Laura studied him and noted the almost-pleading look on his face. She sighed. 'It better be good,' she told him. He nodded.

'Are you OK in the wheelchair, or do you want me to lift you onto the sofa?' he said, more because he wanted to hold her and hug her than anything else. Laura could see through the guise and shook her head.

'Just tell me what the emergency is,' she said tersely.

'OK but don't interrupt, or I'll be here all day. I know what you're like.' Laura nodded and raised her eyes to the ceiling.

When Ed had finished - giving her the long version with all the gory details - he got the usual slack-jawed disbelief.

'Wow, that's some story,' was all she managed to say.

'I'm telling you this, just in case the police, probably Blackthorn and Denton, come round here, telling you I'm a murdering thief. I'm neither. If they ask if you've seen me, tell them I dropped the dog off and didn't say where I was going, OK?'

'You're something else, you are. Why the hell did you say you'd work there in the first place? Surely you must have known it was dodgy?' she said, annoyed that Ed could be so naive.

'I was bored and missing you and I thought it would be a bit of fun and a good way of killing time. I thought it might be a bit dodgy, but how could I have known it was so bloody corrupt?'

'Was she pretty?'

'Who, the dancer?' Laura nodded. 'Of course she was. The club wouldn't make much money if the dancers had figures like sacks of potatoes and faces like bags of spanners, would they? Anyway, what's that got to do with anything?' he said quickly, wanting to steer clear of a conversation about TJ. Laura would know he'd been unfaithful. Women had a knack of just knowing. 'Look, I'm in the shit. I've not slept properly for two nights, I'm totally shattered and I'm bloody scared shitless! Just let me know if you can look after

137

the dog for a week or so, please, and I'll be out of here.'

'Of course you can. I'm sorry, Ed. That was a bit insensitive of me. Where are you going to go?'

'Lake District, far enough from London and somewhere vaguely familiar. That's the other favour I need. Can I use your computer to book something?'

Laura gave him a smile and wheeled out into the study. Ed went out to the car and came back with Fat Boy's bedding, food and bowls, and left them in the kitchen. When he walked into the study, the computer was just finishing its start-up routine. Ed took up position, opened up the internet browser, and began to type. Laura watched as Ed found a website and a vacant cottage in Ambleside. When it came to paying he checked his back pocket and didn't have his wallet on him, as he'd thrown it into his holdall. Laura got her purse and he paid, using her credit card. Ed promised to pay her back as soon as he had sorted out his current predicament.

'If you stay a bit longer, you can say hello to mum and Bob,' she told him.

'Bob's here? I'm not sure I want to speak to him. I spoke to him on the phone a few days ago and he wasn't exactly thrilled about my choice of temporary employment, so I'll give that a miss if you don't mind. I don't need an ear-bashing from him. Shame I'll miss Raechael, though. I still think she's sweet on me,' he said, trying to wind her up.

'Very funny, and I'm not going to bite. Ed, I know it's a bit late to say it, but don't do anything stupid.'

'I won't, and do me a favour. Don't tell Bob where I am.'

'I'll try not to, but you know what he's like,' she said, smiling weakly.

'Yeah, I know. I'd better go now. Thanks for looking after Fat Boy and I'll see you in a week or hopefully before, when I pick him up.' He bent down and kissed her on the cheek again. This time she held his hand and leaned forward and kissed him on the lips. Chancing his luck, he asked, 'Are you going to tell me when the operation is?'

She shook her head. 'Nothing's changed, Ed. We've been through all this and this is something I have to do. When I've had the operation, I'll let you know and we can talk about it, not before.'

She gave him a sad smile. Ed looked down at her. Today her long dark brown hair was pulled back in a ponytail, rather than cascading over her shoulders. She was also wearing her glasses, rather than her contact lenses, slightly obscuring her eyes. She looked as stunning as usual. The urge to give her a hug was overwhelming but he knew it would be unwelcome. She had made her position clear and had driven a wedge between them. Although he didn't like it, he had to respect her decision to put their relationship on hold until after her operation. Laura's decision changed nothing for Ed but he had become increasingly worried that for Laura the operation, successful or not, had changed everything. Ed smiled, made a huge fuss of Fat Boy, closed the door behind him and set off for Ambleside.

# Chapter 23

Denton had been busy contacting the bank, arranging alerts each time Ed used his bank and credit cards. The bank official wanted paperwork and authorisation, which Denton had brushed aside. A few white lies on how dangerous Ed was and how he was likely to strike again without provocation got him halfway there. The clincher was asking the bank official if he wanted another death on his conscience, just because the paperwork wasn't ready. Now, each time Ed used his card Denton would be called personally and advised where it was used.

It was a similar story with the mobile phone company. Denton would have loved to get a tap on Ed's mobile but that was difficult and, without the right authorisation from a very senior level, would put him in a lot of trouble. There would also be a public outcry given recent adverse publicity around the News of the World phone tapping scandal. He satisfied himself with a tag on the phone, where the phone company would send him updates on where the phone was as Ed moved around the country and the mobile passed from cell to cell on the network.

Denton was quite pleased with his morning's work and now knew that Ed was currently heading north out of St Albans. He made a call to Johnny to tell him Ed had been located. Johnny in turn rang Dave, who was sitting in a lay-by on the A10 on the outskirts of London with Paul and Andy, waiting for directions. Andy and Paul were not Dave's first choice of teammates but Johnny wanted Jim and Spike with him, just in case Ed decided to turn up at the club. Dave grinned at the thought of Johnny sitting in his office, half scared to death, fretting that Ed might come back to finish the job. He seemed to be more frightened of

Ed turning up unannounced than he was of Mo or Blackthorn. Having seen the state of Jim's face, maybe he had reason to be. Ed must have a punch like a freight train, he thought; not that you would know that by looking at him. Dave made a mental note to keep his wits about him when he caught up with Ed; which he would, in good time.

Ed was on the M1 with his iPod plugged in and set to shuffle. The complete randomness of track selection was OK in some respects, in that the next track to be played was always a complete surprise, but was also frustrating. Having listened to a string of late 70s punk classics, it would be rudely interrupted by an obscure piece of classical music by Wagner and he'd have to lean across and skip to the next track.

The M1 gave way to the M6 and Ed was flagging. His lack of sleep over the last two weeks and the last few days in particular, coupled with the stress he was under, was taking its toll. He decided that he would stop at the next services and take a break and take the opportunity to fill up with petrol. The thirteen miles to the services as indicated by the road sign dragged, as his eyes became grittier and tiredness began to take a firm hold.

He filled up with petrol first and paid cash. Having paid to have his car stolen, it didn't leave a lot left and a top-up was required. The services were busy and he had to search for a parking space but finally found one. It was a tight squeeze, nestled in between two ridiculously large people-carriers, where he only just had room to open the door to exit the car. Maybe it was a good thing that the government was trying to tax them out of existence.

The main building at the services was heaving with bodies and was incredibly noisy. Quite why service stations felt the need to have amusement arcades was something Ed couldn't understand. After driving for miles on the motorway, why did anyone want to jump into the seat of a computer generated arcade game? Driving on the motorway was challenging enough for Ed and in some instances a lot more dangerous. Arcade games didn't have drivers falling asleep at the wheel and caravans that lurched dangerously at the slightest of breezes.

Ed made his way through the crowds and located the cash machines and replenished his wallet, unaware that this simple task was placing him in danger. He then queued up to pay for a cardboard sandwich and bottle of water, which millilitre for millilitre was more expensive than vintage champagne. Finding somewhere to eat his purchases was more difficult than finding a parking spot. He finally managed to find a space in the far corner, but it was standing room only. From where he was he had a good vantage point and could see the entire eating area and beyond, and he was able to keep a watchful eye on his surroundings, just in case.

Halfway through his sandwich, the noise level suddenly increased as a coach load of football fans came marching in, drunk and singing "I'm forever blowing bubbles," very loudly. Ed looked up at the sea of claret and blue that was descending upon the cafeteria, much to the horror of some of the current patrons. Many of them quickly finished their coffees and lunches and departed. A group of the supporters made their way over to the tables recently vacated, next to where Ed was standing. They pulled open their cardboard sandwiches and ate them with more enthusiasm than Ed thought possible and washed them down with beers they produced from a large carrier bag stashed under the table with equal, if not more, enthusiasm.

Ed finished his sandwich, which was so dry it sapped every last drop of moisture from his mouth, and washed it down with some water.

'These sarnies are fucking shit, eh, mate?' one of the West Ham fans said to him.

'They're OK, if you've got a fetish for expensive cardboard,' Ed replied.

'Too right. Three and a half quid for this shit. It's bloody daylight robbery! Who do you support, mate?' he asked.

'You won't like the answer, but it's Chelsea,' Ed said, grinning.

'Bunch of wankers. Stole all our best players.'

'We sold you a few duff ones in return,' Ed said laughing.

'I'd rather have Joe Cole than Carlton Cole,' he replied. And so the conversation continued. They were travelling to Manchester and were pessimistic about picking up anything from the game against United but it was always a good day out, away from the wife and kids. The good-humoured banter was a nice respite for Ed, taking his mind off his current and dire situation. It didn't last long.

Ed looked up and saw Dave enter, followed by Andy and Paul, obviously looking for him. How the hell did they know he was here? Ed panicked. His heart raced and his legs trembled slightly. Were Jim and Spike here as well? They hadn't seen him yet but it was only a matter of time. He needed to get out, and quickly. The supporter he had been talking to, who he only knew as 'mate', noticed Ed looking agitated.

'What's up, mate?' he asked. Ed crouched down to avoid being seen.

'I need a favour. Can I borrow your hat and scarf?' 'Mate' looked at him suspiciously.

'What the fuck for?'

'There's three blokes just walked in and they're looking for me. I pissed off some seriously dodgy people in London and they want to measure me up for a pair of concrete boots. I need to get out of here a bit sharpish.' Mate took off his hat and gave it to Ed, who donned it quickly. Mate then pulled a scarf off his startled friend opposite and handed it to Ed, who draped it round his neck.

'Right, let's go,' he said, picking up his beer can. Ed snatched up one of the empties on the table and they filed out en-masse, to another raucous chorus of "I'm forever blowing bubbles". Like a flock of sheep, it seemed to be the catalyst for all the other supporters to follow. Ed made sure he was in the middle of the crowd and kept his head down. Dave paid them little attention, his eyes scanning the other occupants of the eating area. Nonetheless, walking by within touching distance was a nerve-wracking experience. Ed's pulse was going off the scale and sweat trickled down his back, making him shudder involuntarily.

Outside, Ed was about to remove his hat and run to his car, when he saw Asif, Abdul and Mo, watching the entrance. Ed's heart sank further. How the hell did they know he was here as well? Was his car bugged? That would explain why it was so easy to get it back. If that was the case, then surely they would have followed him in the early hours of the morning, where they could have grabbed him under cover of darkness. Clearly, that wasn't how they had tracked him. Right now wasn't the time to be worrying about that. Right now was the time to be thinking about getting away, and quickly. Six to one was not the type of odds Ed liked; even less so, knowing they were all likely to be carrying guns.

'Mate. My car's over there,' Ed said pointing. 'Can you cover me to the car, please? Those three Asian

144

guys are part of the same gang,' he added, shifting his eyes to the right, towards Mo. Mate nodded and he and four of his companions veered off from the main crowd and headed to Ed's car. Ed was relieved when they reached it, and apart from a quick glance over his shoulder to see that Mo and his sidekicks were still guarding the entrance to the building, he kept his back to them. Ed pulled the hat and scarf off and handed them back. He pulled out his wallet and gave the guy a couple of twenty pound notes.

'Thanks mate. Have a drink on me to celebrate your three points,' he said with a grin, knowing it was extremely unlikely.

'Yeah, right. More like drowning our sorrows, but thanks and good luck. You know, I always thought all Chelsea fans were a bunch of wankers, but you're OK.' Ed laughed. Coming from a West Ham fan, that was quite a compliment.

# Chapter 24

Denton rang Johnny, advising him that Ed was on the move and heading north. Johnny slammed the phone down and looked across at Jim.

'The little bastard's given Dave the slip. Give him a call and tell him to get back on the road. Tell him to put his foot down. If it means he loses his licence, I don't give a shit. I want that briefcase back ASAP! Fucking amateurs.'

'He's obviously got somewhere in mind that he's going to. When he gets there, it'll be easy enough to find him,' Jim said, trying to put a positive slant on the situation.

Johnny looked thoughtful and slammed his fist down on the table. He picked the phone up and dialled. 'Blackthorn, it's Johnny. See if you can get credit card statements for our mutual friend. I think he's booked in somewhere, and to do that you need a credit card,' he said, pleased with his suggestion.

'Johnny, it's going to be difficult. It's all very well getting an alert put on the use of the card, but getting statements is going to need higher authorisation.'

'You're supposed to be running a murder enquiry. You've got a murder weapon with his prints all over it. Surely it can't be that difficult to get some pen pusher to put a cross on a piece of paper. Why is it I feel like I'm doing everyone's fucking job here? Just do it!'

He slammed the phone down and kicked over the wastepaper basket in frustration. He needed to go easy with Blackthorn. He might be bent but he didn't trust him, and he knew the feeling was mutual. They had plenty of reasons to distrust each other. If he pushed too hard, it might prove to be a mistake; another one. Johnny silently cursed Ed. How one insignificant person could have stirred up so much trouble was a mystery. Johnny blamed himself for underestimating him so badly. Part of him admired Ed's tenacity, but the rest of him wanted to see him beg for his life, as he inflicted more pain on him than he could believe possible, before slowly killing him. Johnny poured himself another whisky and knocked it back in one, finding the burning sensation satisfying. He lit yet another cigarette, inhaled deeply, and let out a hacking cough. He clutched his chest, taken by surprise by the sharp pain, which made him gasp. Jim smiled to himself, amused by Johnny's discomfort.

The two and a half hour drive had given Ed plenty of time to think. He picked up the keys for the cottage from the holiday agency office, passing himself off as Mr Jacobs, husband of Laura, which was the name on the credit card booking. After unloading his few belongings, he drove round to the town car park and left the car there. He was working on the assumption that if his friends from London could track him down to a service station, they could find him here in Ambleside. He made a mental note to stock up on change for the car park. The last thing he wanted was a clamp, when he might need to make a quick getaway. He would also look for other options but assumed that a lot of the parking in the side streets would be permit-holders only. He would check that out later.

First on his list of things to do was to get a haircut. Ed hoped that nestled in amongst the outdoor wear and tea shops he would find one. He wandered round and eventually found one in St Mary's Lane. It wasn't exactly a salubrious affair but for what Ed had in mind, it would suffice. It was also empty, apart from two bored-looking women, who were talking animatedly. They both turned to look at Ed when he walked in. The one nearest indicated to a chair, with a welcoming smile.

'What would you like, love?' she asked.

'I want a skinhead. Take the lot off, please,' Ed said smiling.

'Wrong time of year for that, isn't it? Need all the insulation you can get up here, this time of year,' she said, chuckling at her own joke.

'Probably, but go for it. I've got a woolly hat.'

'How short do you want it, number one, number two?'

'Dunno. Just take it down to the bone. Whatever, that is.'

She picked up the clippers and turned them on, but paused before starting to shear. 'Are you sure about this, love?' she asked.

'Go for it,' Ed said happily. He had no idea what it would look like and whether it would suit him, but he didn't care. He just wanted to look different. When she had finished and stood back to admire her work, he certainly looked different.

'Do you want me to do anything with the whiskers?' she asked. 'It looks a bit like your head's on upside down,' she added, and she and her colleague, burst into laughter.

Ed stared back at his unfamiliar reflection in the mirror, both horrified and pleased with the results. 'I'll sort the face fungus out later, thanks,' he finally replied.

'Anything for the weekend, sir?' she asked. Both of them laughed raucously again.

'With this look, I don't think I'll be needing anything else, do you?' he replied, joining in their laughter.

They both declined to answer. 'That'll be six pounds please, love,' she said, suppressing more laughter.

Ed handed her a ten pound note and told her to keep the change. With a final look in the mirror and a shake of the head, he walked towards the door. The cold northern air hit him immediately. It felt like he had immersed his head in a bucket of dry ice. He stepped up his pace and went in search of glasses and some new clothes. He found a ridiculous pair of round, reactolite, John Lennon style sunglasses, which he paid for and donned immediately. He chose reactolite as he could wear them during the day and in the evening, to further enhance his new look.

He found a menswear shop and bought a couple of loud shirts. One was a mustard colour, which Ed hated immediately, and the other a nasty shade of green, which he also hated on sight. Next he found a couple of equally hideous jumpers, which wouldn't have looked out of place on a golfing green. There was a pair of particularly offensive trousers but he thought that might be overdoing things a little. He would stick to jeans.

# Chapter 25

The cottage was situated in a small courtyard of five purpose-built holiday lets, just off the one way system. The front door opened into a spacious living room, which was neutrally decorated with numerous prints of Lake District scenes on the walls, as seemed the norm with holiday lets in the area. There was an open wooden staircase on the left and at the back a door to the kitchen, which ran the width of the cottage. Upstairs there were two reasonably-sized double bedrooms and a functional bathroom with a shower over the bath. It was in there that Ed got to work on his whiskers. Initially he thought about shaving them all off, but decided to experiment. He left the sideburns long and combined that with a goatee, but he decided he looked too much like a paedophile. The beard was shaved off and the sideburns shortened to a sensible length, just leaving the moustache. Ed stared back and barely recognised himself, which was the effect he wanted. If he couldn't, neither would anyone else. He showered and changed into his hideous cream cable knit jumper, and donned his new glasses. A look in the full length mirror made him laugh. It was a very camp look and he hoped it didn't attract too much attention, from either homophobic or homosexual males. The last thing he needed right now was a fight - or a fuck, come to that.

Extremely pleased with his transformation but not especially happy with looking so overtly gay, he ventured out to the supermarket to get some essentials. It was appreciably colder than it was an hour ago and his recently-acquired bald head was having trouble acclimatising. He had contemplated putting his woolly hat on but decided that it might make him more recognisable and so braved the inclement weather, commando style. The streets were relatively empty which made it easy for Ed to spot his pursuers, should they have followed him to Ambleside. He pushed the thought to the back of his mind but deep down, he knew that he had or that they were not far behind him, hot on his trail.

On the way back, laden with two full carrier bags, he thought he was going to get into a fight when one of two young lads took offence to Ed's new look. He called him a few names but his companion suggested he leave it. Fortunately for Ed, he took his friend's advice. Brawling in the street would be a bit of a giveaway, should he be spotted by Dave or Mo.

Back at the cottage, Ed cracked open a bottle of lager and some peanuts and sat on the floor with the TV on, just for some background noise. He pulled the silver attaché case towards him and tried to open it. The two locks remained firm. He thought it would be too easy for the two, three digit combination locks to be set to the open code. He set both barrels to 000 and tried again and, as expected, it remained firmly shut. Starting with the left hand lock, he flicked over the last barrel one digit, to 001 and tried again. A quick calculation, assuming around a second to change the number, Ed reckoned he could crack each lock in about twenty minutes. That was assuming he had to try each one, the full thousand combinations. That would mean each lock being set to 999, which surely was unlikely. He tried it just in case and drew a blank. Would a dishonest bastard like Johnny choose 999? It seemed unlikely, unless he chose it in a moment of irony.

The first lock sprung open on 748, fifteen minutes and two beers later. He quickly tried the same number on the right hand but the lock remained firm. He reset it to 000 and started the laborious task of incrementing and trying again. It took him slightly longer but the lock opened on 847. It was an obvious choice in hindsight and Ed cursed himself for not trying all the obvious ones first. The important thing was it was open, and his heart was pounding. The excitement of finding out what he was being pursued up and down the country for was mounting.

Ed slowly lifted the lid. The stench hit him like a wall and he closed the lid again. 'Jesus Christ,' he said aloud. The smell was awful and somehow familiar, but he couldn't put his finger on it. He opened the lid again, peered inside, and laughed. Nestling on top of what appeared to be a large amount of cash were Johnny's sandwiches. Tightly packed in clingfilm and stinking to high heavens. Out of curiosity, he peeled back the packaging and flipped over the top slice of bread. He studied the contents, which revealed themselves as tuna chunks and onion. Ed wrapped it back up and put it in the rubbish bin, outside the front of the property.

Back inside, Ed started to take the cash out of the attaché case and began counting it. There were bundles of twenty and fifty pound notes. Each one contained a thousand pounds, or so he assumed as he only counted a few, selected at random. All the notes were used, which ruled out Ed's first guess that they were counterfeit. No wonder Johnny was so keen to get his attaché case back. Ed sat there staring at the pile of cash, wondering what to do with it. He ran his hand over his freshly shaved head, smiled, and turned his attention back to the attaché case. The two pockets revealed nothing, other than a small calculator and a nice monogrammed Mount Blanc pen. He'd keep that too, he decided. Hopefully, it had a high sentimental value to Johnny and he'd miss it. Ed picked up the case and gave it a shake. Something heavy moved inside, knocking against the sides of the case, which surprised him as it appeared to be empty. Ed turned it upside down and two A4 ledgers, held together by a rubber band, fell out between his legs. Ed looked inside the attaché case and realised it had a false bottom. Now satisfied it was completely empty, after giving it a further shake, he pushed it to one side.

Ed picked up the ledgers and removed the elastic band that held them together. He opened the top one and searched for the last entry. Ed whistled, now fully understanding why Johnny was so pissed off with him. The ledger contained names and dates, showing payments and, in some entries, weights. Next to the weights was a letter, either a C or H, which Ed assumed would denote either cocaine or heroin. Ed didn't have much of a clue on drug quantities but the amounts in the ledger varied, between eight and twenty kilos. In Ed's mind, twenty kilos was twenty bags of sugar, which seemed quite a lot. Most of the recent entries indicating the weights were against Blackthorn and Mohamed, as were most of the large payments out. Interestingly enough, there were regular monthly payments to Blackthorn and Denton of a thousand and five hundred pounds, respectively. If Blackthorn knew about Ed's find it could be interesting, unless he already did. Ed now had another dilemma; what to do with the ledgers, which were probably a lot more valuable to certain people than the three quarters of a million cash. Ed smiled, thinking that he was now in a good bargaining position, assuming he stayed alive long enough to bargain.

# Chapter 26

After making short work of a sad meal for one and washing it down with a bottle of wine, Ed decided on an early night, the events of the last two days finally catching up with him. The beer and a whole bottle of red wine also played their part. He slept soundly and woke early, feeling refreshed and ready to face the world. To his delight he didn't have a hangover, and felt rather smug about it.

He checked the loose change situation and was happy to find he had enough for the car park for the day. That would be his first call, before setting off on a long walk. He walked towards the car park, remaining vigilant whilst in the town, just in case. There was no guarantee that he had been followed all the way to Ambleside, but instinct told him otherwise. He stopped off at the bank, having spent most of his cash on clothes that he hated and his few provisions. He inserted his card but only statements and balance requests were available. Ed looked in his wallet and decided he had enough cash for lunch, and for anything else there was his credit card. He put his card back in his wallet and headed off through town, making a mental note to find another bank on his return to Ambleside later that day. Right now, he needed get his head together and the best way to do that was a long, peaceful walk around the lakes and fells.

The bank immediately contacted Denton, to inform him of the recent transaction. Denton finally got something other than Johnny's answering machine and he in turn had woken Dave up, telling him to get his arse in gear and get his money back. Time could have been saved if Johnny allowed Denton to speak directly with Dave, but Johnny wanted to know everything that was going on. By the time Dave had left his hotel, Ed was well on his way to Rydal water, en-route to Grasmere.

Once past the outskirts of the town, Ed pulled on his woolly hat, to keep the chill off his head. The wind was biting but the sun was shining, gradually warming the air, on what looked to be a perfect day for walking. Ed wasn't counting his chickens. He knew how quickly the weather could change in this area. He had been caught out before and ended up stuck for two hours, waiting for the mist and drizzle to disperse so he could find his way back. Now he packed a waterproof jacket and trousers whenever he went walking, even in the summer when the sun was blazing.

He walked through the park and up a long winding road, which seemed to go on for ever. By the time Ed reached the end of the road, which turned into a footpath above Rydal water, he was sweating and his legs were aching. The result, he decided, of not enough exercise and too many fry-ups. When this latest episode in his life was finally over, he was going on a strict exercise regime and diet. If Blackthorn got his way, he wouldn't have a choice; prison food would be his only option and an hour walking round the exercise yard each day.

Ed found a nice flat rock to sit on and took off his rucksack, to take in the view and work out what to do about his current predicament. Would the money and the two ledgers that went back to the mid-seventies be of any use to him? Sure, he could use it as a bargaining chip with Johnny and Blackthorn, but what would happen once he handed them over? Surely they would just go back on their word and he would be no further forward. If Ed copied them and kept them with a solicitor, would that make a difference? Ed thought perhaps not, and that only the originals would be of any value. There was always the option of taking them straight to the police. Who in the police he could trust to use them and not destroy them, he didn't know, and that was a risk. If he walked into a police station and told them his story, it was unlikely that he would be believed. The clincher would be his prints all over the gun that killed Barry.

The other complication was Mo. Did he just want his money back or did he have a hidden agenda, after their run-in at the club just over a week ago? The way Ed's luck was going, it was probably personal as well as the money, so handing it over to Mo wouldn't achieve a great deal. If he killed Johnny and handed over the ledgers to Blackthorn and split the money between him and Mo, would that work? Ed thought it might, but the one problem he had was that he couldn't kill Johnny in cold blood. He liked to think he could, but deep down the only way he could kill Johnny would be in the heat of the moment, like what happened on Friday night. The bottom line was Ed was in deep shit and there was no obvious way out. He put his head in his hands and stared out across Rydal water, wishing for his life back.

TJ, like Ed, was feeling sorry for herself, sitting on the sofa, hugging a cushion to her chest. She was staring across the room, looking at the flowers that she had placed in three vases with the card positioned in front of them on the sideboard. She felt guilty and that she was somehow responsible for Ed's current predicament, because she had talked him into working at Johnny's in the first place. She was worried that she hadn't heard from him and wondered if she should call him to thank him for the flowers, knowing that was just an excuse to hear his voice. She knew he was alright. If anything had happened, it would have been the talk of the club. Ed was the talk of the club, but not because

Johnny had caught up with him. TJ knew deep down in her heart that Ed had told the truth, no matter what the others at the club were telling her. Bizarrely, Pandora was the only other person at the club who shared her view, and even stood up for Ed when she overheard Debbie and Suzanne calling him a murdering, thieving bastard, which surprised TJ; Pandora was the most unlikely of allies. She hugged the pillow tighter, praying that Ed was safe and had worked out how to put an end to it all.

Johnny, having been woken early by Denton, was in a state of heightened agitation. He had spent most of the morning pacing nervously, when he wasn't on the phone to Dave, asking for updates. How could he have disappeared into thin air? The mobile phone was still registering in Ambleside, unless he had dropped it, having worked out it was partly the reason he had been followed. Johnny didn't think so, he wasn't that clever; or was he underestimating him again? He tried Blackthorn's phone again, which was still going straight to voicemail. He threw the phone onto the sofa and lit another cigarette. He let out a rattling cough and spat the phlegm he brought up into his handkerchief. Slightly worried, he poured himself another scotch, his third of the morning - and it wasn't even ten o'clock.

Blackthorn had been busy. He had managed to get the credit card company to email him copies of Ed's transactions over the last two weeks, which he was looking over. Nothing really stood out apart from a bill for just under a thousand pounds at the Ritz, the previous Wednesday. He would look into that later, to see if that yielded anything of interest. The phone company had been less willing to part with any call details, but he would resolve that on Monday. The search of Ed's house had been pointless and he found nothing of interest. It wasn't what he expected of a millionaire, which he now knew to be true, from bank and Inland Revenue searches. Johnny's house was bigger and nicer than his, and he wasn't a millionaire. The neighbours had been next to useless or had been lying, and claimed to know next to nothing about him. They'd known him for years and looked after his dog once in a while. He bought up houses, renovated them and sold them on, and had a girlfriend who was disabled but didn't live locally. It was all very uninteresting and absolutely no bloody use to him at all. Not that it really mattered; the murder charge was trumped up and if it went to court, based on the flimsy evidence he had, it would undoubtedly result in the little shit getting off. Blackthorn didn't intend it to get that far. If Ed did give evidence, it could open up a whole can of worms and end up with himself being investigated. Therefore, the only option was to find him and make him disappear.

# Chapter 28

Ed's quiet contemplation was broken by a brace of Golden Retrievers approaching from his left, followed by their owners. They were the first people Ed had seen all day. The retrievers wandered over to Ed to be made a fuss of, and he duly obliged. They were lighter in colour than Fat Boy but had similar big fat heads, with too much skin, which seemed to give them a multitude of expressions. The one to his left, bored of being stroked, turned his attention to Ed's rucksack, hoping to find a tasty snack. He did have a packet of crisps in there but didn't think the owners would take too kindly to him feeding their dogs. After a short while, it gave up on the rucksack and picked up Ed's woolly hat, tossed it in the air and ran after it. The second one, which Ed was still stroking, became more interested in the fun his mate was having and ran after him. A tug of war ensued between the two, which Ed found highly amusing.

The owners, an elderly couple who Ed guessed to be in their early seventies, were horrified and began calling the dogs back, but they were having far too much fun to take any notice. Both dogs had a mouthful of Ed's hat and stood facing each other, paws firmly planted, pulling and tugging to win the prize of the entire hat. When the owners caught up with Ed, they couldn't stop apologising.

'We're so sorry. It's so unlike them, they're usually so well behaved,' the woman said, horrified at their dogs' behaviour. The husband was doing his best to get the dogs to let go of the hat but they were having none of it. Ed pulled his mobile out of his rucksack and took a few snaps of them.

'It's exactly the sort of thing a retriever does. I've got one myself. Let them have it, it's only a woolly hat.

159

It's really not important and besides, it's about as much fun as I've had all week.'

The husband was still doing his best to persuade the dogs to let go, but he just seemed to be spurring them into pulling harder. With an audible tearing sound, the woolly hat finally gave up the struggle of holding itself together and both dogs ran round excitedly, holding their respective prizes. Ed howled with laughter. It wasn't just the dogs; it was the look of indignation on the husband's face as he wandered back, cursing his pets and apologising profusely once again.

'Like I said to your wife, it isn't a problem.' The husband pulled out his wallet and offered Ed a ten pound note. Ed looked at it and thought, I've got seventy five thousand of those in a carrier bag in my cottage. 'Look, the hat only cost about two quid and I should be paying you for the entertainment.' he said, wiping away tears of laughter.

'I suppose it was rather funny,' the woman said, putting her hand over her mouth and tittering. She received a stern look from the husband, who looked like he just wanted a hole to appear and swallow him up. With a final flurry of apologies and a further offer of payment, they departed with their dogs. Ed was sure the dogs looked at each other and sniggered.

He sat there a while longer, trying to blank out any further thoughts of his current situation, which was altogether rather depressing. Instead he took in the beautiful view of Rydal water, laid out in front of him. Despite the view being stunning, the glassy surface of the lake reflecting the tree-strewn hills opposite, it did little or nothing to lift his spirits. Sufficiently rested but rather depressed and now missing Fat Boy, just to add to his misery, he decided it was time to press on. Maybe walking would help snap him out of his doldrums.

Ed was walking briskly now, as the wind had picked up and his head was bloody freezing; poxy dogs. He was still chuckling to himself over the incident with the retrievers, despite his discomfort. He would buy a replacement hat when he reached Grasmere. The fresh air was doing him good with the exception of freezing his head and he was finally thinking straight. He had been worrying about his car being spotted. To get round the problem, he would take it to a garage for a service or to get the brakes looked at or some other minor, fictitious problem that he knew would take a couple of days.

He was also thinking about the murder charge and how it might not be as bad as he first thought. His fingerprints on the gun was pretty damning evidence, but would that alone stand up in court? If Ed was on the jury, then it probably would. He had always held the opinion that the police didn't arrest innocent people. Anyone in court on trial was obviously a criminal and known to the police. If they were innocent of that charge, then there was a good chance they were guilty of others but had been lucky. His bigoted opinion on this was changing, surprisingly.

If his murder charge went to court, his version of events, coupled with the ledgers and money he had, would surely swing the pendulum in his favour. The result would have to be a full investigation into Blackthorn, Denton and Johnny Gold. Wouldn't it? This line of thought cheered him up more than the two retrievers. He stopped dead in his tracks and cursed himself again for being so bloody naive. Of course, Blackthorn knew the murder charge was bollocks and would never get to court, which meant that the only reason he was pursuing the matter was to make sure it didn't go to court. That, of course, left only one other possibility. Johnny, Mo and Blackthorn all wanted him dead. Life was just getting better and better.

He walked moodily into Grasmere and arrived just before midday. At the first outdoor shop he came to he purchased a new hat, and then made for the pub to get a pint and a sandwich. The sandwich was cheaper than the one he had purchased at the service station and tasted a thousand times better. It was even served with a crisp green salad and a good handful of salted crisps. Now that was class. You wouldn't get that at the Ritz, he thought.

Ed was nursing his pint and contemplating a second, when he looked up and noticed that the pub was now full. A group of four were looking in his direction, clearly waiting for him to leave so they could order lunch. Ed got the hint and downed the last few dregs of his drink. Before he had even picked up his rucksack, they were taking position, making sure that changing his mind and ordering a second pint wasn't an option.

Ed strolled around Grasmere, going into the art galleries but finding nothing that he would want to hang on his wall or nothing different from what he already had. Disappointed, he walked out of the village on the main road, heading for Dove Cottage. On the way out, he noticed that kids had messed with the road signs and on one side of the road it announced the speed limit as twenty miles per hour and on the opposite, thirty. Ed smiled and wondered if that would hold up in court, if you were caught speeding. When he passed them, he turned around to see the same thing going into the village, and paused to take a photo.

The road, which took him past Dove Cottage, was steep and heavy going. When he reached the top he sat down on an empty bench and took in the magnificent views over Grasmere and the hills beyond; it was stunning. Ed was trying to decide whether it was better than Cornwall or not. It was a difficult call, as the two were so different. Cornwall had the rugged granite coastline and beautiful sandy beaches, which were as good as any found in the Caribbean. In comparison to the Lake District, it was relatively flat and couldn't compete with the views from the top of Coniston or the Haystacks. Cornwall edged it, Ed decided, on account of having a lot of friends there and the clincher - the Cornish pasty. Satisfied with his conclusion and rested sufficiently, he continued his journey in the direction of Ambleside.

Before reaching Ambleside, he took off his hat as a precaution and once again became vigilant, despite the day turning to dusk. Again, there was no sign of his pursuers and, not for the first time, he wondered if he was just paranoid. Once he reached the cottage, he had a final look around before inserting the key and opening the door. Satisfied he wasn't being watched, he entered the cottage and locked the door behind him.

Ed froze as a familiar voice from behind him said, 'Hello, mate.'

# Chapter 29

Ed reached up and switched on the light and turned round to see the unsmiling face of DCI Bob Brown.

'Bloody hell, Bob. You frightened the life out of me! How did you get in, anyway?'

'Oh, that's great that is. I come all the way up here to save your sorry arse, wasting my week's holiday, which I was looking forward to spending with Raechael, and that's the greeting I get,' he said abrasively.

'Sorry, Bob. You took me by surprise,' Ed said defensively.

'You need to be more careful. I could've been one of your mates from London and put a hole in your back.'

Ed nodded almost apologetically. 'So, how did you get in? More to the point, how did you know I was here?' Ed asked, going on the offensive.

Bob grinned back at him. 'When Raechael and I got in and found Fat Boy there, it was obvious you'd been round. Laura gave me all the details of why he was there and then cracked under pressure and told me where you were.' He seemed rather pleased with himself. 'Getting in was easy. Standard Yale lock; they're a piece of piss to pick. When you've got the right tools, that is,' he said, patting his jacket pocket. 'So, do you want to tell me all about it?'

'Didn't Laura tell you everything?' Ed asked sarcastically.

'I want to hear it from you and I want to know everything. Sounds like you've got yourself into some really deep shit this time, you cretin.'

'Can I grab a shower first? Look, there's beer and peanuts in the kitchen. Help yourself while I go and get cleaned up.'

'There isn't any,' he replied smiling.

'You mean you've drunk all my beer and scoffed all my nuts.'

Bob nodded and smiled, obviously pleased with having annoyed him. 'I didn't think you'd mind.'

'Same old Bob,' Ed replied exasperatedly, and trudged up the stairs.


Ed showered and shaved, leaving behind the moustache, which was now getting quite established. He put on his new mustard shirt, looked in the mirror, and wondered what Bob would make of his new look. He didn't have to wait long to find out.

'What the fucking hell do you look like?' were Bob's first comments, when Ed came down the stairs.

'I take it you don't like it, then?' Ed said grinning.

'You look like a bloody great nancy boy.'

'I needed a change of appearance, because I've been followed up here. I thought that a skinhead would do the trick. The glasses were an afterthought and the clothes; well, they sort of went with the camp look. Don't worry, I've not come out the closet, if that's what you're thinking. Your arse is safe with me.'

'Right then, Ed - or should I call you Edwina?' he said, laughing at his own joke. 'Now sit down and tell me everything, from the beginning, and don't leave anything out.'

Ed held up his hand and went into the kitchen and returned with a bottle of red wine and a bowl of crisps, in the absence of any beer and peanuts, and sat down in the armchair opposite Bob. He took a deep breath and told him everything, from the first Saturday night at Johnny's, through to evading Dave and Mo at the service station.

'Anything you've missed?' Bob asked, sensing something had been held back.

'There is the attaché case,' he replied, giving Bob a sly grin. 'I inadvertently ran out with it on the last night at the club. I'd used it to batter Johnny round the head and forgot to let go.'

'Where is it now?'

'I brought it up here, obviously. It's in the cupboard under the stairs.'

'Have you opened it yet?' he asked, his curiosity piqued.

'I have. It contained a tuna and onion sandwich, a bit of money, and a couple of ledgers,' Ed said, smiling, deliberately holding back.

'I'm assuming Johnny didn't send out a posse just to get his packed lunch back, so it must be the money and the ledgers. How much are we talking about?'

'Seven hundred and fifty,' Ed said, grinning broadly. 'Thousand.'

'Fuck me!' Bob exclaimed. 'That's probably not the best expression to use, with you looking like a raving woofter. What about the ledgers?'

'There's two of them and they contain a record of just about everything. Regular payments to Blackthorn and Denton, going back years, listed as DI Blackthorn and DS Denton. Quantities of drugs received from them and from Mo, and money paid to them for the goods received.' Ed gave Bob a wide grin.

'Ed. Your capacity for making friends and influencing people never ceases to amaze me. You've excelled yourself this time.' Bob leaned forward and ran his fingers through his hair and sat staring at Ed, deep in thought. 'OK, what's your take on the situation?'

'Funny you should ask that, I worked it all out earlier,' Ed replied. Bob gave him an exasperated look and nodded for him to continue. 'Mo wants his money and Asif wants to get even with me for the incident in the club. He doesn't give a monkeys about the ledgers, unless he knows about them, but my guess is, it's all about the money and revenge.' Bob nodded, which Ed took as agreement. 'Johnny also wants his money and revenge but also needs the ledgers back, as that could send him down for a long time. It's the same story for Blackthorn. He wants his money and the ledgers back, which will cost him his job and send him down for a long time if they become public. I think Johnny told him about the ledgers and is using that as leverage to get me in the frame for Barry's murder. That's about as far as I got.'

Bob nodded and gave him an approving look. 'Not bad, Sherlock. I reckon you're right. Blackthorn's arse must be twitching like a rabbit's nose. The prints on the gun would ensure the case got to court. That is, once they have you under arrest but he can't risk it going to court, now you have the ledgers. Using the ledgers as a bargaining chip might work but I think he's more likely to take the ledgers and kill you anyway. Also, if he has the ledgers, he's got Johnny in his pocket, rather than the other way round. Whatever way you look at this, you've got three sets of bad guys looking for you, and they all want to see you dead. Way to go, Ed.'

'So what do we do next then, Mister Big-shot?' Ed said angrily.

Bob sniffed. 'I don't know about you, matey, but I'm starving and dying of thirst, so you can buy me dinner.'

'Great plan, Bob. I wish I'd come up with something that brilliant,' Ed replied sarcastically. 'You come all the way up here and break into my cottage, just to tell me I'm in deep shit and to buy you dinner. Well thanks a lot, Bob. That's just the kind of help I need.' Ed stared at Bob angrily, feeling better for having vented his spleen at him. Bob grinned back and laughed.

'Oh shut up you tart,' he replied, 'and don't forget your handbag.'

# Chapter 30

They left the cottage and turned right onto the ring road, walking in the opposite direction to the one-way traffic, onto the main road. Ed was edgy and was constantly looking left, right and behind for signs of his pursuers. Bob found it amusing and told him he looked a prat and that he was drawing attention to himself, and suggested being a little more subtle. Ed glared at him and walked on in a moody silence.

'The pub's here,' Bob said, as Ed strolled past it.

'I haven't got any money, or not enough for the amount you drink. I'm off to the bank,' he replied curtly.

'Stroppy bastard. Haven't you stopped to think that they might have an alert on your card? Haven't you stopped and wondered about how they knew you were at the service station?'

Ed stopped and looked at Bob 'You know, I never really thought about it. You think they might have?'

'If it was my murder investigation I would, and I'd have one on your mobile. You know they can trace it, even if you don't use it? Every time you move it connects to the nearest base station, and that can be monitored. Just a thought, knuckle head.'

'I haven't even looked at my phone,' Ed shrugged. 'Well, if I can't use my card, then it looks like dinner's on you,' Ed said with a grin.

'Well, unless your phone's switched off, you might as well use it,' Bob replied smugly.

'You're putting me at risk just to get a free dinner - how low can you go?' Ed said, baiting him.

'Just get your cash out so we can get to the pub, I'm starving. Anyway, I've known you for years and didn't recognise you. How the hell are they going to with you looking like an extra from a gay porn film?'

Ed conceded the point and withdrew his maximum daily allowance, and they headed back towards the pub. Bob argued that the one over the road from the bank was nearer but Ed knew it didn't serve food and reluctantly Bob passed a pub, which was a first.

As they were heading back to the pub, Denton made his call to Johnny, having been alerted by the bank who in turn alerted Dave. He galvanised Andy and Paul into action and they drove into the centre of Ambleside from their hotel in the outskirts of town. Once parked, Dave suggested they split up to cover the ground more quickly. They headed off in separate directions to check every pub, restaurant and shop that was still open. Dave gave them strict instructions that they needed Ed alive and if any of them found him, they would phone the others and tackle Ed en-masse. They knew he was dangerous and it would probably take all three of them to subdue him. Dave was concerned that with the history between them, Andy and Paul would be out for revenge and he didn't want them shooting him, at least until they had recovered the briefcase. He deliberately didn't mention the money and the ledgers; he didn't trust them.

Bob and Ed took a table and browsed the menu in silence. Ed was conscious that he was receiving a few funny looks, which made him smile. He ordered at the bar, in as butch a voice as he could muster and wandered back to the table.

'I feel like a dirty old man, sitting here with you looking like that,' Bob hissed. Ed smiled and put his hand on Bob's forearm, which he shook off violently 'Get off, you cretin,' he barked, making Ed laugh, and one or two of the other patrons turn their heads and stare. This made Bob even more uncomfortable, and he scowled at Ed across the table.

'So, come on then, what's your big plan then. I'm buggered if I know what to do next,' Ed said, a little more relaxed.

'Well, we've got the ledgers, which gives us a bit of leverage. Basically, they need you alive until they get them. I've still got a few contacts fairly high up in the Met and as far as I know, they're straight. I'll give them a call and see if I can get Blackthorn out the way.'

'Thanks,' Ed replied 'That helps in the long run but in the short term, we've got six of London's biggest arseholes up here looking for me. What do we do about them?'

'I haven't worked that out yet. We could always leave your phone in the cottage and bugger off back South,' Bob said with a shrug.

'Sounds like a plan to me. I'll go with that in the absence of anything else.'

Bob raised his glass and finished his pint and went to the bar to get another round in. Ed was pleased that Bob had turned up. Despite their abrasive relationship, they had a good laugh and both had a lot of respect for each other. Not that either would admit it and they both rubbed along, happy to wind each other up as much as possible. It wasn't dissimilar to marriage really, in Ed's brief knowledge of such things.

The food arrived and they ate in silence. Ed hadn't realised how hungry he was, and ate his steak and chips quickly and with a lot of enthusiasm. Over the last two weeks, the only real meals he had eaten were the two occasions he had dined out with TJ. His diet had been poor and was mainly fast food, greasy fry-ups or whatever he managed to rustle up before leaving for work, which usually didn't amount to a great deal.

After finishing the second pint, Ed went to the gents. He felt a lot happier than he had done since everything had come tumbling down around him. What he would give to turn back the clock two weeks and do things much differently. His thoughts turned to TJ, who he was missing; he hoped she was safe and that Johnny hadn't worked out that she had helped him. The fact that he had thought of TJ and not Laura took him by surprise, and he immediately pushed the thought to one side. He had enough to deal with at present and a guilty conscience wasn't going to help his situation.

Ed walked out of the gents and headed back towards Bob. His heart skipped a beat. Andy was walking towards Ed, looking everywhere but at him; obviously, he didn't recognise him. The fact that his new look made him unrecognisable cheered him, but seeing Andy filled him with a hatred he didn't know he was capable of. When he got within touching distance, Ed launched a savage kick to his groin. Andy lurched forward, a look of disbelief in his eyes. He dropped to his knees, his hands instinctively cupping his crotch. Ed was on him like a flash, grabbing his head and smashing his knee into his face, once, twice and a third time, before taking a step back and kicking him in the side of the head. Andy slammed into the wall and lay on the floor, stunned and breathing heavily through his pulverised mouth. Blood was gushing from his flattened nose and split lips. He looked up at Ed with eyes barely able to focus, as Ed kicked him twice in the ribs.

Bob was running towards him, his eyes blazing with anger. Everyone else in the pub remained like statues, gawping at Ed and wondering how a four-eyed wiry poof could have taken out a man mountain like Andy with such ease. Ed looked at Andy, the hatred for him still coursing though his veins, and stamped down on

172

his ankle with as much force as he could muster. Ed heard the loud crack, as did many of the other patrons in the pub. A woman sitting at the nearest table jumped up with her hand over her mouth, and ran for the ladies.

Bob grabbed Ed and spun him round, slamming him roughly against the wall and deftly handcuffing him. 'You're fucking nicked.' he said loudly. Then turning round to the barman shouted 'You. Call an ambulance. Now!' He then pushed Ed towards the back entrance and the car park beyond. Ed staggered out and tripped on the step down to the car park. Bob grabbed him and stopped him going over on his face.

'I'm gonna be sick,' Ed told him shakily and rushed over to the perimeter wall and heaved, bringing up his dinner.

'What the bloody hell was that all about?' Bob shouted.

'That was Andy. He's one of Johnny's men,' Ed replied, his voice quavering

'Jesus, Ed. That was bloody spiteful by anyone's standards. He'll be limping for the rest of his life, that's for sure.'

Ed nodded and looked guilty. 'He didn't think about me walking with a permanent dribble the night he tried to take my head off with a baseball bat. I agree it was a bit uncalled for, but I'm not losing any sleep over that bastard.'

Bob steered him to the car park exit and removed the cuffs. 'You OK?' he asked, with a hint of concern.

'Yeah, fine, a bit shaky. To be honest, Bob, I didn't think I was capable of something like that. It came as a bit of a shock.'

Bob patted him on the back and gave him a sympathetic look. 'On the bright side, one down, five to go. Come on, let's get you home.'

'We can't yet,' Ed replied, receiving a confused look from Bob. 'We've no beer or peanuts in the house. You pigged the lot if you can remember, and I need to get drunk. The off-licence is this way.' Ed pointed back up towards the high street and began walking.

# Chapter 31

They stepped out of the off-licence and turned left, heading back to the cottage, but stopped to look at the ambulance outside the pub. Dave and Paul were there, talking animatedly as the paramedics put the stretcher into the back of the ambulance. The three Asians who had approached from the other end of the street joined them. Ed glanced at Bob, who was staring intently at what was taking place.

'I take it the whole gang's there, now?' Bob asked.

'That's all that I know of. I didn't notice Blackthorn or Denton at the service station so assume they're still back in London. Nasty looking bunch, aren't they?'

'Who's the guy in the leather jacket? He looks familiar.'

'Dave Carter, he's one of the regular bouncers at the club. Don't know too much about him, to tell you the truth. In fact, I think I only ever spoke to him once. Well, it was more of a run in with him, really. He thought I was wheedling my way in and was working for someone else. It was a load of hot air really, just Dave reaffirming the pecking order. Jim was in charge and Spike seemed to be his right hand man. Dave was just there and seemed to keep himself pretty much to himself. You probably nicked him once upon a time, when you were doing real police work and not just catching sheep-shaggers.'

'Funny bastard. Maybe I did nick him but why would I remember him, unless he was a right bastard? Never mind, a few beers and good night's sleep might jog the memory. Come on,' he replied, giving Dave one last lingering look.

Ed took a final look as Dave walked a few feet away from the others and made a phone call on his mobile. It started to drizzle with rain when they were about halfway back to the cottage, the way it only does in the Lake District. By the time they closed the front door it was hammering down, and they were soaked.

They hung up their sodden coats and slumped into the armchairs, and opened a couple of bottles of beer and unwrapped one of the packets of cigarettes Ed had purchased. Ed offered them to Bob, who hesitated before taking one. Ed gave him a wry smile as he lit his and threw the lighter over to Bob.

'Still only smoking when you're stressed or pissed off?' Ed enquired.

'I am. This is the first one I had since the last time I saw you. Doesn't that tell you something?'

'So, I've either pissed you off or stressed you out. What one is it?' Ed said grinning.

'Both,' he said, not elaborating. 'So, what's she like then, this TJ?' He asked, changing the subject. Ed took a breath and held it, thinking of how to answer.

'She's really nice. Although, I know you find it hard to believe that anyone who does what she does for a living could be nice.'

Bob shrugged. 'A tart with a heart, how touching.'

'Maybe,' Ed shrugged. 'Like I said to you on the phone, she's spent half her life looking for Johnny to somehow get revenge because he killed her mother. She took lap-dancing and pole dancing classes to get work in his club. Wasted years and now she's there, she can't get anything on him. It's sad really.'

'It's sad that she played you for a mug, to do her dirty work,' Bob said caustically.

'That's a bit unfair, Bob. I got sucked in because I gave one of the punters a slap and then fended off the bouncers. She had nothing to do with it,' he said defensively.

'Why didn't you just leave it to the bouncers?' he asked, although he already knew the answer. Ed was a sucker for a damsel in distress.

'They weren't around, or certainly not interested in intervening. I found out later from one of the other girls, Pandora, they have to give the bouncers sexual favours or they won't help you out when you need them. TJ didn't play ball, no pun intended, so she didn't get looked after. Anyway, the bloke was a real prick. Full of himself with a stupid beard and a watch the size of a wall clock. You know the sort.'

Bob laughed. 'You mean to tell me that the whole reason you're up to your neck in shit, is because of a beard and a watch! You're something else, you really are.' Ed looked at Bob and nodded and they both burst out laughing. 'Have you slept with her?' Bob asked, once they'd stopped laughing and Ed had brushed away his tears.

Ed nodded nervously. 'I feel guilty about it but it happened, OK. Don't get all judgemental on me. We'd both had a few drinks, and it happened.'

'I'm not judging you. That's between you and your conscience. What about Laura?' Bob knew it was a cruel question to ask, but he wanted Ed to think about the consequences and what he could be throwing away.

'I don't know. I know she has her reasons for not wanting to see me but when I dropped the dog off, she was cold and distant. I don't know if it was an act or whether she really is having second thoughts. I love her to bits but I have a feeling there's no future there, even if her operation is a success. What do you think? You see more of her than I do,' he replied sadly.

'I've no idea. I can't work her out. Raechael's not saying anything either way and avoids the subject if I bring it up. She knows I'll be on the phone to you if she told me anything. I'm sure it'll work itself out. Assuming you want her back?'

'Of course I do,' he replied, a bit too quickly. Bob noticed and raised an eyebrow. The honest answer was that he didn't know. TJ was so different from Laura and he would be lying if he said he didn't have strong feelings towards her. He wasn't sure if TJ was just using him to get what she wanted, or if she did genuinely like him. He didn't think he was being used, but what did he know.

'Is she pretty?' Bob asked, interrupting his thoughts. Ed nodded and pulled his phone from his pocket. No missed calls and no text messages, no surprise there. He browsed through the menu and pulled up the picture of TJ, which he had taken before she left for work on Friday, and passed the phone to Bob, who whistled. 'I can see why you like her. She's bloody gorgeous. Don't suppose she's got an older sister?'

'That picture doesn't really do her justice. In the flesh, she's even better. She's also a lot of fun to be with and I can't help but like her. Even though I know it's wrong, because of Laura.'

'You're a lucky bastard. Pass me another of those beers.'

Ed picked up a bottle from the floor and passed it to Bob. 'Can I borrow your mobile, Bob, to send a text? Only you said mine might be tapped and I don't want to put TJ in any danger if it is. I said I'd let her know I was OK and I'd like to do it before I get too pissed.' Ed said sheepishly. Bob grinned and threw him his phone. Ed sent a short text. Doing OK. 1-0 to the good guys XXX Ed. He thought about adding more but decided that what he had sent was enough, just to let her know he was alive and well and holding his own. He smiled and pushed the send button.

Bob looked on as Ed stared thoughtfully at the phone and began tapping out his text message. In truth he was worried; not just for Ed's safety, as he was sure that between the two of them they could work things out. What concerned him was Ed's state of mind. The attack on Andy was brutal and malicious and completely out of character. He'd seen Ed fight before but it had been in self-defence, and he had been in control the whole time. What he had witnessed tonight ranked as one of the most savage, unprovoked attacks he had seen and in his time in the force and he'd seen a lot. Aware of Ed's past, he knew that under the surface he was actually quite fragile; his attempted suicide a few years ago was testament to that. What he didn't need now was Ed spiralling out of control or going into self-destruct mode, the consequences of which he didn't even want to begin to contemplate. He lit another cigarette, tossed the packet to Ed, and raised his bottle in a silent toast.

Dave was waiting for Johnny to pick up, dreading the conversation that would take place.

'You'd better be ringing me to give me some good news, Dave,' Johnny said, when he finally answered.

'Not quite, boss. Andy's in hospital,' he replied meekly.

'How did that happen?' he said shouting angrily.

'He got beaten up in a pub. He looks like a bus has hit him. His nose is smashed and his teeth are on the wrong side of his lips. Well, those that are still left. The paramedic thinks he might have a couple of broken ribs and his ankle's been snapped.'

'Where the hell were you and Paul when his happened? Don't tell me he was on his own. Tell me you're not that fucking dumb.'

179

'We got the call saying his card had been used again and thought if we split up, we would cover all the pubs and restaurants quicker. He was only supposed to look and see if he was there and if he was, he was supposed to call in for back up.'

'I take it Case is responsible for this,' Johnny barked. Dave was certain he detected a hint of fear in his voice, and smiled.

'I asked the barman and he said the guy who attacked him was about Ed's height and build but looked like a right poof, with cropped hair, moustache and glasses. Either he's got a great disguise or it was someone else,' Dave replied, beginning to enjoy Johnny's discomfort.

'I've seen what that bastard can do. He's off his trolley, and I think it's him. What happened to him afterwards?'

'Strange, really. This guy jumps up and waves his warrant card around, slaps the cuffs on Case, tells the barman to phone an ambulance and marches him out the back.' Dave couldn't help but admire Ed's survival instincts and was grinning broadly.

'What do you make of that; was he legit?'

'Haven't a clue, boss. He could be. My bet would be he's got a bit of help.' Johnny was silent for a while but Dave could hear him, pacing up and down inside his office.

'Next time you see him, just shoot him,' he finally replied.

'What about the briefcase?'

'OK, shoot him in the leg and torture the bastard until he coughs. Then kill him.' It was Dave's turn to be silent this time. 'And no more splitting up, you and Paul stay together - and no more fuck ups!' Johnny hung up, lit another cigarette and poured a large measure of whisky. With a trembling hand, he mopped his sweaty brow and downed the whisky, immediately pouring another. He swirled the liquid around in the crystal tumbler, studying it intently, before hurling it at the wall, cursing the day that Ed walked into his club and he had offered him a job. He had read him all wrong. Perhaps if he had been completely honest with him, things would have turned out differently.

# Chapter 32

The sun was shining brightly through a crack in the curtains, directly into Ed's eyes. He turned away from it onto his stomach, but the pressure on his bladder made it impossible for him to stay that way. He reluctantly got up and padded across to the bathroom. He walked in, unaware that Bob was showering, which wasn't something he wanted to see first thing in the morning. Bob shouted at him to piss off but Ed ignored him and urinated copiously, with a grin on his face. Bob informed him he pissed like a horse and shouted obscenities at him from behind the shower screen. Ed smiled broadly, flushed the chain, and waited.

Bob screamed loudly as the cold water supply dwindled as the cistern filled up, and scalded him. 'You malicious little bastard,' he shouted. Ed laughed loudly and went down to put the kettle on. He heard Bob's second scream from the kitchen as he filled the kettle up, and laughed even louder. Feeling guilty, he made Bob a cup of tea.

Ed sat in the armchair, picked up his mobile and looked at the picture of TJ, and not for the first time in the last few days, hoped that she wasn't in any danger. The only reason she would be, he reasoned, was if somehow Johnny found out he had stayed with her on that Thursday night. How they would find that out, he didn't know, but it preyed on his mind. Once again, he thought about phoning her but if they did have a tap on his mobile, then that would definitely put her in danger. He reluctantly put the phone down, keeping temptation at arms length. He just hoped that she didn't phone him or if she did, used Bob's number from which he'd sent the text last night.

Bob walked down the stairs and sat down sulkily in the opposite armchair. 'Tell me this, Ed. Why did you go to the bank yesterday?'

'I needed some money to buy you dinner, obviously,' Ed said, looking at him like he was stupid.

'I only ask, because you've best part of a million quid in a carrier bag under the stairs.'

'It's not mine and I don't want anything to do with it. Do you want it?' he asked with a smile.

'It's tempting, but no. It's dirty money. Find another home for it.'

'I'll give it to a worthy cause. I'm certainly not giving it back to that big-nosed bastard or his cronies. Anyway, Bob, have you got a plan?'

'I'm going to make a few calls and see if I can pull in a few favours. To be honest, mate, I really don't know what to do. Staying here isn't a good idea but then running away back south isn't going to achieve anything. Tell you what, you buy me breakfast, I'll make a few calls and see where that leads.'

'Better than anything I can come up with. I'll grab a shower first. I need to move my car too. It's sitting in the public car park and to be honest, I'm surprised it hasn't been found yet. I was thinking of maybe taking it to a garage to get the brakes looked at to get it out the way.' He looked at Bob to seek approval.

'Seems like a good idea. Right, go and get that shower while I play with the taps down here and then we can get some breakfast, I'm bloody famished.'

Ed showered and Bob played with the taps to get his own back and then they headed out to get breakfast and to move the car. Ed took a circuitous route to the car park, avoiding the main streets as much as possible. By the time they got there Bob was in a foul mood, complaining bitterly that he if didn't get breakfast soon, the Red Cross would be sending him food parcels.

They entered the car park from the rear and Ed was glad to see that his car was still there and in once piece. They drove out of the car park onto the A594 and turned right, heading back into the town centre. Ed picked up the one way system and the road back towards Windermere, where he knew there was a garage. Traffic was light due to the time of year and Ed was able to turn right, across the main road, without too much of a wait, and into the garage opposite.

It was only a small concern but by the amount of cars on the premise, it was clearly very good or they got the work through default, by being the only garage in town. Ed wasn't bothered by this as he didn't really want any work done. It was just a convenient place to leave the car out of sight. He stood there with Bob, who began tapping his foot impatiently, waiting for the owner who was talking with another customer. Bob wasn't known for his enduring patience so Ed nudged him in the ribs and shot him an angry glance, implying that he should calm down and just wait his turn. Bob stopped but stared daggers at the owner, willing him to get a move on so they could get on with finding somewhere to eat breakfast.

Ed was concerned about being so exposed on the main road. Not so much his appearance or Bob's, but the car. He was confident that both Dave and Mo's gang would have a description of his car and number plate. Bob's impatience wasn't helping Ed's own nerves any.

They both turned and stared at the main road as they heard the screeching of rubber, as someone braked too hard. Directly across the road from them was a silver Mercedes with Mo behind the wheel, staring though the open window. Ed locked eyes with him and in that instance saw the recognition register in him.

'Shit. Come on, Bob, let's go!' Ed said, trying to remain calm but failing miserably as panic set in. Mo was already getting out the car and crossing the road followed by Asif and Abdul.

'Give me the keys, I'm driving,' Bob ordered. Ed threw him the keys without hesitation, and jumped into the passenger seat. Before he even had a chance to pull the door to, Bob had floored the accelerator and shot out into the main road in a squeal of rubber. Ed turned round and saw that the Asians were hastily getting back into their car. Without indicating, they spun the car round - receiving a blast of horns from cars in either direction - and began their pursuit.

'How come you get to drive, Bob?' Ed asked out of curiosity.

'Because you drive like my granny and I've done all the advanced driving courses, that's why.' Ed shrugged and sat looking into the passenger mirror on the sun visor as Mo began to make up ground.

Bob was driving way over the speed limit and showed no signs of slowing down, even when there were pedestrians crossing the road. He blasted the horn and grimaced as pedestrians scurried across the road to the safety of the pavement.

'Right, you know the area, tell me where to go,' Bob barked.

'OK, go screw yourself,' Ed replied, laughing nervously at his own joke.

'Very funny. What way, you cretin?'

'Turn left at the lights, then swing a right a few yards further on.'

Ed looked over his shoulder and saw that Mo was only a few yards behind. He turned round and concentrated on the road ahead, not knowing what was worse - Mo catching them up or Bob scattering pedestrians to the four corners of the earth. Bob ignored the red light, incurring a cacophony of blaring horns in the process. Ed turned again, hoping Mo was more law abiding. Bob swung right, Ed's poor Mondeo almost up on two wheels as he hurtled up Smithy Brow, faster than seemed possible. Ed squeezed his eyes closed as a car coming from the opposite direction took evasive action and mounted the kerb.

'I think I was better off taking my chances with Mo the way you're going. Take it easy, Bob, this road is called "The Struggle" for a reason!'

'Oh shut up, you tart. I'm an expert. You know, I'm actually enjoying this. It's been a long time since I was in a good car chase. Must admit though, it's the first time I've been the one being chased.'

With that, Bob took a corner too wide and the passenger wing mirror flew into the air as it hit the drystone wall that lined the aptly named Struggle. Bob just laughed.

'Bob, the bends get a bit sharper and the road narrows further up,' Ed said nervously.

'Stop worrying. I told you, I've done more driving courses that you've had hot dinners. This is a walk in the park.'

A car approached in the opposite direction, taking a lot more care than Bob. Ed prayed silently as Bob swerved at the last minute into a small passing space, scraping the wall, trim and bits of bumper flying in all directions and the driver's side wing mirror disintegrating on impact with the other vehicle. Just hearing the screech of metal on stone made Ed recoil and screw his eyes up, praying for his life.

'You might need a bit of a re-spray after this,' Bob said, grinning like a lunatic.

'The way you're going it won't cost much, because there'll be fuck all left of it,' Ed said angrily.

Mo was still keeping up with them and was also minus both wing mirrors, Ed noticed, as he looked at them through the mirror on the sun visor. He also noticed Asif hanging out the window, taking aim with his handgun.

'Fucking hell, Bob, he's gonna bloody shoot us!' Ed informed him. Bob grinned and accelerated as the rear window was obliterated, showering glass everywhere. Ed instinctively ducked, although it was far too late for that. He slunk lower in the seat, adrenaline coursing through his veins.

"Where the bloody hell does this road go to?' Bob asked. Ed marvelled that he was so calm, when Ed was feeling physically sick with worry.

'It joins up with the Kirkstone Pass. That's the A592 to you. It starts getting a bit steeper as well. When you get to the T-junction at the top, turn right,' he said nervously, peering over the dashboard.

'Why right? Why not left?'

'If you go right it gives us a few more options and leads back into Ambleside. Left it's a straight road and a bit wider, which gives those bastards a chance to catch up.'

Bob nodded. 'Cheer up. You're supposed to be having fun. Look at it this way, it's better than getting your head blown off by those maniacs,' he said, taking his hand off the wheel and pointing over his shoulder.

'Put your bloody hand back on the wheel!' Ed shouted.

'Oh ye of little faith,' he replied, as a couple more bullets tore into the rear of the car.

At the top of the Struggle, where it met the Kirkstone Pass, Bob barely slowed and slew the car to the right onto the main road, which was fortunately empty. Ed was going to say something about looking after the tyres but with the state the rest of the car was in, it seemed pointless.

The road was slightly wider and less windy, and Bob increased the speed again. Ed took another glance in the mirror and saw they had gained a few yards on Mo, and breathed a sigh of relief.

'How far behind are they, mate?' Bob asked. Ed turned and took another look.

'About twenty yards or so, I'd say.'

'Right, then, time for a bit of fun. Brace yourself - this is either going to be a stroke of brilliance, or spectacularly disastrous,' Bob advised him, chuckling.

'Why don't I like the sound of this? Have I ever told you I how much I hate you?' Ed told him angrily. Bob just laughed, as they flew over the brow of the hill and he slammed the brakes on, skidding to a halt and reversing back a few yards, into the smoke that lingered in the air from his tyres. Before Ed even had a chance to ask what the hell he was playing at, he saw the silver Mercedes take off over the crest of the hill. He sat looking in the visor mirror as it landed and swerved to avoid them. Mo had overcompensated, and the Mercedes bounced and skidded, clipping the rear of Ed's Mondeo. The heavier car took out his rear light and what remained of the bumper, before shooting across the road. It was going way too fast and Ed watched as it crashed through the drystone wall and took off into the air. It turned over one hundred and eighty degrees, and landed with an almighty crash on its roof, skidding to a halt into a prominent rocky outcrop.

'Watch and learn, Ed, watch and learn,' Bob said excitedly.

Ed stared at him open-mouthed and Bob smiled back, reaching across and pushing his jaw shut. Ed pulled open the passenger door and began to walk briskly across the road.

'Where the bloody hell do you think you're going?' Bob shouted.

'Off to see if those three need an ambulance.'

'Don't be bloody daft. Two minutes ago they were trying to kill you and now you want to see if they're OK? You must be a bit touched. Let the bastards rot in hell.'

Ed ignored him and walked across the road and stepped over the ruined wall. As he did, the Mercedes exploded in a fireball, blowing Ed clean off his feet and onto his backside. He landed heavily and painfully on the remains of the wall. Seconds later, Bob was beside him, pulling him away.

'I thought that only happened in American movies?' Ed said, shocked and bewildered. Bob just shrugged and helped him to his feet.

'Are you OK?' he asked, genuinely concerned.

'Nothing that a drink and a change of underpants won't cure,' Ed said, trying to make light of it.

'My thoughts exactly. Sorry about the car, mate,' he said with a smirk. Ed looked at it and gave a short laugh. What remained of the rear bumper was hanging off and the light nearest was smashed to pieces. The rear windscreen was gone and there were two bullet holes in the side. Both wing mirrors were missing in action and he knew from the sound as it scraped the wall, that the entire passenger side was a mess.

'I think I'll scrap it and get a new one. I don't fancy having to explain that to the insurance company.'

Bob patted him on the shoulder and nodded. 'Look on the bright side. It was for a worthy cause and there are three more bad guys out of the picture. Four down, two to go.'

'That makes me so much happier,' Ed said dryly. 'Where did you learn that trick, anyway?'

'I think I saw it in a film once and thought it was worth a try.'

'You're something else, Bob, I give you that. Come on, get me back to civilisation so I can have that drink and calm my nerves. You OK, by the way?'

'Me? Never felt better. Want me to drive back?' he said, giving Ed another of his grins. Ed smiled, nodded, and got in the passenger seat.

On the drive back to Ambleside, which was at a much more sedate and less stressful pace, they discussed what to do about the car. They couldn't very well leave it in the car park and didn't want to leave it outside the cottage, just in case Dave and Paul spotted it. The only option was to take it back to the garage and ask the guy to scrap it or do what he wanted with it.

They got some very strange looks driving through Ambleside, and Ed was glad when they pulled up into the garage. The owner came out the office, took one look at the car, took of his baseball cap and scratched his head in disbelief. Bob and Ed stood there, grinning like naughty schoolboys as he walked up to them.

'Hello mate,' Ed said smiling. 'Don't suppose there's anything you can do about this, is there?'

The owner shook his head and stared. 'Reckon it's about had it. Complete write-off, if you ask me,' he said, walking round the car, still shaking his head.

'That's what I thought. I'm on holiday up here and go home tomorrow,' he lied. 'I know it's had it but I don't know where the scrap merchant is. Can I leave it with you to deal with? The engine's sound so you might be able to salvage some of the parts. I'll pay you for your trouble.'

The owner scratched his head again and gave it some thought. 'It ain't no use to me, son. I don't use second hand parts and the bodywork's too far gone to repair. Tell you what. I'll take it to the scrappy for you for a hundred quid.'

Ed looked at him and knew he was lying, but didn't really care. He was just about to agree, when a young lad came out of the workshop, cleaning his hands on a greasy rag and began looking round the car.

'How much do you want for it, mate?' he asked.

'It's yours if you want it,' Ed said, giving the owner an up yours smile.

'You bet I do. Won't take me long to get that back on the road,' he said, genuinely pleased.

'In that case, you can have it with my compliments. It's got thirteen thousand miles on the clock and it's only three years old. I've had it from new and can honestly say, it's had one careful owner and five minutes with a complete lunatic. Enjoy,' Ed replied, slightly bitter.

He opened up the passenger door, which protested loudly, and pulled the registration documents from the glove box. After fishing out a pen, he filled in his details and handed the paperwork over to the mechanic and shook his hand.

Everyone who knew Ed made fun out of his Mondeo. Just because he was a millionaire, they expected him to drive a Ferrari or a Rolls Royce. Maybe he would buy one just to shut them up. Maybe he would just buy a new Mondeo.

# Chapter 33

By the time they reached the cottage, it was lunchtime. Bob had grumbled and whined that he was famished, having sacrificed breakfast for a high-speed car chase - or pursuit, as would be more appropriate. Ed was tempted just to go back to bed and put the terrifying memory of the morning behind him, hopefully waking up in his own bed at home and finding the last two weeks were all a bad dream. Bob had other ideas and insisted on a pub lunch. The only redeeming factor in this was Bob insisting lunch was on him, by way of compensation for trashing Ed's car. Ed was tempted to ask if the price of a ploughman's was fair compensation for a three year old car with only just under thirteen thousand miles on the clock, but held his tongue.

Ed had known Bob for around five years and had met him through Jacqui, one of Ed's oldest friends, who had been shot dead in May. Ed still blamed himself for this and always would. Jacqui had been Bob's DS when Bob first arrived in Cornwall. Bob had been exiled from the Metropolitan police for his unorthodox methods, which were deemed far too politically incorrect to fit into the new image the Met wanted to portray. Since the day they first met, their relationship had been very confrontational and abrasive. Deep down, there was a lot of mutual respect and although neither would admit it, they were actually quite alike. Both had a strong belief in what was right and what was wrong. The only difference being, Ed had a conscience and Bob didn't, or if he did, it was hidden so deep a team of Welsh miners would have difficulty digging it back out.

As a general rule, whenever Ed was in Cornwall - where he owned a caravan, a legacy from his parents - he always made time to have at least one night on the town with Bob. It was always the same course of events. After a few beers they would both do their best to wind each other up, get completely plastered and at the end of the night, slap each other on the backs and say what a great night they had. Since May, things had changed and Ed had, until recently, seen a lot more of Bob. This was because he was now in a relationship with Laura's mother, Raechael, and was a frequent visitor to their St Albans home. Ed took great delight in reminding Bob that there was a good chance he could be his father-in-law. Bob did likewise and constantly reminded Ed he would be his son-in-law. Both told each other they could think of nothing worse. Secretly both were pleased, but of course would never admit that either. The way things were between him and Laura at the moment, being a son-in-law to Bob was a looking to be a very remote possibility. Ed hoped he was wrong, but usually his instincts were pretty good.

Ed's reminiscing was abruptly interrupted as Bob grabbed him by the shoulder and hurried him past the pub where Ed had so viciously assaulted Andy, putting him in hospital. Ed looked through the window and felt a self-loathing for his brutal attack. Despite his talent with his fists, he rarely lost his temper and never started a fight. Equally, he never backed down but his actions last night, still made him feel physically sick. The thought of how easily he had lost control frightened him. Maybe he would sign up to one of those anger management courses when this was all over. Then again, perhaps not. In Ed's view, to understand someone with a mental disorder you had to be a bit unbalanced yourself, and he didn't like the idea of being treated by a fruit cake. It was bound to be run by some bearded psychologist who had no real life experience, but had a certificate that said he had been to university and attended a few lectures, therefore

193

making him an expert. That would wind him up and he'd probably end up giving the guy a slap, which would be a little counter-productive.

They walked on quickly and Bob pushed him into the next pub they came to. Bob began rubbing his hands together as the blackboard on the wall announced that all-day breakfast was served. Ed didn't have much of an appetite but his stomach was growling, due to a bellyful of beer the night before and not having eaten that day. Bob ordered two all-day breakfasts and two pints of lager. Ed would have preferred a mug of tea, which complimented a fry-up much better, but went with the flow. It was the path of least resistance and he wasn't in the mood to engage in caustic banter with Bob. They picked up their pints and chinked their glasses together in a silent toast. Bob gulped his pint and belched into a clenched fist, before picking up his glass again and finishing the contents in two massive swallows. Bob slammed his glass down noisily on the table, which Ed chose to ignore. Irritated, Bob picked up the empty glass and waved it in Ed's face, a subtle reminder that it was Ed's round. Ed frowned and finished his own drink, and wandered over to the bar for two more.

When the food was placed on the table, the smell perked up Ed's appetite and he ate it with relish. Bob seemed to be deep in thought and Ed didn't feel inclined to interrupt. Not that he had anything to say; in fact, neither had said a great deal since leaving the car with a very happy mechanic. Bob finished his food first, pushed his plate away and leaned back, patting his stomach appreciatively. Once he had finished his second pint he got up and ordered two more, and placed them on the table.

'Right, I'm off outside to make a couple of calls,' he informed Ed, checking the battery level on his phone and looking pleased that it was still reasonably charged. Before Ed could reply, he walked outside with his pint and left him sitting there with the remains of his meal.

'Jack, long time no speak. Bob Brown, how the devil are you?' Bob said cheerily, when the phone was picked up after three rings.

'That'll be Superintendent Griggs to you, DI Brown,' he replied stonily.

'That'll be DCI Brown to you, Jack.'

'Congratulations on your promotion. What can I do for you? Make it quick, I've got a meeting in fifteen minutes.'

'I'm after some information. I thought you might be able to help. You always did keep your nose to the ground.'

'Cut the crap, Bob. What do you want from me that could possibly affect anything that goes on in Cornwall?'

'What can you tell me about DI Roger Blackthorn and his trusty sidekick, DS Mike Denton? I believe they both work for you, indirectly of course.'

There was a long silence. Too long, Bob thought, before Griggs replied. 'What do you want to know about them and why?' Griggs asked suspiciously. It was Bob's turn at melodramatics, and he mentally counted to five before answering.

'Well, for a start, are they straight?' he asked and again received a pregnant pause before Griggs answered.

'Bob, I don't see that that's any of your business. You still haven't told me why you're asking.'

'I know,' Bob replied and thought he'd throw in a few more snippets, to see what the response was. 'OK. What about a dodgy character by the name of Johnny Gold? He runs a lap-dancing club up Soho. I know him from days of old. Always was a scumbag. The club's probably a legit front, for his other less legit activities.'

'Bob, where's this leading to?' Griggs replied. Bob wasn't slow to pick up on the slightly nervous response and looked to exploit the situation.

'So, you're aware of their relationship then? Are they under investigation by any chance?' Bob was now smiling, believing that Griggs was on the back foot. Once again, there was a satisfying silence.

'I can't tell you that Bob, and you know it. Whatever you think you know, you don't. OK?' Griggs hissed, angrily into the receiver.

'Unfortunately Jack, I do know and I've seen the hard evidence that those two bent bastards are taking backhanders and supplying Johnny with drugs,' Bob said calmly. He heard Griggs swear under his breath and chuckled down the phone at him.

'I'll call you back in five minutes, Bob,' Griggs replied, quickly. Bob ended the connection, took a few gulps of beer and grinned broadly.

When his mobile rang a few minutes later, he deliberately left it to ring and only picked up just before the answering service cut in.

'Hello Jack, that was quick. I thought you had a meeting to go to?' he said sarcastically.

'You always were an annoying bastard, Bob. Just tell me what you know?' he replied calmly.

'It doesn't work like that, Jack. The way I see it and from the tone of your voice, I or should I say a friend of mine, has something you might want. You tell me what's going on and I'll tell you what I know,' Bob said evenly.

'Look Bob, I don't have time to play games. Blackthorn is under investigation. He has been for a few months but so far we've got nothing to go on or nothing we can prove. We know he's on Gold's books but he's being very canny with the money. No extravagant spending, nothing out the ordinary in his bank accounts. We've got someone on the inside and I don't want him compromised. Do you understand? If anything happens to him, I'll hold you entirely responsible and make sure you're kicked off the force. Have you got that? So what have you got for me?'

'A very good friend of mine managed to get hold of a couple of ledgers while he was working there. They contain names, dates and amounts, going back years. Who supplied him with drugs, amounts and what he paid. Enough to put Blackthorn, Denton and Gold down for a very long time, I'd say. How does that sound?' Bob said, pleased with what he had heard.

'You're talking about Mr Case, then? I hear he's been a complete pain in the arse. It seems the two of you are very much alike. Knowing he's a friend of yours explains a lot.'

'I'll take that as a compliment,' Bob replied cheerily.

'Tell Case, I want those ledgers delivered to me personally, ASAP.'

'That might be a bit difficult as he's not in town at the moment. But you already know that, don't you? Still, he seems to be managing very nicely without your help. One of Johnny's gorillas is in hospital and I don't think he'll be coming out any time soon. Oh, and do you know three Asians by the name of Mo, Abdul and Asif? They supplied drugs to Johnny as well. It's all in the ledgers. Well, they won't be supplying any more. They had a bit of a nasty car accident this morning.' Bob gave a short laugh.

'Bob, I want you to get his arse back down to London now, before he does any more damage. And that's an order!' Griggs shouted.

Bob laughed again at Griggs's discomfort. 'I'll do what I can but he hasn't broken any laws as such, so I can't arrest him, and officially, I'm on leave. We'll be down soon. Doesn't seem to be much point in staying here anyway, there's no more bad guys left. Anyway, you should be pleased. He's got a better clean-up rate than you have.'

'I'm warning you Bob, if he jeopardises my operation, I'll have your bloody job. Just do it,' Griggs shouted, before hanging up and reaching for his painkillers to ease the throbbing in his temple.

Bob walked back into the pub with an exaggerated swagger. Ed looked at him and gave him an inquisitive look. Bob smiled and beckoned him outside. Ed followed, wondering what he was so pleased about, and eventually asked. It was clear Bob was going to be his usual antagonistic self, and wasn't going to volunteer any information. God, he could be an annoying bastard sometimes; make that most of the time, Ed thought to himself.

'Come on then, Mister Smug Twat, spill the beans. You've got a face like you've just rogered the neighbour's cat.'

'Well, to cut a long story short, my contact in the Met is keen to see your ledgers. Blackthorn's been under investigation for some time and they have a man on the inside.' Bob gave him a what do you think of that? look and grinned.

'I hope it wasn't Andy! He's not going to be too happy with that. If it's not, I don't know who it is. It's not Spike - that bastard shot Barry. At least I assume it was Spike. Jim's too much of a bastard and he's been with Johnny years. Dave's the only one it could be, unless it's the new barman or someone I don't know.'

'It doesn't matter. Tomorrow we go home and hand those ledgers over to the police.'

'How do we know, they're not going to make them disappear?' Ed said suspiciously.

'Jack Griggs is a superintendent and straight as they come. He's one hundred percent trustworthy.' Ed shrugged and carried on walking. 'You've got a text, by the way. At least I assume it's for you. It's not the sort of thing Raechael would send,' he informed Ed and handed him the phone. Ed found the inbox and looked at the last message received. It was short and to the point and read, Miss you, love you and don't do anything stupid. XXX. Ed smiled and handed the phone back to Bob. 'Where are we going by the way?' Bob asked.

They had just walked by the post office and turned left, heading up a steep, winding road.

'I fancy a bit of fresh air and there's a nice waterfall up there. Should be worth seeing after all the rain we had last night. Last time I walked up to see it, it had been sunny for weeks and was nothing but a trickle of piss. I like waterfalls,' he replied lamely.

'Not only do you look like a bloody great big poofta, you're beginning to act like one,' Bob replied, laughing, clearly pleased with himself.

# Chapter 34

Dave was talking secretively once again, a few yards from where Paul was standing, and it was beginning to seriously wind him up. They were supposed to be a team and right now, he didn't feel part of one. When this was all over, he was going to get even and bring him down a peg or two. For now they had work to do, and if he put Dave in a hospital bed next to Andy, Johnny would go ballistic. Not that Johnny would get his hands dirty. He'd get Jim or Spike to do it, the spineless prick.

While he was pacing up and down the street, cursing Dave for his secrecy, he caught site of Ed and Bob disappearing down a side street, a little further down the main road. He shouted to Dave as loudly as he thought he could, without alerting Ed. Dave dismissed him with a curt wave of the hand. Well, fuck you, Paul thought. He didn't need him anyway. He was perfectly capable of killing the big bloke, maiming Ed and getting information out of him. He'd enjoy doing it too, for making him spend days in this godforsaken town, with its rain, bitter wind and hordes of bloody tourists, and for what he'd done to Andy. Christ, he'd done some damage to him. He had visited him in hospital last night and he could barely look at him. His face was a mass of cuts, bruises and stitches. OK, Andy was no angel. He had dished out a lot of punishment himself, some of it gratuitously, and even killed a few men in his time but he'd never seen anyone look as bad as he did; anyone alive, that is. The ankle was worse. It looked like some demented child had been experimenting with a Meccano set. Thinking about it made him shudder as he hurried up the hill, keeping his quarry just in sight, biding his time to strike.

Dave finished his call and looked round to see that Paul was nowhere in sight. He began to panic and cursed under his breath for not being more vigilant. Paul hadn't passed him, he knew that, so he headed back up the street, just catching site of him disappearing round the back of the post office and up the hill. He crossed the road and followed, wondering where the hell he was going to. Logic said the only reason that he had wandered off was because he had seen Ed and had gone in pursuit on his own; the stupid bastard. He was fired up after seeing Andy in hospital last night and was likely to do something stupid. He didn't give a toss about Ed, but he needed the ledgers; without them the whole trip would have been a waste of time. He resisted the urge to shout out or use his mobile, knowing that it could possibly alert Ed and he would go on the run. He wanted to avoid that. All he wanted to do was to bring this whole affair to a close. He'd had enough of chasing that pain in the arse around the Lake District and wanted to get back to London. He laboured up the steep hill, trying to make up ground, on his lumbering oaf of a so-called partner.

Ed ignored the first signpost to his left indicating the footpath to the waterfall, which they could hear in the background, thundering down the ravine, knowing there was a second signpost further up. The footpath ran parallel to the narrow tarmac track they were walking up, separated by a strip of woodland. Beyond this was a deep ravine and the raging river, which eventually snaked its way down into Ambleside.

When they reached the second signpost, Ed turned off the track and looked over his shoulder at a frowning Bob.

'Are you coming or what?' Ed asked impatiently.

'Not in these shoes, I'm not. They're brand new and I don't want to get them covered in mud and sheep shit. If I wanted to do that, I would have stayed in Cornwall.'

'Suit yourself,' Ed replied and continued down the footpath. The roar of the waterfall increased with every step, which pleased Ed. Waterfalls had always fascinated him, ever since he was a child. He could stand and watch a waterfall for hours. The sheer power of the water, the sound of it thundering over the rocks, and the wonderful dank smell that you only found around waterfalls was spellbinding.

When he finally reached the small clearing, offering uninterrupted views of the ravine and the waterfall, he wasn't disappointed. Last night's rain had swollen the river as it gathered water from the surrounding hills and thundered relentlessly onwards, before crashing noisily onto the rocks below. Ed was mesmerised and stared at it in awe. His mind was closed to anything else, which was why he didn't notice when Paul crept up and stood a few feet away, with his gun aimed at Ed's head.

Paul had seen Ed turn off down the footpath but was unable to follow, as his companion had stayed on the track. Remembering the signpost he had passed earlier, he doubled back and crept into the woods, pleased that the thundering waterfall masked his clumsy footsteps. His excitement gathered as he saw Ed in the distance with his back to him, gawping at the water like a big kid. The noise was so great now that he didn't even need to try to creep up stealthily and strode up to him confidently, knowing it was now all over. He pulled back the slide on his automatic and aimed. The metallic sound carried and was audible, even over the waterfall. Paul was almost in touching distance of Ed, who turned and stared into Paul's hate-filled eyes.

'Tell me where the briefcase is and I'll kill you quickly. If you don't, I'll make it a slow and painful death for you. It's your choice,' Paul said, fixing Ed with an icy glare and a twisted smile. Ed looked around for Bob, who was nowhere to be found, and cursed him for not wanting to get his precious shoes dirty. He stared back blankly, desperately looking for a way out, once again being forced to think fast. He elected to try the nonchalant approach.

'And how do you propose to do that? Last time you tried, back in the club, you ended up on your arse,' Ed replied, trying to sound confident, while his stomach was turning cartwheels.

'You think you're so fucking invincible. Well, let's see how well you fight with your kneecap missing.' He lowered the aim of his gun, and grinncd broadly.

'Probably not the best idea you've ever come up with. As soon as my mate up there hears that shot, he'll call the police. I'll probably writhe around on the floor and scream like a big girl's blouse, and you'll get nothing at all out of me. You'll still be no nearer getting the briefcase and Johnny will be pissed off. He'll probably take it out on you, no doubt.' Ed gave him an "I couldn't care less" shrug and waited for something to happen. God, he hoped his blasé attitude would work. It didn't.

Paul took a step forward and raised the pistol, directly in line with Ed's face, and pulled back the hammer. Ed's legs filled with lead and he shuffled backwards as Paul continued to edge forward, grinning manically. A quick look down at this feet confirmed he had run out of room. He was almost balanced on the edge of the clearing, inches from the deep ravine and the raging torrent of water below, with Paul still advancing.

'Do you actually know what's in the attaché case, Paul?' Ed asked, stalling for as much time as possible, hoping Bob would come to his rescue.

'It's none of my business. My job's to get it back and give it to Johnny. I don't really care what's in it.'

'What about if I told you it's three quarters of a million pounds? Would you care then? Andy's out the frame, Mo and his mates are all dead.' Ed noticed the look of surprise on Paul's face, and smiled. 'Didn't know about that, then? They had a little accident in their car. Keep me alive and the money's yours.' Ed was taking a chance, but anything to bide his time was worth a shot. Paul studied him and was obviously thinking about what Ed had told him, buying Ed precious time he needed.

'So, why haven't you disappeared with it then?' he asked tersely.

'Believe it or not, I'm already a millionaire. That money won't make any difference to my life. I've only got that bloody briefcase because I forgot to drop it, after giving Johnny a wallop round the head with it. It's yours, as long as you keep me alive. What about it? With that sort of money you could disappear abroad and live like a king. Johnny wouldn't have a clue where you were. You'd be home and dry.'

'Nice try, but not good enough. Say goodbye to your kneecap. Have you got any preference - which one?' Paul asked coldly.

Ed gave a shrug. 'The one in the middle?'

'Paul!' came a shout from behind. 'Put the gun down, it's all over now.' Ed turned and saw Bob walking down with Dave behind him, with his gun in his back. Bob looked angry and pissed off. 'Put the gun away. He won't try anything, or I'll shoot his friend.' He looked like he meant it. Bob gave an almost imperceptible nod and a half a wink. Paul put his gun in his waistband and looked over towards Dave. Ed seized the moment, grabbing Paul and turning him around in one fluid movement before giving him an almighty shove, sending him over the edge of the ravine. His arms flailed uselessly, trying to grasp thin air as he tumbled backwards, his face frozen in a rictus of fear. His head smashed on the rocks below, followed shortly after by his back, before the raging torrent picked him up and swept down-river. Ed turned round, hoping that Bob had also taken the initiative, poised to run to his defence. Instead he saw them both standing side by side staring at him, not a gun in sight.

'Fucking hell, Case!' Dave said 'You're turning out to be a right pain the arse. I'm gonna be filling in paperwork for the next fortnight because of you.'

'Can someone tell me what the bloody hell is going on?' Ed asked, confused.

'I'm an undercover cop, trying to get Blackthorn and Gold put away. That's what's going on,' Dave said angrily. That explained a lot, Ed thought, about Dave's attitude towards him at the club. Ed tilted his head back and looked at the sky, the reality that he had probably just killed Paul unnecessarily dawning on him. He turned and ran down the path, looking into the river for Paul. He spotted him through the trees, slumped over an outcrop of rocks where the ravine had dropped away, petering out into sandy banks. Ed slid down the slippery bank onto the rough sand, and waded out into the water. The ice cold water lapped at his calves as he tried to drag the body from the water. Ed knew from looking Paul's cold, lifeless eyes that he was dead. He managed to get his hands under Paul's arms and hauled him to the bank and laid him on his back. He checked for a pulse on his neck. Not finding one, he slumped down heavily on the bank, and put his head in his hands.

Dave and Bob followed him down. Dave also checked for a pulse and shook his head, looking at Bob. Dave took out his mobile and called for an ambulance and Bob slipped the gun from Paul's waistband, which miraculously hadn't fallen out, and tucked it into his jacket pocket. Dave had wandered off to the side and was now giving an update to his superiors. Ed remained sitting on the bank, feeling guilty and pissed off with himself for acting so rashly. It didn't matter that Paul would most likely have blown his kneecap off. In Ed's view, Paul's death was totally avoidable, but once again he had acted without thinking. Bob put a hand on his shoulder and patted him sympathetically, before hauling him up on his feet and leading him away, back up to the track.

The ambulance arrived, blue light flashing, and Ed chuckled at the irony of it. It was followed by a dark blue BMW and a black Lexus. The ambulance team stepped out and made no attempt to approach the body, leaving that to the doctor, who emerged from the Lexus and pronounced him dead. Dave pulled out his warrant card and spoke to the two detectives who stepped out of the BMW. Ed watched as they looked over in his direction on more than one occasion, making him nervous. He was half expecting to be arrested but Dave patted the officer who appeared to be in charge on the back, and they climbed back into their BMW and left. Dave walked over to where Bob and Ed were standing, deliberately having kept out the way.

'Don't look so bloody terrified,' he said to Ed. 'I've squared it all away. I told them the situation and that there was no foul play involved, so you're in the clear. I'll get it all written up in my report and if their boss has a problem with that, he can speak to mine. I'm more than confident my boss carries a lot more clout than his.' He smiled and looked at Ed again. 'It looks like it's all over for you now - well, almost.'

'Almost?' Ed echoed. 'What else is left?'

'I just need the ledgers and that's it. You can get back to a normal life or whatever passes as normal for you.'

'To be honest I've forgotten what normal is. But I'm not giving the ledgers to anyone, other than whoever is in charge. No offence Dave but I've risked my life over this. I want to make sure they don't get lost.'

'Are you suggesting I'm in on this, too?' he asked angrily and obviously offended.

'No. I want to hand them over to your boss or whoever is running this operation so I can vent my spleen on them. This could have ended days ago. He could've sent in a bunch of her majesty's finest and rounded up Andy, Paul and Mo and his lot, but he didn't. As a result he put my life in danger, and didn't give a flying toss about it. He can wait for his precious ledgers. Right now I'm going to get pissed, and then I'll think about going home,' Ed said defiantly. Bob was grinning broadly, used to Ed's belligerent streak. Even Dave gave him a wry smile.

'You really are a pain in the arse, Case. Have it your way. I'll let my boss know and I'll join you down the pub.'

Ed smiled, pleased with himself.

# Chapter 35

They walked back down the hill into town, Ed's feet freezing from jumping in the river to pull Paul out, and his trousers wet up to the thighs. Rather than the pub, they opted for a carry-out and made a stop at the off-licence, picking up as much booze as they could carry.

On arriving back at the cottage, Ed changed into dry clothes and joined the party, which had started without him. Bob and Dave had commandeered the two armchairs so Ed sat down on the sofa in between and selected the end nearest to Bob, thinking that he might need some moral support.

'I think I owe you an apology for coming on a bit strong in the club last week,' Dave said. Ed gave a shrug as if it didn't matter. 'I was only doing it for your own good. Mo isn't the sort of person you want to have as an enemy, as you found out. I thought I might be able to scare you off. It appears you take a lot of scaring.'

Ed smiled. 'I'm just pig-headed, always have been. I just put it down to you wanting to establish the pecking order. Wanting to let me know I was the new boy and was therefore, bottom of the food chain. No need to apologise.' Dave raised his bottle of lager in a silent acknowledgement.

'Tell me. Why did you agree to work for Johnny? Didn't you have any idea what you might be letting yourself in for?' he asked, giving him a smile that implied he was naive or stupid.

'I was bored and wanted something to occupy my mind for a couple of weeks. I thought it might be a bit of a laugh working there. Had I realised how obnoxious most of the people who worked there were, I wouldn't have bothered. I was under no illusion that it wasn't as clean-cut as Johnny made it out to be. I'm not that bloody daft. I have to admit though, I had no idea just how corrupt it was.'

'I still don't know why Johnny wanted you. No offence, but you don't look the part and there's no shortage of muscle looking for work.'

'Initially, he told me he was short-staffed. Later in the week he seemed to think he could turn me into some psychopath to use as he saw fit. That's why he set me up with Barry's murder. If I didn't shoot Barry, he'd get Jim to shoot me. If I did shoot him, I would need his protection and be in his pocket. Either way, I lost. That's why I lost it and went on the run. The briefcase was just a bit of luck - or not, depending on how you want to look at it.'

'Well, you've certainly got some balls. I don't think there's too many people out there who would have done what you did.'

'Not too many people out there are as pig-headed as I am,' Ed replied smiling.

'I'll drink to that,' Bob chipped in, raising his bottle in an attempt to provoke him. Ed gave him a shrug but refused to give him the satisfaction of taking the bait. He was feeling altogether a lot more relaxed now that it was all over, and he wasn't going to let Bob or anyone else get to him. He was going to unwind and get slowly drunk, and put the last two weeks behind him.

Dave was keen to at least see the ledgers, even if Ed had no intention of handing them over. Ed went to the cupboard under the stairs and pulled the ledgers out of his rucksack and handed them to Dave. He started with the most recent and opened it on the last entries and worked back, nodding and smiling to himself.

'Well, it looks like we've got enough here to put the lot of them away. I rang Johnny and told him about Mo, and he was quite pleased. It means one person less to pay off. Just Blackthorn and Denton now.' He gave Ed a sly grin 'What's to stop me walking out with these now?' he said.

'Me,' Ed said calmly. 'I'd rip your head off and ram it up your arse.'

'Aren't you forgetting, I'm the one with the gun?' he replied, just as calmly.

'And aren't you forgetting, so am I?' Bob stated from the armchair opposite, patting his jacket pocket. Dave raised his bottle of beer in salute.

'Don't worry. As long as they get to my boss tomorrow, I don't really care,' Dave replied.

'So what's next for you, then?' Ed asked.

'Back to the club and keep an eye on things, until we're ready to pull them in. Hopefully, that will be in a few days or so. Blackthorn and Denton will be out of the frame first and then we'll close in on Johnny. After that, I'll move on to my next assignment. What about you?'

Ed thought for a few seconds and replied 'I don't really know. Hand over these ledgers. I'll go and see TJ, just to let her know I'm OK and then get back to normality. Maybe take a holiday, dunno. I haven't given it much thought, really. I need to keep busy, that's for sure. It was boredom that got me into this mess in the first place.'

'Are you and TJ an item?'

'No. We're mates, of course. She's Johnny's daughter. Did you know that?' Ed replied, addressing Dave only, knowing that Bob's eyes were boring into the back of his head. Dave raised his eyebrows. 'She wasted years of her life trying to find him. She only learnt how to lap-dance and pole dance just so she could get a job in his club. He murdered her mother and she wants to get even. Hopefully, what I've done will

210

see him behind bars for a while and she can get back to a normal life, too.'

'What a bloody waste. You know, we'll probably never be able to prove he killed her mother, but maybe seeing him behind bars will be enough for her.'

'I'll drink to that,' Ed replied, raising his bottle.

Blackthorn was nervous. The news from Johnny was not encouraging. Andy was in hospital and was going to be out of action for a long time. Paul was dead, as was Mo and his two right-hand men. Not that he gave a toss about them. He only cared about getting the ledgers back, and his money. Even the money wasn't really an issue. That was Johnny's problem. If he didn't get it back from Case, then he'd have to find the money from somewhere else. Dave was still on Ed's tail, which was something, but the others had been brushed off so easily that he didn't rate his chances of getting the ledgers back. He contemplated going to the Lake District himself but couldn't do that, not without raising too much suspicion. He had to find another way.

Ed's credit card statements were interesting. There was a meal at the Ritz, with a bill for the best part of a grand and a cash withdrawal in Borough. He had his suspicions but needed proof. A phone call to the Ritz, confirmed it was a reservation for a table for two. Blackthorn had confirmed with the duty manager that CCTV footage was kept for three months and that he could come down to view them at any time. Blackthorn had a feeling that Ed would not have risked travelling to the lakes with the briefcase and would have left them with someone. He just had to find out his movements prior to heading North and pay a visit to everyone he saw. Once he had the ledgers, Johnny had no proof of his involvement in any clandestine deals, and he no longer needed him. Then he could tie up a few loose ends.

Johnny was smoking and drinking far too much. He knew this, but drink was the only thing that seemed to calm his nerves. His doctor wouldn't be too pleased, especially if he knew that the pains in his chest had returned with alarming frequency. At the club he spent all his time in the office, fretting. Blackthorn and Denton had been next to bloody useless and so far had come up with nothing, or if they had, they were keeping it to themselves. In Johnny's view they were becoming a liability. Perhaps he should hire someone to arrange for an accident. Maybe he would when this was all resolved. Right now, no matter how useless he thought they were, he needed all the help he could get.

When Dave had called to inform him of Mo's death, he hadn't really cared. Partly it was the drink, but also relief. He only had to worry about getting Blackthorn and Denton's money now. Once he had the ledgers back, Blackthorn was back in his pocket being controlled, rather than as he was now, trying to call the shots. The temptation to arrange an accident was overwhelming. He'd give that some more thought.

News of Mo, Asif, Abdul and Paul's death, and Andy's hospitalisation, was the talk of the club. TJ, who had spent the last few days worried sick for Ed's safety, was now slightly more at ease now that only Dave was on his tail. She knew very little about Dave. He was either quiet and intelligent and therefore remained a danger to Ed, or he was uncommunicative due to an inability to string a sentence together, and would hopefully end up the same way as Andy and Paul.

Since his departure on Friday, TJ had missed Ed more than she thought she would. Work just wasn't the same. Partly because she didn't feel as safe without knowing Ed was watching her every move. Ready to leap to her defence like a knight in shining armour, and because he was one of the only people she could talk to or wanted to talk to. Pandora had been much friendlier since Ed had intervened between her and Mo. She actually seemed to like him. TJ was surprised that she was actually jealous that Pandora now saw him as a friend, rather than a foe. She just hoped he was still safe and that she would see him again, when it was safe to do so. Not that she saw that as likely. Once this was all over, Ed would go back to Laura and once again she would be alone in the world.

Blackthorn had been acting strangely earlier when he had visited Johnny, and she had seen him staring at her on several occasions. He gave her the creeps at the best of times; his staring just made it worse. She wasn't sure if it was her own paranoia or not but it was almost as if Blackthorn knew that she and Ed had a relationship of sorts and that she had given him a safe base after leaving the club on Thursday. She put it down to paranoia, as there was no way he could know - or was there? She decided not to dwell on the subject.

Ed, Bob and Dave were getting nicely drunk and were now tucking into a curry, which they had ordered from the Indian restaurant in Ambleside. It was adequate but they all agreed the best curry was their respective local Indian restaurants. Dave thought that because his local was on Brick Lane his must be the best, because it was the most famous street in London for curry houses. Ed disagreed; he had eaten in two curry houses on Brick Lane and thought that they were overpriced, not spicy enough, and not hot enough. Bob's only contribution was that he was usually drunk when he ate curry and could never remember in the morning if it was good or not. In his opinion, they all gave him an arsehole like a blood orange and bad breath. In the end they agreed to differ and got back to serious eating and drinking.

Eventually even Bob had given up on drinking, which was a first and a relief to Ed, who had been sitting there listening in on the conversation with eyes like two piss-holes in the snow. Bob had known Dave vaguely from his days in the Met and for the last two hours they had been reminiscing about past cases and past colleagues. At first Ed found it interesting and sometimes amusing but after a while he became bored, which made him even more tired.

Before leaving, Dave made one last attempt to charm the ledgers off Ed and failed. Ed was glad he didn't mention the gun or pull it out. Bob seemed to have become alert, and looked like he might pull his own recently-acquired gun if he did. The last thing Ed needed now was to see another corpse. In the end, Dave shrugged and departed without further protest. Ed, relieved, dragged himself up the stairs to bed, taking the ledgers with him and placing them under the mattress, just in case. He still didn't trust Dave - well, not completely. If Bob could break into the cottage with ease, he was sure Dave could. Returning to the cottage in the dead of night to steal them was something that Ed thought was well within Dave's capabilities.

# Chapter 36

The morning arrived far too soon for Ed. The same chink of sunlight seeped through the crack in the curtains as it had yesterday morning. When it reached his eyes it was like having acid poured onto his retinas, and he recoiled violently in his bed. Further sleep was not an option, as once again his bladder protested at being squashed, and by this time he was wide awake. He shaved with a shaky hand and, fortunately, managed to do this without cutting any major arteries. He decided to leave the moustache until after he had handed over the ledgers. He told himself it was just for a laugh but in truth, he was getting quite used to the look and he was really quite proud of it.

Bob wasn't too far behind Ed and walked unsteadily into the living room, grateful that Ed had made him a strong black coffee.

'I don't suppose there's anything for breakfast?' Bob asked quietly, but even that made his head hurt.

'Sorry mate, nothing but bread. I can do you some toast or we can go to one of the cafes and get something. I'm assuming you're up for a big greasy fry-up?'

Bob nodded but stopped abruptly as the sharp movement didn't agree with him, sending waves of pain coursing through his temples. He grimaced and sipped at his coffee.

Whilst Bob was showering, Ed packed up his few belongings into his holdall and stuffed the money into his rucksack, which only just fitted. The ledgers, which he retrieved form under the mattress, were put to the bottom of his holdall. The silver attaché case he deposited in the dustbin outside the front of the cottage. Putting the lid back on he hoped was symbolic of being the closure of this latest episode in his life. He was going to make a promise to himself to keep busy and keep out of trouble but knew that it was one he could never keep. Life never seemed to be that simple for Ed. For as long as he could remember, he had lurched from one disaster to another. This was just another one to add to the long list, which as sure as night follows day would continue, until one day his luck would run out.

Bob came down the stairs tentatively and dumped his holdall on the floor. After rubbing his temples and letting out a long weary breath, he declared it was time for breakfast. Ed nodded, and they headed out into the bright sunlight. Ed's glasses darkened, taking the edge off the sun, and Bob hastily pulled out his sunglasses. Together they made their way slowly to the cafe.

Bob rang Dave from the cafe to be informed he was halfway down the M6 and hoping to be in London in time to beat the lunchtime crowd to his favourite greasy spoon. Bob told him that the plan for them was to head back to St Albans and bring the ledgers to Scotland Yard, first thing Wednesday morning. Dave protested that they should do it today but Bob hung up, telling him to get lost.

The greasy fry-up, strong tea and short walk back to the cottage in the bracing northern wind seemed to revive them, albeit only slightly. Ed climbed into the passenger seat, glad that he wasn't the one driving the four hours back to St Albans. He was pleased they were going to St Albans first, as it gave him an opportunity to work on Laura. Hopefully she would take sympathy with his plight and let him back into her life. Right now he needed a bit of stability, and Laura always seemed to have a calming influence on him. With his heart full of optimism, he buckled up the seatbelt, wriggled into a comfortable position, and closed his eyes. A hard punch in the arm made him open his eyes.

'If you think you're sleeping all the way while I do the driving, then think again, sunshine. Get that iPod of yours plugged into the stereo and stick the Clash on. And make it bloody loud!' Bob shouted, as he started the engine. Ed did as he was told and they pulled out onto the main road with Tommy Gun blaring out and Bob singing at the top of his voice. Ed was already missing not having his own car.

The traffic was appalling and they encountered more road works than seemed feasibly possible, plus the obligatory tailbacks, for no apparent reason. Ed offered to swap driving when they were around Birmingham, where they stopped for a comfort break. It was met with the barrage of derisory comments from Bob that Ed had fully expected. Apparently, Ed still drove worse than Bob's granny and he couldn't trust him to sit the right way up on a lavatory, so there was no way he would trust him behind the wheel of his car. That suited Ed, who stretched out in the passenger seat and watched Bob wriggle to alleviate the cramp in his legs and pain in his shoulder from sitting in the same position. Unfortunately, the driving hadn't affected Bob's appetite for singing, and he was now murdering his way through Billy Idol's greatest hits. Ed switched off and turned his thoughts inwards to block out the din from the drivers seat. It was a great relief when they pulled up onto the drive of Raechael and Laura's house, a little after six in the evening. Bob switching off the engine, killing the stereo and subsequently his singing, was music to his ears.

They rang the door bell and were greeted by Raechael, who threw her arms around them both and gave them a hug. Fat Boy squeezed through the gap and jumped up at Ed, licking his face. Ed gave him a hug and made a huge fuss of him. Laura wheeled down the corridor and Ed moved past Raechael, who was now surgically attached to Bob, and knelt down and kissed her on the cheek and hugged her; it felt good.

'I'm not sure I like the new look,' Laura said. 'It's a bit camp.'

'I know, but it served a purpose. I'll lose the moustache and the glasses when this is all over and let the hair grow back.'

'I would. It's not a good look. The clothes are disgusting and the glasses are awful. Never did like moustaches.'

'Me neither, but I must admit I've kind of got used to it,' he replied, giving it a stroke.

They all stood there in awkward silence, until Raechael suggested they go through to the living room while she put the kettle on. Bob suggested something stronger and as nobody disagreed, Raechael came back into the living room, carrying a tray with two bottles of red wine. Bob poured and handed everyone a glass, raising his glass and saying 'Cheers.'

Laura wanted to know the ins and outs of their stay in the Lakes, and Ed asked if she wanted the warts and all version or just the bare bones - warning her that one wasn't very pleasant. Laura wanted the full unabridged version and sat forward in her chair in anticipation. Raechael didn't seem to want to know anything and looked nervously at Bob, who smiled back awkwardly.

Ed proceeded to tell the story, right from the very beginning from the first time he walked into Johnny's, for the benefit of Raechael. When Ed got to the last part of the story, narrating their exploits in the Lakes, Bob chipped in to make sure his expert driving and quick thinking came over much better than Ed would have told it. Raechael and Laura remained silent throughout, letting their facial expressions do the talking for them.

At the end of his narration, they stared at him unblinking.

'Somebody say something, for Christ's sake,' Ed said. The silence was making him decidedly nervous.

'But you're both OK?' Raechael finally said, embarrassed her question seemed so lame.

'I am,' Bob replied, 'although still a little hungover,' he added, grinning.

'What about you, Ed?' Laura asked.

'I've no idea, really. Better now it's nearly over, I think,' he said, giving her a weak smile. 'I feel a bit guilty about killing Paul, even though he would have killed me had it not been for the briefcase, and I'm not happy that I lost it completely in the pub - but other than a bit of self-loathing, I'm sure I'll be all right.' Ed shrugged. 'I'll survive,' he added solemnly.

'You could get counselling,' Raechael suggested.

Ed laughed. 'I'd probably end up getting committed and spend the rest of my life screaming for my medication. I'll be OK.'

'I need some fresh air,' Laura said angrily, spinning round in her chair and heading for the patio doors and the garden beyond. Ed looked at Bob and Raechael, who were holding hands on the sofa, and decided he should go and see Laura. Bob and Raechael getting amorous wasn't something he wanted to see.

Laura was sitting in her wheelchair next to the bench on the patio, staring out across the lawn to the conifers and shrubs beyond that marked the boundary of the garden. Ed sat down on the bench as close as he could get to her and stared silently ahead, with Fat Boy curled up at his feet. Unable to bear the awkward silence any longer, Ed reached out tentatively and held her hand. Rather than pull away she squeezed it gently and turned and looked at him. Ed stared into her sad smoky eyes that he always found so captivating and smiled, waiting for her to say whatever was clearly on her mind.

'Why do you keep getting yourself into these situations, Ed?' she asked, looking at him earnestly.

'I don't know. Shit just seems to happen to me,' he replied, not really knowing how to answer her.

'I've been worried sick for the last few days. Not knowing if you're all right. You could've been dead for all I knew! You just don't think about anything before you get involved, do you? You don't stop and think about those closest to you and how they feel!'

'That's a bit unfair. OK, I can be a bit impetuous, but I do think about those closest to me. Not a day goes by when I don't think about you. I've really missed you these last few weeks.' He felt a little fraudulent telling her this. The truth was he had thought more about TJ during his time in Ambleside. Laura was more of a guilty afterthought, which intruded whenever his thoughts turned to TJ.

Laura turned her head away and looked down the garden. 'Ed, in the short time we've been together, Jacqui was killed. Both you and the dog were stabbed and ended up in hospital and now four more people are dead and another one is in hospital. Plus God knows how many others walking around with cuts and bruises because of you! I can't go on like this, Ed. Knowing that perhaps one day it's going to be you who ends up dead.'

'I only got involved in all this because I was bored and missing you. Let's get back to how it was before and I'll promise things will be different. No more adventures, no more getting involved with bent coppers and dodgy nightclub owners.'

'Ed, you'll never change, that's the point. You'll always feel the need to be the knight in shining armour for every damsel in distress and underdog. That's just the way you are and that's never going to change.'

'I can change and I will change. Let's get this relationship back to normal and give me a reason to change. I don't want to lose you. I only got involved in this because I thought it would kill a couple of weeks and stop me moping about the house. If things hadn't changed between us, none of this would have happened.' He knew as soon as he had said it that it was nothing more than emotional blackmail but thought it was worth a try, even if he hated himself for it.

'Ed, it's not going to happen, OK. The last six months with you have been the best in my life. You're the kindest, sweetest, most generous man I've ever known and you have an uncanny knack of making me happy and feel so special. I love you to bits, but I can't carry on like this. I don't want you to change; you are what you are and that's what makes you so special, but I just can't carry on like this any more. It's just not fair on me.' Tears were flowing down her cheeks and Ed knew that whatever he said wasn't going to change anything. The end of the line had been reached. Ed nodded, reached over and pulled her to him, hugging her for what could be the last time.

'Just promise one thing,' he whispered in her ear. Laura nodded and wiped away her tears. 'Don't get involved with anyone like that ex of yours, Greg. You deserve a lot better than that, OK?' She nodded again 'Also, promise me you'll keep in touch and tell me how the operation went, and promise me we'll still be friends.'

'That's three things,' she said quietly.

'I know, but we've already established that I'm full of shit. So do we have a deal?'

Laura stared at him intently and leaned forward and kissed him passionately on the lips. Ed was surprised, but responded with enthusiasm. It was certainly the nicest and strangest break up he had been on the receiving end of. It beat the usual phone call, with the line It isn't you, it's me.

'That's the first time I've kissed anyone with a moustache,' she said, when they stopped kissing.

'First for me, too. How was it?'

'It tickled,' she said, smiling. Ed leaned forward and kissed her lightly on the neck, making her giggle and squirm in her chair. 'Pack it in, will you,' she said, pushing him away.

Ed put his arm around her and slipped the other under her legs, and lifted her out of her wheelchair and sat her next to him on the bench. Laura leaned against him and they sat in silence, staring down the garden. After what seemed a long time but still not long enough, Raechael poked her head through the patio door and announced she was going to bed. Ed hadn't paid much thought to that. Normally he would sleep with Laura, but wasn't sure if that was appropriate. Laura sensed his discomfort and looked up at him and smiled.

'Don't worry. I'm not going to make you sleep on the couch. You can come in with me.'

'OK. As long as you're OK with that?'

'It would be rude not to say goodbye properly and besides, I want to see what you can do with that moustache of yours.'

Ed laughed, lifted her into her wheelchair, and wheeled her back into the house.

# Chapter 37

Bob and Ed set off early to get to Scotland Yard and hand over the ledgers, which had been the cause of so much trouble. Ed was just pleased that Johnny was going to be brought to justice. He could then say he had kept his promise to TJ to do all he could to help her. It was a pity that the murder of her mother was effectively going to go unpunished but Johnny was going to be put away for a long time, which was a good compromise. Once the ledgers were in safe hands, Bob had agreed to take him round to see her and give her the good news. Fortunately it was a Wednesday and it would be her day off, so there was a good chance she would be at home; at least, he hoped so. He was looking forward to seeing the look on her face. She was excitable at the best of times and could just imagine how she would react, especially when he gave her the other good news he had planned. He thought about phoning her but decided that he would prefer to surprise her. He was also unsure if his phone was still being tagged as Bob suggested it would be, and whether phoning TJ might put her in trouble with Blackthorn. Despite being about to hand over the ledgers, nothing had really changed. Blackthorn and Johnny were still out there and presumably were unaware that the game was up. They were still a threat, until the police had read the ledgers and decided they had enough to bring them in - whenever that might be.

Bob seemed to be in a buoyant mood, once again singing along to the Clash, which he had insisted Ed put on – yet again. Ed would rather have listened to something a little mellower or anything other than the Clash again but wasn't in the mood for an argument with Bob, not this early in the morning. They had set off at half-past seven, when Raechael and Laura left for work, Ed saying goodbye to Laura for the last time. Last night had been a strange experience, making love, having been jilted only minutes before. However, it was a nice way of saying goodbye and Ed was sure they would keep in touch, as their parting had been amicable.

'You're very quiet this morning. Did she wear you out?' Bob said, breaking the silence.

'Very funny. As it happens, she broke off the relationship last night. Not just a temporary halt to proceedings until after her operation, but finished for good. End of, thank you very much, and goodbye.'

'Why the bloody hell did she do that? I got the impression she worshiped the ground you walked on,' Bob said with genuine surprise.

'She does in a way but she can't deal with my inability to keep out of trouble. Doesn't want to be sitting at home and getting a call from someone, saying sorry, but his luck ran out. I can't say I blame her. I promised to change but deep down, we both know that trouble just seems to stick to me like shit to a blanket. We're still friends and hopefully always will be but nothing more than just good friends.'

'You know, if I live to be a hundred, I don't think I'll ever understand a woman's mind. Surely, if you both love each other, if you end up dead it's going to be just as painful to hear - whether you're in a relationship or not?'

'Well, that's what I thought, but she was adamant and all I can do is respect her wishes. I can't say I'm happy about it but I don't have a choice. Bloody strange, being given the elbow and then sleeping together, but there you go.'

'Just don't go doing anything too stupid. I know what you're like, and going into self-destruct mode again isn't going to help anyone. OK?'

'Don't worry, I don't intend to,' Ed replied. 'Once we've handed the ledgers over and I've gone to make sure TJ's OK and try to persuade her to find a new job, I'm taking a holiday. There's nothing quite like a few weeks in Cornwall, tucked up in my caravan, to sort me out.'

'If you're coming down to my manor, you better bloody behave yourself.'

'I'll be good as gold, Bob. You won't even know I'm there.'

'Why is it I don't believe you for one minute?'

Ed laughed.

As they approached the outskirts of London the traffic became heavier, with the thousands of people commuting into the city to start the daily grind. Bob had insisted on getting an early start, saying he wanted to be in and out of London and back in St Albans by mid-afternoon. That suited Ed as that would give him enough time to hire a car and get back home, to start getting his life back to normal. Whatever was going to pass as normal from now on was a question he had yet to answer. He also wanted to avoid meeting Laura again. He had accepted the situation with her but didn't want to see her, knowing it wouldn't help with the healing process. She was still the most beautiful woman he knew and she oozed sex appeal. Seeing her again would only make things worse.

After a long and laborious crawl through central London, Bob finally parked the car near to New Scotland Yard. Ed retrieved the ledgers from his holdall and they walked the short distance from the car park to New Scotland Yard. When they arrived outside, Ed looked up at the famous sign that rotated endlessly day and night. Ed had read somewhere that it rotated over fourteen thousand times a day. Quite why he

225

remembered this useless piece of information he didn't know, nor why he had recalled it at this moment in time.

Once inside the building they walked over to the reception desk and waited, while an officious-looking sergeant finished a telephone call and then made a big show of moving some paperwork around, just to keep Ed waiting.

'We're here to see Jack Griggs,' Ed announced in a businesslike manner, a little annoyed at the desk sergeant's deliberate show of self importance.

'Would that be Superintendent Griggs?' the Sergeant replied condescendingly.

'Unless you've got two Jack Griggs in the building, yes it would be,' Ed said curtly, enjoying the fact it seemed to niggle the Sergeant. Bob remained in the background, smirking. The Sergeant picked up the phone and dialled an internal number and turned his back to them. He put the phone down with a smile.

'Superintendent Griggs is in a meeting and won't be available for at least another hour,' he said, obviously pleased.

'Well, in that case, get him out of his meeting,' Ed said raising his voice. 'And tell him that if I'm not sitting in his office in ten minutes with a nice cup of tea, I'm taking what I've come to give him back to its rightful owner.' Ed delighted in the look on the Sergeant's face and the colour it went. Bob was stifling a laugh behind him.

'And who should I say is calling?' he asked, through gritted teeth

'Ed Case. He'll want to see me.'

'Do you have any proof of ID on you, sir?' he asked, wanting somehow to gain the upper hand in the exchange. Ed gave him his driving licence, that no longer looked anything like him, and waited for the inevitable question.

'Looks nothing like you, sir and the name on this drivers licence is James Case.'

'Look, it's me. I was christened James. Everyone calls me Ed, and you don't want to find out why. Now, in seven minutes, I'm walking out of here and I wouldn't want to be in your shoes when Jack finds out. So make the call!' Ed turned and walked with Bob to some visitor seats.

'A bit hard on him, weren't you?' Bob said grinning broadly.

'Bloody jobs-worth. And I don't intend to sit here all day waiting until some guy decides he wants to see me, not with the price of parking round here.'

'Fair enough,' Bob said still grinning.

They were collected by a good-looking middle-aged woman, in a tight grey business suit. Bob seemed to approve of her, or at least her outfit, and ogled her taut buttocks all the way down the corridor. She said nothing as she led them to the door at the end of the long corridor. Without waiting for an answer after she tapped lightly on the door, she opened it and stood to one side, letting Ed and Bob through. Jack Griggs was sitting behind a large mahogany desk and, as Ed expected, was making a point of reading a document. They sat down in front of him while he continued to read, which irritated Ed. He looked at Bob, and frowned.

'Sod this, Bob, I'm out of here. If I wanted to watch someone read, I'd take a ride on a train,' Ed said, annoyed by Jack's arrogance. Ed stood and towards the door, not in the mood to play mind games.

'Sit down, Mister Case!' Jack said loudly and authoritatively, with the self-assuredness of someone used to getting what they asked for. Ed turned and walked back to his seat and sat back down, next to a smirking Bob.

'OK, if you stop reading. I'll give you the ledgers and then I'm out of here.'

'I'm just reading your file, Mister Case - or can I call you Ed? Or is it James?' he replied, looking up from the file in front of him.

'Call me what you like. I don't particularly care,' Ed replied nonchalantly. 'I didn't even know I had a file?' he added, perplexed at having never been in any real trouble.

'I can see that you're a very tenacious young man and have a certain way with people. You've been in the building five minutes and you've already upset the desk sergeant in reception and been rude to me.' He stared directly into Ed's eyes. Ed assumed to intimidate him but it didn't work, and he stared back. Jack was the first to look away and Ed took that as a small moral victory.

'Sorry about upsetting the desk sergeant. However, I don't like being treated like a second-class citizen by officious little men who get a kick out of pretending their time is more important than mine. Especially when that person is there to provide a service to the public and indirectly, through taxation, I'm paying his bloody wages,' Ed replied, feeling better for his outburst. 'So what's in the file then, I didn't think I had a record?' he added, his curiosity piqued. Griggs gave him a bored look.

'When it came to light that you were involved in our investigation into Johnny Gold, I made it my business to get some background information on you. I can see that your parents died when you were twenty-nine and left you some money, which you invested in shares, and subsequently became a millionaire. Your wife of eighteen months died two years later. I believe she was

228

- how should I say - having extramarital relations with a floor fitter, and the van they were making love in rolled down a gully and burst into flames. What else do we have - let me see. Oh yes, in May this year in Cornwall, you were involved in a series of altercations with a local thug called Mack, who you beat so severely he ended up in hospital; as did you, with a knife wound. This you justified, because he had stabbed your dog. He ended up shooting a friend of yours whilst trying to kill you and then shot himself, despite DCI Brown's best efforts to stop him.' He paused dramatically and gave Bob a knowing look, letting him know he thought that was bullshit, which of course it was. 'The next thing we have on you is the latest episode at Johnny's. It's quite interesting reading, Mister Case.'

Ed was quite shocked that he had so much information on him and looked at Bob, who just shrugged and pulled a don't ask me face.

'Lost for words, Ed?' Griggs said smiling unpleasantly.
'What do you want me to say? Nothing in there I don't know, and it's all true.'

'Tell me what you know about your time at Johnny's. Please don't leave anything out,' Griggs asked calmly, as if he knew that he had taken the wind out of Ed's sail.

Ed told him his version of events, from his first night in Johnny's to the last, and his escape to Ambleside and the events that unfolded there. Griggs listened intently, taking notes but not interrupting. When Ed finished, Griggs looked up and gave him another of his unpleasant smiles.

'Who killed Barry, if it wasn't you?' he asked.
'I think it was Spike. He drove down with Barry in another car but it could have been someone else, I

suppose. I'm guessing, but that's where my money would be.'

'How do I know it wasn't you?'

'You don't, but whatever you may or may not think about me, there's no way I could have killed him in cold blood. I shot into the ground, threw the gun down and walked away, just like I told you. It was only the next day at Johnny's that I found out he'd been shot in the back of the head.'

'You killed Paul in cold blood, so why should I believe that you didn't do the same to Barry?

'Because Paul was holding a gun to my head and was a scumbag. Barry was unarmed and harmless. I'm not even sure he was fiddling the books. I think Johnny just fabricated it as an excuse to set me up. Where are we going with this, by the way?' Ed asked, just wanting to hand over the ledgers and go.

'I'm just trying to ascertain your integrity. I'm also trying to find out if you have any more information that may help us with our investigations. If it makes you feel any better, I believe you. Anything else you saw that might help?'

'I saw Blackthorn and Denton handing over a briefcase full of drugs to Johnny. He's got CCTV in his office and has the private rooms covered. I assume he keeps the tapes as he kept a ledger, so if you get those, it might help. Other than that, the only other thing I learnt is that the bouncers only look after the dancers if they give them sexual favours. Not that that's really anything you'll be interested in.' Ed placed the ledgers on the desk and pushed them towards Griggs, who opened them and browsed through them quickly. 'Right, if that's everything then, I'm out of here,' Ed said, wanting to get away. Griggs looked at him, silently appraising him.

'I trust that your involvement with Johnny is now over and you won't be interfering in our investigation further?' he said in a tone even more condescending than the desk sergeant's, getting Ed's back up.

'You're an ungrateful bastard. Do you know that?' Ed said with venom. 'The way I see it, I've done you a favour, so cut the superiority bullshit with me. If it wasn't for me, you'd still have five more bad guys out there and you'd be nowhere near prosecuting Johnny or those two bent coppers you employ.' Ed stood and looked at Bob, who followed suit, nodding to Griggs as he walked behind Ed towards the door.

'I'm warning you, Case. I don't want to hear your name come up again in this investigation. Do you hear?'

Ed turned and looked at Griggs in the eye. 'Go screw yourself,' he said, slamming the door behind him. Griggs laughed at the closed door, thinking that Ed was right and he had done more in a week than his undercover operation had yielded in months. He even admired his complete lack of respect - make that total lack of respect - for authority, his self-belief and strong sense of right and wrong. He was tempted to call him back and offer him a job.

# Chapter 38

About the same time as Bob and Ed were arriving at New Scotland Yard, Blackthorn was arriving at the Ritz. He walked up to the reception desk and asked to see the manager, showing his warrant card. The duty manager arrived at the desk, smiled, and offered his assistance.

'I'd like to see your CCTV footage from two weeks ago. Wednesday evening to be precise, from about seven o'clock onwards,' Blackthorn informed the duty manager, whose badge identified him as Colin. Colin was obviously thinking about this and trying to remember the official line. Blackthorn decided to up the stakes. 'It's in connection with a murder enquiry. Of course, I can come back with a search warrant and arrive with blue lights flashing if you like, but I'm sure that will be unnecessary.'

'Of course, please come through to the security office,' Colin replied, flustered. The last thing he needed was any adverse publicity.

Colin sat down in front of a computer, typed in the access code and opened the digitally stored CCTV programme.

'Was there any particular area you wanted to see?' he asked Blackthorn.

'Let's start with the foyer and the entrance. If I don't get what I want from those, I'll have a look at the restaurant areas.'

Colin gave him a quick overview of the controls; how to fast forward, rewind, zoom in and out, freeze frame, print and change cameras. He vacated his position and advised Blackthorn he would remain in the room in case he encountered any technical problems. Blackthorn thanked him and took up position in front of the terminal.

Blackthorn picked up the mouse and moved the footage on to 7pm and began watching intently, stopping when anyone approached or a vehicle pulled up outside. Eventually he saw what he was looking for, and froze the picture. He moved the picture along a frame at a time until he got the best view of the faces. He then zoomed in, on the smiling faces of TJ and Case. They were slightly blurred but there was no doubt about it, it was them. Blackthorn smiled to himself. The lying little whore, he thought. It was time to pay the conniving bitch a visit. He selected 'Print' and waited while document printed out on the laser printer on the adjacent desk. He didn't need a printed copy but didn't want to arouse any suspicion in Colin by not taking physical evidence with him.

He thanked Colin and strode out into the lobby and sat down in a comfortable armchair and opened his briefcase. He pulled out a file and flicked through the contents, finally finding what he was looking for. He nodded to himself, pleased with his morning's work. He took out his mobile and rang Denton, telling him to meet him on Webber Row in half an hour, before hanging up.


'You were a bit stroppy in there, Ed,' Bob said as they walked out of New Scotland Yard.

'I didn't like their attitudes. I was doing them a bloody favour by coming in personally to hand these ledgers over and they give me all this I'm more important than you bollocks, and I can keep you waiting as long as I like. It makes my blood boil,' Ed replied angrily.

'I suppose I'm used to it. Most senior officers are the same. I even do it myself, sometimes. Jack's a good bloke though. I know he came over as a prickly bugger but he's one of the better senior officers I've worked under. You should've seen your face when he gave you your life story, it was an absolute picture!'

'I'm glad you found it amusing. It took me by surprise, I must admit,' Ed replied, smiling.

'It was meant to. I'm sure Dave gave him a quick briefing on what a pain in the arse you can be so he used that to put you on the back foot. I'd say he did just that,' Bob said, laughing at Ed's grumpy face.

'OK. Do you know where Webber Row is?' he asked Bob, who thought about it before replying.

'Just off Blackfriars road, isn't it?' he finally replied.

'I'm impressed. Do you know how to get there, though?'

'Of course I bloody well do. Now get in, and shut up.'


Denton was waiting in his car, when Blackthorn pulled up behind him and got out and banged on his roof, making him jump. Denton folded up his newspaper and exited the car.

'Morning, Boss, what are we doing here?' he asked Blackthorn.

'Paying TJ a visit. She's been a bit economical with the truth. It seems that our mutual friend Case took her to the Ritz for dinner a couple of weeks ago. I also think he stayed with her last Thursday, as he withdrew money from a cash machine on Borough High Street. Now, that's too much of a coincidence for me. He may have even left the briefcase here.'

'OK. I'll turn the place upside down. If it's there, I'll find it,' Denton said, pleased that they might at last be making progress.

They walked up the flight of stairs and knocked hard on TJ's door. TJ opened it in her dressing gown, having just showered, and looked at them nervously.

Blackthorn kicked the door fully open, making TJ stagger back. He walked through, staring at her with hard eyes, a malicious smile playing on the corner of his mouth. TJ backed off into the living room, looking back at Blackthorn, fearfully. Denton closed the door quietly and followed. TJ didn't know what to do and just kept backing off, until she ran out of room and was pressed up against the far wall. She was visibly shaking and her chest was rising and falling with each panicked breath she took.

Blackthorn stood inches from her face and grabbed her jaw, squeezing hard, making her cry out in pain.

'It seems you've not been telling us the truth, TJ,' Blackthorn said, still gripping her jaw in a vice-like hold. Blackthorn tutted three times, released his grip on her jaw, and slapped both her cheeks viciously. TJ whimpered in pain and fear and almost slumped to the floor, her legs having gone to jelly through fear. Blackthorn grabbed the front of her dressing gown, pulled her away from the wall, and hurled her to the floor. TJ sat up and shuffled backwards on her backside, tears welling up in the corners of her eyes. Blackthorn walked to the far side of the small room and picked up a dining table chair and placed it beside TJ. He bent down and pulled her up by the front of her dressing gown, dropping her onto the chair. TJ sat there sobbing and shaking, her dressing gown gaping, exposing her breasts. Blackthorn looked down on her appreciatively and roughly pulled her dressing down off her shoulders, restricting any movement in her arms. TJ's legs turned to lead and she felt dizzy, and had to fight back the urge to throw up. Blackthorn took the belt off his trousers and TJ instinctively tried to shrink away from him, which made him smile. He walked behind her and lifted the belt over her head and brought it down, deliberately brushing her breasts, making her shudder. He positioned the belt around her waist and arms and secured the buckle around the back of the chair, immobilising her. He walked round to face her, smiling and shaking his head, acting disappointed.

TJ stopped sobbing, determined not to give Blackthorn the satisfaction of seeing how afraid she really was. She took a deep breath and looked back, staring daggers at him. Blackthorn just laughed, amused by her futile act of defiance. She could hear Denton in the bedroom and it sounded like he was ransacking the place. He then moved onto the bathroom and she heard him kicking in the bath panel, checking for anything hidden, but finding nothing. A search of the kitchen was equally fruitless but Denton enjoyed smashing crockery and hurling implements and saucepans around. He took a sharp knife with him and headed into the living room to join Blackthorn, shaking his head, when he caught his eye.

TJ caught sight of the knife and feared the worst but Denton turned over the sofa and, using the knife, ripped open the hessian base, again finding nothing. Next to get his attention was the sideboard. He hurled the contents across the floor and found nothing.

'It's not here, Boss,' he informed Blackthorn, slamming the knife point first into the dining room table and leaving it there, much to TJ's relief. He turned and leered at TJ's exposed breasts and felt himself become aroused. He'd do something about that, before they left.

'TJ, you lied to us,' Blackthorn said.

'What do you want?' TJ stuttered.

'I want the ledgers. Where are they?'

'I don't know about any ledgers,' she replied firmly, determined to show courage.

'If you continue to lie, it's going to get a lot worse for you, TJ.' He stepped forward and ran a hand over her left breast. He held her nipple between his thumb and forefinger and squeezed it gently. 'It's amazing how sensitive a woman's nipple is,' he said, staring at her and increasing the pressure. TJ held out as long as she could before crying out in pain. Blackthorn gave it a further quick squeeze before letting go, making her cry out again.

'Did you enjoy your meal at the Ritz with Case, last week?' he asked. TJ now realised where this was leading.

'I didn't think it was important,' she lied.

'Really? What else didn't you deem important enough to tell us?'

'There's nothing else. That was it,' she lied again. Blackthorn had interrogated criminals for years and knew all the telltale signs of lies, and shook his head again.

'Wrong answer, TJ.' He caressed her right breast and grabbed the nipple and began to apply pressure. 'This is what happens when you lie to me, TJ. It hurts. Now, when was the last time you saw Case?' TJ let out a cry of pain and fought back the bile that was beginning to rise. She was determined not to betray Ed.

'At the club, last Thursday,' she said quickly. The pressure on her nipple increased once more to an unbearable level, and she screamed. Blackthorn took his hand away and slapped her round the face, hard. She tasted blood in her mouth and her cheeks felt like they were on fire.

'I'll ask you again, TJ. I know he stayed here on Thursday night so don't lie to me or I'll inflict pain, like you've never experienced in you life. Now, when was the last time you saw him!' he shouted.

'OK, it was Thursday. He was here Thursday,' she said, now sobbing uncontrollably at having let Ed down. Blackthorn smiled and nodded.

'Did he have anything with him? I know he did, but what did he do with it?'

TJ decided that if he knew, then she may as well tell him. 'He had a briefcase... a silver one. He took it with him when he left.'

'And you lied and kept this from us. If you'd told us this on Friday, all this could have been cleared up. Do you realise the trouble you've caused? Do you!' he shouted, causing her to flinch involuntary. 'I just hope he appreciates the sacrifice you made for him. What a pity - you won't be alive to hear him thank you for it.' TJ stared back at Blackthorn, knowing now that whatever she said or did would make no difference. She sat there passively, and wept.

Blackthorn turned to Denton. 'Over to you, Denton. Do your worst, you devious little bastard.' Blackthorn retrieved his belt and walked out of the flat. TJ was too terrified to move as Denton leered and walked towards her.

# Chapter 39

Bob pulled up on Webber Row and switched off the engine. Ed got out the car and stretched. The journey wasn't a long one but the traffic was heavy and Bob got lost, much to Ed's amusement. Bob blamed it on the new one-way systems that weren't in place when he was last working in London. Ed thought it was quite amusing, watching Bob curse and swear until he found a familiar landmark and got back on the right route.

A car pulled out and passed by at speed. Ed caught a glimpse of the driver and could have sworn it was Blackthorn. His heart skipped a beat, thinking the worst. He shouted for Bob to hurry and ran towards TJ's block, with Bob not far behind him. He was about to tap lightly on the door, but instinct told him not to. Where Blackthorn went, Denton went, and he could only recall one person in the car that sped by. He put his ear to the door but could hear nothing. Ed pushed the letterbox open and saw the carnage in the hallway left behind by Denton. His heart skipped another beat, thinking the worst once again. Bob had caught up with him and was breathing hard, just behind him.

'What's the big rush, Ed?' Bob asked, between pants.

'I'm pretty sure that I saw Blackthorn driving off as we pulled up. There's no answer, and I'm worried. It looks like the place has been ransacked.'

'Stand back,' Bob instructed him, and took a step back, ready to kick the door in. Ed put a hand on Bob's chest and fished out the spare key TJ had given him. He dangled it in front of Bob and grinned. Ed inserted the key and opened the door as quietly as possible.

The first thing he noticed was the extent of the mess previously seen through the letterbox, clothes and TJ's belongings everywhere. He looked at Bob, who frowned. Ed was trembling, fearing for TJ's safety; he just hoped he wasn't too late. It was then that he heard a sound from the living room. He walked silently on tiptoes, down the short hallway and looked through the open doorway. What he saw revolted him

TJ was on her back with her dressing gown pulled down off the shoulders so her arms couldn't move, and it was wide open. She was gagged and thrashing her head from side to side, her eyes wide and fearful. On top of her, bare-chested and with his trousers around his knees, was Denton. He was trying to stop TJ from wriggling away, and pulling down his underpants at the same time. Ed felt revolted, and the red mist descended. Denton turned and stared wide-eyed as Ed rushed towards him, and kicked him with all his strength between the legs. Denton screamed. It came out more like a high pitched squeal and he fell on his side, clutching his ruined testicles, crying in agony. Ed picked him up by his hair, which came out in clumps, and hurled him into the corner of the room, smashing heavily against the wall. Denton curled up in a ball, still clutching his balls, and moaned loudly. Ed ignored him and turned his attention to TJ.

He lifted her up and pulled her dressing gown up onto her shoulders, pulling it round to cover her modesty, and removed the gag. She threw her arms around him and hugged him, almost crushing him.

'I told you I'd be back,' he said, not knowing what to say. TJ looked up at him, her face streaked with tears and cheeks burning from the slaps Blackthorn had given her, and tried to smile through trembling lips. She stretched up and kissed him on the lips. 'Are you OK? He didn't...' She shook her head and continued to smother his face with kisses.

'No, you got here just in time. I'm so glad to see you. Although, I'm not sure I like the hair. Not enough on top and too much on the lip.' She buried her head in his chest and hugged him, sobbing uncontrollably. Ed looked over at Bob, who smiled back and gave him a thumbs-up. 'I'd better get some clothes on,' she said between sobs, sniffing loudly. 'Assuming I can find any. I think they turned the place over looking for those ledgers.'

'The police have them now, non-corrupt ones,' Ed said, trying to sound cheerful. 'This is Bob, TJ. He came up to the Lake District to look after me.'

'Looks like he's done a good job. Nice to meet you, Bob,' she said, sniffing and wiping her nose on the sleeve of her dressing gown, laughing nervously.

'Likewise. Are you sure you're OK, love?' he asked, concerned.

'Yeah, I'll be fine now. Look, I'll put some clothes on. You can put the kettle on and make some coffee. That is, if you can find any cups that aren't smashed.' TJ left them standing there, looking at the half-naked Denton, curled up in the corner, still clutching his ruptured testicles and crying like a baby.

'What are we going to do about him?' Bob asked. Ed smiled

'I've got an idea,' Ed said, grinning like a Cheshire cat.

'Why is it I don't like the sound of that?' Bob said. Ed shrugged.

'Get up, Denton!' Ed said angrily and kicked him in the ribs when he didn't move. Denton reluctantly got to his feet and made to pull his pants and trousers up. 'You won't be needing those. Get 'em off. Do it!' Ed shouted, and Denton began taking them off with shaking hands.

Ed turned to Bob and asked him for a pen. Bob produced one from his jacket pocket and handed it to Ed, who smiled and wrote 'I AM A CORRUPT

POLICE OFFICER AND A RAPIST' on Denton's back, making sure he applied more pressure than was absolutely necessary. Denton hissed in pain as the pen gouged his flesh.

Ed searched Denton's jacket and found the handcuffs he was looking for and cuffed Denton's right wrist, leaving the other end dangling. Bob looked on, wondering what Ed had in mind.

'Get out,' Ed told him, and shoved him towards the door. Denton turned and looked at Ed with a pleading look on his face. Ed stared at him with hatred, and pushed him out onto the landing. Denton grabbed hold of the railing but removed it when Ed smashed his fist down on it as hard as he could, breaking two fingers, and shoved him down the stairs. He stumbled and fell down the remaining stairs, landing heavily. He turned to Ed again and looked up at him, pleading, tears rolling down his cheeks. He tried to talk but through pain and fear, all that came out was an unintelligible burbling. Ed felt nothing but revulsion and hatred for him, and kicked him hard. Denton clattered down the stairs, hitting his head and cutting his brow. Ed dragged him out into the street by his hair and threw him down by the nearest lamp post. He pulled his arms around it and cuffed the other wrist. Denton begged him to let him go but Ed just sneered at him and punched him hard in the mouth, splitting his lips. Satisfied, he walked back to TJ's flat.

When he walked in TJ was sitting on the sofa, which Bob had turned upright, drinking tea and looking better than he had expected. She wore jeans and a lilac jumper and had combed her hair and put her make up on. Ed once again marvelled at her resiliency. Even after going through a traumatic ordeal, she was still thinking clearly enough to ensure she looked her best. She put her tea down, and ran up to him and threw her arms around him. Ed gave her a hug, lifting her off the ground, and kissed her.

'What did you do with Denton?' she asked, with a mischievous look in her eye.

'Take a look out the window.'

Both TJ and Bob walked over to the window and looked out at Denton. Some of the locals had gathered round and were spitting on him and jeering him. One woman even threw some dog shit at him, much to the delight of the crowd.

'That was a little bit vindictive, wasn't it?' Bob said.

'A corrupt copper, who just tried to rape TJ, I think that's letting him off lightly. With any luck the locals will tear him to shreds. Do you think I should call the police?' Ed asked, having second thoughts.

'I think you should. If the mob turns angry, do you want his death on your conscience?'

Ed nodded and dialled 999 on his mobile, not giving a name or address.

'So, what happened today, TJ?' he asked, as she sat down on the sofa next to him and leaned into him.

TJ told them about her ordeal and what Blackthorn was after, and Ed felt more than a little guilty.

'I'm sorry, TJ. If I hadn't come here, this would never have happened.' TJ drew her legs up under her and put her arm behind him, and leant into his chest.

'He knew about the Ritz, so it would have happened anyway,' she said happily. Bob raised his eyebrow at the mention of the Ritz, and Ed grinned back in return.

'Are you sure you're OK, TJ? You don't need a doctor?' Ed asked, still concerned.

'I'll be fine now. What's with the skinhead and the hairy top lip? God, you look so gay!'

'I was followed up the motorway by a few of Johnny's men. I managed to borrow a hat and scarf from some West Ham fans and sneaked away. When I got to the Lake District, I decided I needed a disguise, in case they followed me up there,' Ed told her grinning.

'I know they did. It's been the talk of the club,' she said, both concerned and excited.

Ed nodded. 'Dave with Andy and Paul, and Mo, with Asif and Abdul,' he replied, hoping she wouldn't ask any more questions.

'And what happened?' she asked.

'Only Dave made it back,' Ed replied flatly. 'Andy's in hospital somewhere. Probably Kendal or Penrith, and he won't be going anywhere for a while. Paul drowned and Mo and the other two died in a car crash. Dave turned out to be an undercover cop, investigating Johnny and Blackthorn.'

TJ stared at him open-mouthed before finally speaking. 'Did you kill them?' she asked, with no hint of emotion.

'I put Andy in hospital with a broken ankle,' he replied, not wanting to elaborate on how he completely lost control and did it out of pure malice. 'I pushed Paul into a river but he was holding a gun to my head at the time.' It was a white lie, but not far from the truth. He looked at Bob, who scowled at him. 'Mo spotted us in a garage and we had a car chase. Bob stopped the car over the brow of a hill and they swerved to avoid us and ended up going through a dry stone wall upside-down, and the car exploded.'

'I thought they only did that in American movies?' she said, with a hint of a smile. Ed nodded and smiled back. 'Sounds like you had a lot more fun than I did.' Ed looked at her and smiled. 'I'm just so glad you're alive. I've been worried sick about you. Not knowing if you're OK or not.'

'How's it been at Johnny's, then?'

'Pretty crappy, to be honest. Johnny tried to poison everyone and told them you robbed him and killed Barry. About the only person who didn't believe him was Pandora, would you believe? We've actually become friends of sorts.'

'Bob would like Pandora. He's a bit of a tit man,' Ed said, never tiring of trying to wind Bob up.

'There's nothing wrong with that,' he replied defensively. 'I'm just not into these skinny things you tend to go for.' TJ pouted at him 'Sorry, no offence TJ, you're quite well-proportioned,' he added, colouring slightly. TJ smiled back broadly at the compliment.

Ed excused himself to pay a visit to the bathroom, hoping that Denton and Blackthorn hadn't destroyed that as well. TJ seemed reluctant to let go of him and he had to prise her off, warning her that if she didn't let go she would end up with a wet sofa, which seemed to do the trick.

'Ed told me you could end up being his father in law. I bet that's going to be a little strange?' TJ said to Bob, once Ed had gone.

'Not any more I won't. Laura broke it off completely. She couldn't be doing with his knack of getting himself into bother and worrying herself sick. Did Ed tell you about the circumstances of how they met?' TJ nodded 'Well, I think Laura thought that was a one-off, and this episode was just too much for her. Seems to think that he's still got a self destructive nature and one day will get himself killed, and she doesn't want to be around when that happens. I think he's a bit upset about it. He may seem a roughty-toughty type but he's actually quite vulnerable, when you scratch under the surface. Did he tell you about his ex-wife?'

TJ nodded. 'And his attempted suicide and the death of his parents. He's had quite a hard life, really.'

Bob nodded 'Harder than most. Although, yours hasn't been all that easy from what he told me.'

TJ smiled and gave a shrug. 'I feel I've wasted my life, trying to prove Johnny killed my mother, giving up a reasonable job to get a job lap-dancing in his club - and all for nothing.'

'Well, at least it looks like your father is going down. Unlikely to be able to prove he killed your mother but he's going down anyway, if it's any consolation?' Bob said sympathetically.

'I'm glad he's going down for something. It'll have to do.'

'What are you going to do when he does - carry on dancing?'

'I haven't thought that far ahead. I really don't know,' she replied, the question taking her by surprise.

'I'm sure you'll think of something,' Bob said encouragingly.

'What's that?' Ed asked, catching the tail-end of the conversation as he entered the room.

'What I'll do next, once Johnny gets put away. I expect the club will close,' TJ replied.

'I thought you were only doing that work as a way to get nearer Johnny. You can get a proper job now.'

'Yeah right, with my CV, I'll be lucky to get a job. Not many jobs require jiggling your tits in someone's face as a qualification,' she said angrily.

'Well, maybe it won't be a problem when this is all over,' Ed replied, giving her a mischievous smile.

TJ have him a quizzical look. 'What do you mean by that?' she asked. The sound of a police car approaching with its siren blaring stopped him from answering. As one they rose and walked over to the window, to watch the events below unfold. The police turning up seemed to be a huge disappointment for the growing crowd below. Ed, Bob and TJ looked out the

246

window as the naked Denton was un-cuffed and bundled unceremoniously into the back of the police car with a blanket over him. The crowd booed, shook their fists and spat on the car as it sped off down the street with its blue light flashing.

'Will you be OK on your own for a couple of hours, TJ?' Ed asked.

TJ sat up and looked at him wide eyed. 'Where are you going?'

'I'm off to get myself a lap-dance.'

'Ed, don't be bloody stupid!' Bob shouted at him 'It's over. Let the police do the mopping up and don't get involved.'

'Bob's right, Ed. It could be dangerous. Don't go. Stay here with me,' TJ said pleadingly.

'I can't, it's eating away at me. All I want to do is go in there and give your old man a wallop on that great big, fat bugle of his and let him know his time's up. Then I'll come back here.'

'Well, if you're going then so am I,' Bob told him. 'TJ, there's no point in arguing with him when he's like this. Once he's made his mind up, that's it. I'll go along and look out for him and bring him back in one piece. Come on, Ed, let's get this over with.'

TJ held onto Ed and wouldn't let him get up. Ed looked at her and she kissed him again, passionately, on the lips. Ed pulled back and smiled. 'It's not enough to stop me going but it gives me a reason to come back,' he said, smiling broadly over his deliberately corny reply.

'I'm coming with you,' she replied, smiling back at him and still holding onto him. 'I don't want to stay here on my own, I don't feel safe here. To be honest, I don't think I'll ever feel safe here again,' she added. Ed looked at Bob, who shook his head and gave him a stern look. Ed felt guilty about leaving her here on her own, after the ordeal she had just been through. It was risky enough going back to the club himself and there was no way TJ could go in, not without increasing the risk to all of them. He was banking on his newly acquired camp disguise to get him through the door. Bob was unknown and wouldn't be a problem, but TJ would arouse suspicion immediately, especially if Jim or Spike were around.

'What about if TJ comes along but stays in the car, Bob?' Ed said, thinking it was a fair compromise. He looked at Bob and raised his eyebrows, looking for agreement.

'I don't see that I have much choice but to agree,' Bob replied resignedly. 'Come on, then, before I change my mind. But you stay in the car and wait. OK? And you,' he said, pointing at Ed. 'Go in, do what you have to do, and out. No sodding about. Got it?'

They both nodded in unison, TJ smiling broadly at getting her own way.

# Chapter 40

In the car, Bob was staring moodily through the windscreen. He knew that going to the club was something he would regret. It also meant not getting back to St Albans without having to crawl through the rush hour traffic. He silently cursed Ed, but knew how he must be feeling. If his life had been turned upside down by an arsehole like Johnny, he'd be doing exactly the same now - it was personal.

'Thanks, Bob. You don't have to come,' Ed said, knowing that Bob would wave it off and not be able to resist coming along for the action.

'We go in and you go rub it in with Johnny, then we come straight back out again. No pissing around, trying to give everyone in there a bloody good slap before you leave, OK. Just in and out,' Bob replied, giving Ed a stern look, which became even sterner when Ed grinned back. 'I'm only coming along so that I can make sure I hand you back to TJ in one piece, as I said I would.'

'Oh yeah? You're coming along because you don't want to miss out on anything and you know if it does kick off, it'll piss Griggs off - and there's nothing more you like better than to piss off the hierarchy.'

Bob smiled. 'You know me too well,' he replied and pulled out, heading towards Waterloo Bridge.

Bob parked in another NCP car park, which were doing quite well out of him today, and gave TJ strict instructions to stay in the car and wait. She nodded, gave him a sulky pout, and leaned through the gap between the front seats and threw her arms around Ed's neck, and kissed him. Ed gave her a broad grin and exited the car with Bob, and walked round to the club. Ed was confident that his new look would make him unrecognisable to everyone who knew him in the club, with the exception of Dave. Bob was an unknown so, all in all, Ed thought going into the club was relatively risk-free, as long as he kept his cool.

'What do you think of TJ?' he asked Bob.

'She seems very nice and very likeable. I see what you mean about the photo not doing her justice; she's stunning.' Ed nodded. 'She seems to like you. Quite a lot, I'd say,' Bob added.

'I know. The feeling's mutual. She always seems to be happy. The way she was today, you wouldn't have guessed what she had just been through, just seconds before we turned up.'

'Is this the start of a beautiful relationship?' Bob asked sarcastically.

Ed gave a shrug. 'I don't know. I'm not sure her father would approve of me,' Ed said, making them both laugh.

They walked round to the entrance, where there were no girls on the pavement touting for business, but then it was a Wednesday afternoon. Bob gave the outside of Johnny's a once over and seemed unimpressed. He turned to Ed and nodded, signalling it was time to go. They walked down the short flight of steps and through the door. The little booth where you would normally pay for entry was empty, but as it was free entry before ten o'clock, it was to be expected. They entered the main bar and seating area and were greeted with a curt nod from a bouncer, one who Ed didn't recognise. He and Bob took a seat near the bar, as near as possible to the doors leading to the corridor and the stairs beyond to Johnny's office. They could have sat anywhere as the club was virtually empty, with the exception of one or two punters.

Debbie began walking towards them with a broad smile, and an exaggerated swing of the hips. She asked if they wanted a drink and Bob ordered two pints of lager, declining the offer of a dance when she returned, saying he'd have one later once he'd quenched his thirst. Ed noticed that he visibly winced when he handed her a ten pound note for the drinks and Debbie walked off, giving no indication of coming back with change.

'That was Debbie,' Ed informed him. 'We never really got on. The girl up on stage is Suzanne. She is awesome on that pole. Have a watch, it's really something. The girl on the far side lap-dancing is Pandora. The bouncer down the far end is Spike. I don't know the bloke we just walked by, and that's our mate Dave on the far side, who we both know.'

'Just in case we need to make a quick exit, what's the layout of this place?'

'Beyond the bar there,' Ed said indicating with a nod of his head to the far end of the bar, 'is a door that leads to a canteen area and the changing rooms for the girls and staff toilets. The door at this end leads to Johnny's office via a set of stairs on the left, and the right set of stairs leads to two private rooms. At the end of the corridor is an exit into the back yard,' Ed explained.

'Thanks. You're right about that bird on stage, she's giving me the bloody horn,' Bob exclaimed.

'You could always have a dance?' Ed suggested.

'The day I have to pay for it, is the day I die,' Bob replied hastily.

Ed looked up as Pandora made her way through the tables and made a direct line towards Bob and Ed, hips and breasts swinging provocatively.

'I may make an exception for that, though. That is very tasty,' Bob whispered excitedly.

'That's Pandora. I told you you'd like her.'

Pandora arrived at the table and looked down on them, licking her glossed lips with her hand resting on

251

her hip. 'I don't suppose you want a dance do you, love?' she said, looking at Ed.

'Why not?' he replied, putting on his best Irish accent.

'Wouldn't have thought I'd be your type, would I?'

'Too right, darlin' - I'm silicone intolerant,' Ed replied, with a grin.

Pandora stared at him for several seconds, before whispering 'Ed?'

Ed smiled and said 'That's me. Larger than life and camper than Boy George.'

Pandora smiled broadly and bent down and kissed him on the cheek. 'You're still alive then?' she said rhetorically. 'You can have this one for free,' she told him. Ed shrugged and sat back. 'I don't like the new look, by the way. You look very gay, and the glasses look stupid. And that shirt should be illegal.'

'It'll all be gone by morning. It came in handy at the time, but it's served its purpose,' Ed said.

'I didn't believe them when they said you killed Barry and stole Johnny's money,' she said over her shoulder, grinding her buttocks into Ed's groin.

'Spike shot him,' he said in a strained voice. 'At least, I'm pretty sure it was. I did pinch his cash, though. Not deliberately, mind you. I hit him over the head with it and in my panic to get out, forgot to drop it. I'm not a thief - well, only on a technicality. Jesus, Pandora, you're quite good at this, aren't you?' he said, feeling that familiar stirring in his loins.

Pandora turned round and held his head and pushed it into her ample cleavage. 'I'm the best. I told you. So, what did you do with the money?' she whispered in his ear.

'Nothing yet. I'll find a worthy cause, though. I won't be keeping it for myself, I've got enough. Is

252

Johnny in today?' he asked, shifting uncomfortably in his seat

'He's in his office. Why, are you going to pay him a visit?'

'That was the intention. Just to rub it in and let him know it's all over for him and for Blackthorn. Have you seen him today?'

'He's not been in today, and before you ask, Jim's out on an errand.' She crouched down and began rubbing herself along Ed's thigh, and began purring.

'Thanks Pandora, but you can stop now. I think I've had enough. I don't want to walk into Johnny's office with a hard-on,' he said, but rather too late.

'I think I'll know when you've had enough,' she replied, lifting his head from her cleavage and giving him a salacious smile. Ed glanced at Bob, who was gawping and gave him an excited thumbs-up.

'I think you should save some for my friend, Bob,' Ed said, almost pleadingly. 'Pandora, say hello to Bob.'

'Hello, Bob,' she said in a sexy, breathy voice. 'Don't worry, I've got plenty left for you.'

Bob gulped and stared at her like a little boy with money to blow in a sweet shop. Pandora turned round and began pushing her buttocks into Ed's groin again, which was getting to be too much. She really was very good.

'I think we're all done here, aren't we?' she said, turning around, lifting Ed's chin and kissing him lightly on the lips. Ed rolled his eyes and Pandora giggled and moved onto Bob, who was all but rubbing his hands in anticipation. Unfortunately it was not to be, as Dave came over and whispered in Pandora's ear. She pouted, blew Ed a kiss, and walked off.

'What the hell are you two doing here?' Dave wanted to know.

'I've just come to say hello to Johnny. Don't worry, I'm not going to start any trouble. I'm just going to say what I want to say and leave. That's it,' Ed said defensively.

'You two just don't know when to stop, do you? I thought Griggs made it clear when you saw him this morning. I think you've caused enough trouble as it is,' he hissed.

'Dave, I'm gonna tell you what I told him. I've done more to further your undercover operation in two weeks than you or anyone else has in bloody months. So don't go giving me all this bullshit about jeopardising your operation, because it ain't gonna wash with me. Besides, this is personal, and more so since this morning. Did you hear about Blackthorn and Denton?'

'No,' he replied meekly.

'They paid TJ a visit and roughed her up a bit. When they got what they wanted to know, Blackthorn left her with Denton. Nice bloke trussed her up and tried to rape her. He probably would've done if we hadn't turned up. I left him with bollocks the size of watermelons and tied him naked to a lamppost. The police have him now, unless they've taken him to hospital. That's why this just got a lot more personal,' Ed said, angrily but keeping his voice just above a whisper.

'Jesus Christ. Look, I'm sorry about that, Ed, I really am, but being here isn't going to help. Just leave and forget about Johnny, all right?'

Ed looked at Bob, who shrugged, making it perfectly clear it was Ed's call. Ed knew that the best course of action would be to leave but now he was here, he really wanted to give Johnny a piece of his mind. Still undecided, he blew out a long breath, delaying a decision. It was a delay that changed

254

everything. Ed looked up as Spike was making his way towards them, having seen Dave talking animatedly and thinking there was a problem.

Spike was nearly upon them, and once again Ed was thinking on his feet and decided on a course of action. He got up, acting drunk, and barged into Spike - calling him a 'fucking moron' - and staggered towards the gents. He knew instinctively that Spike would rise to the bait, and heard him following. Ed grinned to himself and lurched through the door of the gents. Once inside he stepped into the first vacant cubicle, and waited.

He didn't have to wait long as Spike slammed the door back, almost taking it off its hinges. Ed put his arms up and held onto the supporting strut over the cubicle door, and braced himself. Just as Spike came level with the door, Ed pulled back and swung, lifting his legs as high as possible, bending his knees and launching a savage two-footed kick towards Spike's head. He made contact and pushed the kick through, straightening his knees. The blow was massive and nearly lifted Spike off his feet, sending him crashing into the wall, head-first. The sound of the back of his head connecting with the lavatory wall was like the sound of a block of wood being hit with a sledgehammer. Spike's eyes glazed over and he slumped to the floor, blood trickling down the back of his head, leaving a red smear down the white tiled wall.

Ed pulled off Spike's shoes and removed his socks, which were sweaty and unpleasant to the touch. Fighting back his nausea, he pulled Spike's arms behind his back and used one of the socks to bind his wrists. He used the second to bind his ankles and then pulled his trousers and boxer shorts to his ankles. Ed couldn't resist a quick look and was satisfied that he was called Spike because of his haircut, and not because he had an amusingly-shaped penis. Ed then dragged him into the cubicle and sat him on the lavatory, with the lid and seat up. Satisfied that he was wedged in nicely, Ed locked the door and, using Spike as a makeshift ladder, slipped over the cubicle partition and dropped down into the adjacent cubicle. It was a lot easier than the last time he had tried to do that some months back, when he had got his belt caught on a rogue screw and became stuck. He smiled at the memory of happier times.

Ed walked back out and gave Dave and Bob a thumbs-up and indicated he would be five minutes, before heading through the doors into the corridor and onwards to Johnny's office.

Bob looked at Dave, who was clearly not happy, and shot him an irritable glance. He looked at his watch and scowled at Bob, and walked off angrily. Pandora, ever the opportunist, walked over to Bob and smiled. 'You're next,' she said huskily. 'Sit back and enjoy the ride.'

# Chapter 41

Sitting in the car in the multi-storey car park, TJ was bored and getting cold. She wished she had found a jacket amongst the carnage left behind by Denton in her flat. She didn't have a watch on and hadn't looked at the clock on the dash when Ed and Bob had left her so couldn't say how long it had been, but it seemed like ages ago. TJ decided a quick trip to Starbucks would relieve the boredom and give her something to warm her hands on. Bob had given her strict instructions to stay in the car, but she decided that the risk of bumping into anyone from the club was remote. Even if she did, it wouldn't raise any suspicion, unless of course it was Blackthorn - but she reasoned the chances of that happening were also remote.

She left the car and was faced with a dilemma. Should she leave it unlocked and risk the car being stolen, or lock it and not be able to get back in when she returned, as Bob had taken the key with him? Bob and Ed had, in her opinion, been gone some time, so by the time she got back to the car with her coffee, they would be on their way back. Reluctantly she locked the car, thinking that Bob would be mightily pissed off with her if it did get stolen. She paused before pushing the door to, having second thoughts. Finally, she slammed the door shut with a shrug, and set off to find coffee.

Starbucks was busy, as it always was. After what seemed a very long wait she finally got to order a black Americano. She preferred latte but decided that a black coffee would stay warmer longer. Now that she was locked out of the car, she would need a bit of extra warmth. Rather pleased with her clear thinking, she began walking briskly back to the car.

Blackthorn was on his way to Johnny's when he stopped suddenly in the street, much to the annoyance of the woman behind him who wasn't paying attention and walked straight into the back of him. Blackthorn shot her such a menacing glare that it took the tirade of abuse she was about to hurl at him out of her mouth. He blinked and narrowed his eyes at the petite blonde, leaving the Starbucks across the road from him. It couldn't be TJ, he reasoned; he'd left her in the capable hands of Denton. Even if she had somehow survived that sadistic, depraved bastard, surely she wouldn't be wandering around Soho? He needed to make sure. If it was her, she could lead him to Case. He patted his jacket pocket, checking his gun was still there, already knowing that it was, and crossed the road, following her at a safe distance.

TJ was oblivious of her surroundings, content with having the coffee to keep her hands warm. Had she been more vigilant, things may have turned out very differently. Blackthorn was biding his time, wanting to avoid any unnecessary scenes in full view of the public. Not that it was a particular problem. A quick flash of his warrant card would deter even the most curious. When TJ turned down the deserted side street where the car park entrance was located, he stepped up his pace. Within a few long strides he was directly behind her. He placed his strong hand on her shoulder and spun her around. One look at the terrified face confirmed he was right. TJ stared back wide-eyed and open-mouthed at Blackthorn, who was grinning malevolently.

The scream of panic she had building never left her throat, as Blackthorn clamped his hand over her mouth and pushed her roughly against the wall. She panicked and began to hyperventilate, cursing her stupidity at not heeding Bob's warning.

'Hello, TJ,' Blackthorn said menacingly through gritted teeth. 'Where the fuck is Case?'

Unable to answer as his hand was still clamped over her mouth, all she could do was stare back and shake her head from side to side. She felt she had betrayed Ed on her last encounter with Blackthorn and there was no way she would do it again. She was still holding her coffee and tipped it over the hand that Blackthorn had over her wrist. The coffee only dribbled out of the small hole in the top of the carrying lid, but it was enough. Blackthorn hissed in pain as the piping hot coffee scalded the back of his hand and wrist. He did what anyone else would do and let go of TJ's wrist to shake of the liquid off, exactly what TJ had hoped he would do. She took flight and ran as fast as she could, throwing the coffee in Blackthorn's direction. Being a dancer, she was fit, but was hampered by her slip-on shoes. Her body ached from her earlier encounter with Denton and Blackthorn, particularly her nipples which chaffed painfully against the lace of her bra, still sore from Blackthorn's improvised torture. She pushed the pain out of her mind and concentrated on her escape. Blackthorn was closing. He too was fit and had a much longer stride. She dared not look behind her as she darted into the entrance to the multi-storey car park. Blackthorn followed, knowing she had made a mistake.

TJ stopped on the third floor and ducked down behind a people-carrier, trying to keep her breathing under control, hoping Blackthorn would continue up to the fourth floor, allowing her to quietly escape. She was sure her heart was pounding so loudly that Blackthorn would hear it from the first floor. She put her hand over her chest, in an attempt to muffle the noise.

Blackthorn became aware that TJ had stopped, no longer hearing her tiny footsteps. He stopped and listened. He heard nothing so crouched down to look under the cars. He caught sight of a white shoe, sticking out from behind the wheel of the blue Ford Galaxy, and smiled. He approached stealthily, taking out his gun when he got nearer, after ensuring that there was nobody around.

TJ froze when she heard the sound of Blackthorn, cocking his weapon by pulling the slide back; she gasped involuntarily. She had only ever heard that sound in films but she knew what it was, and she knew what it meant. Her only option was to run for it. The thought of her life ending, crouching behind a car, was not something she wanted to contemplate. She edged around the back of the Galaxy and squeezed in behind the adjacent Honda as quietly as she could, and continued along the line of cars. She looked under the car and could see the feet of the approaching Blackthorn. When he reached the front of the Galaxy, he raised his weapon and spun round, aiming down the side, which was now empty.

TJ seized the moment and ran up the ramp to the next floor, the down ramp being too far away and, she reasoned, it would leave her exposed and vulnerable to being shot. Blackthorn cursed and followed. He wasn't overly concerned as after the fourth floor there was only the roof left and from there, there was nowhere else to go. TJ realised this, but too late. She reached the top, bursting through into daylight ,and for a moment was disorientated and began to panic.

Blackthorn reached the top floor seconds behind her and headed her away from the exit ramp. There was only one place left to go, and that was over the perimeter wall that she now found herself backed up against. She took a furtive glance over the top and stared at the five storeys of nothingness, to the pavement below. The end of the road had been reached. Blackthorn walked slowly and purposely towards her, a satisfied grin spreading across his face. TJ's legs began to tremble and tears stung her eyes as Blackthorn stood a few feet in front of her, his gun aimed at her face.

He would have killed her there and then and thought nothing of it, had it not been for the car park security guard, who heard the running and had come to investigate. Brian Jones walked up the exit ramp and confronted Blackthorn. He put his gun away and showed him his warrant card.

'Police,' Blackthorn announced. 'She's wanted in connection with a murder - stay where you are. She could be dangerous.'

Jones regarded Blackthorn and TJ and decided that he didn't like the look of him, and thought the girl looked about as dangerous as his ten year old grandson. However, he'd been brought up to respect the law and did as he was told, but eyed Blackthorn suspiciously. Blackthorn smiled at him and approached TJ, who was too frightened and too exhausted to move. Blackthorn took out his handcuffs and cuffed TJ's right wrist to his left. He would have preferred to have kicked her all the way down to the ground floor, but knew from looking at Jones that he would probably report him for police brutality. This way, he would arouse less suspicion. As it was, Jones followed him all the way down to the ground and watched them leave the premise. Blackthorn headed towards the back entrance to Johnny's, where he could enter unseen and finish the job. TJ was pulled along, just glad that she was still alive; at least for the moment.

# Chapter 42

Ed took a deep breath and looked up at Johnny's office door from the bottom of the stairs. In the car, he had been thinking through what he was going to do or say when he arrived at the club. Events so far hadn't gone as he expected. Not that he really had a plan. The incident with Spike certainly wasn't planned, but he felt more than satisfied the way things had turned out. It was one thing less to worry about now, which left only Jim and Blackthorn, as he didn't see Johnny being too much of a concern.

Ed composed himself and walked up the short flight of steps to Johnny's office. At the top of the short flight he peered through the frosted glass, looking for any signs that Johnny had company. Seeing only the blurred outline of Johnny, sitting behind his desk, Ed knocked and walked through, without waiting for a reply.

The first thing that Ed noticed was Johnny's pallor, which was grey and clammy. He didn't look well at all and for a fleeting moment Ed felt sorry for him, before remembering the events of the last two weeks. The air was thick with stale cigarette smoke, the overflowing ashtray on his desk testament to a full-on habit. Johnny looked up at him and gave him a weary stare, and downed the remains of the whisky from the crystal tumbler he was holding, wincing as he swallowed. Ed smiled back, pleased that all was not well in the world of Johnny Gold.

'I thought you'd turn up. You must be quite pleased with yourself?' Johnny said bitterly. It was almost as if he had been expecting him.

'Not especially so. Your ledgers are with the police now, so I thought I'd pop round to give you a big smug grin and say enjoy your last few days as a free man. I was also going to give you a thump on that big fat hooter of yours,' Ed replied, grinning broadly. Johnny stared back and opened the drawer in his desk. Without taking his eyes off Ed's, he pulled out a bottle of whisky and topped up his glass. Ed noticed his hand was shaking quite badly, the bottle rattling against the side of the glass, another sign that Johnny was under a lot of stress. He lit a cigarette and blew out a long stream of smoke in Ed's direction and gave a hacking cough, causing him to clutch his chest as if he was racked with pain. Beads of sweat appeared on his brow, which he wiped away with the back of his hand.

'As well as being a pain in the arse, you're a tenacious bastard, I'll give you that. It's a real shame things didn't work out as I thought they would. You could have been a real asset to me,' he said with a shake of his head, reaching into his drawer once again and pulling out a handgun, which looked similar to the one that he had given Ed two weeks ago. He still didn't know what make it was, and to be honest he didn't care. They were all bad news and they all killed people, no matter who made them. Johnny gave him a satisfied smile, which Ed noticed looked more like a grimace of pain. Perhaps it was, he thought, as Johnny aimed the gun at him, sweat continuing to bead on his forehead. 'Give me one good reason why I shouldn't just blow you away, right now?'

Ed was trying to find an answer but the adrenaline was pulsing through his veins, making logical thought nearly impossible. It seemed that staring down the barrel of a gun was something that didn't become easier each time it happened, which for Ed's liking had been far too frequent recently. In the end he said the first thing that came into his head. 'I don't think your daughter would be too happy with you if you did.'

The smile dropped from Johnny's face and Ed detected the briefest flicker of emotion in his eyes.

'What the fuck do you know about my daughter?' he hissed, as a fresh wave of pain caused him to clutch his chest.

'Probably a little more than you do,' Ed replied, seeing an advantage to be exploited. 'She's already pissed off with you for killing her mother, so killing me isn't going to make a great deal of difference to how much she despises you,' Ed replied calmly.

'Is this what this is all about? My daughter, who I haven't seen in about thirty years, has sent you to screw up my life.'

'It's been a lot less than thirty years, Johnny. Tell me, what is your daughter's name?' Ed asked grinning.

'Tracey Jane...' he replied, the penny suddenly dropping. 'TJ's my daughter?' he said incredulously, almost in a whisper.

'Give the man a banana!' Ed said sarcastically. 'She gave up her career to learn how to dance, just so that she could get a job working for you. She's thrown away everything, just so she could try and get revenge on you for killing her mother.'

'I didn't kill her mother,' he replied bitterly. 'Like you, she's got it all wrong. I loved Helen. I wouldn't have... I couldn't have killed her,' His eyes glistened at the painful memory and he pulled in a deep breath, causing him to wince in pain once more.

'Well if you didn't, who did?' Ed asked, trying to keep any hint of compassion he felt out of his tone, not to mention surprise at this new revelation.

'Blackthorn did,' he replied with a snort of derision. 'Believe it or not, I'm the good guy in all this. I wanted to run a straight business - well, more or less - but Blackthorn had ambition,' he sighed wearily. With his free hand he wiped away the tears that had spilled down his cheeks. Ed turned away in an effort not to feel any compassion for the man that had turn his world

264

upside-down and made him loathe what he had become.

'That's not what it says in your precious ledgers. It looks to me like you had him in your pocket and used it to your advantage. Got yourself a nice, profitable sideline in drugs.' Ed spat back.

'You know nothing!' Johnny replied angrily. 'Blackthorn killed Helen because she threatened to turn him in. Those ledgers were my insurance policy, for when I needed them. The money I paid to Blackthorn and Denton wasn't because I wanted to keep the law sweet. It was because he was blackmailing me, you stupid bastard.' He stared at Ed. The gun was still aimed at him and he lit another cigarette with his free hand, giving Ed time to digest what he had just told him, before continuing. 'Years ago, I was running a reasonably legit business and there was a bit of a turf war going on. This was back when Soho was rife with corruption and sleaze, even more so than it is now. Blackthorn was young and ambitious and already had a number of the firms in his pocket offering protection - me included. One day he helped me out by covering up an incident, when I shot a rival gang member in self defence. After that, he leaned on me heavily and demanded more and more. It's been like that for years. I suppose I've just come to accept it, and the money from the drugs was good - although, if you read the ledgers, you'll see that Blackthorn was getting the lion's share of it.'

Ed stared back not sure if to believe Johnny or not. 'How do I know this isn't all a load of bullshit?' he eventually asked.

'Because I'm the one with the gun and have no reason to lie. That's why I wanted you on board. I wanted someone with some balls like you, who I could trust, and who could help me bring Blackthorn down without incriminating myself.'

'What about Jim? I thought he was your right hand man.'

Johnny scoffed. 'Jim. He's just as corrupt as Blackthorn. I know he blackmails the girls out there but he's Blackthorn's man, not mine. He's here just to keep an eye on me, to make sure the gravy train doesn't get derailed. He used to be in the force years ago but got kicked out after a string of complaints for using excessive violence. I've got nobody I can trust. When I saw you out there sticking up for TJ, I thought I saw some good in you. I saw someone who was honest and halfway decent who could help me. It seems I was wrong.' He finished by coughing loudly and clutching his chest.

'Maybe if you'd told me all this two weeks ago I would've helped, rather than trying to stitch me up for murder, you daft bastard!'

Johnny gave him a quick smile and shrugged. 'Like I said before, I underestimated you. When you didn't shoot Barry, I had to think on my feet and, well...' he shrugged again and added, 'Perhaps I've been tainted by Blackthorn for too long and am becoming too much like him. I can't say I'm proud of what I've become.'

Ed was beginning to feel sorry for him but didn't want to show any compassion. Even if Johnny was feeling remorse, he'd still been responsible for a sequence of events that had screwed up his chances of reconciling his differences with Laura. On top of that, four people were now dead. One of which Ed had been solely responsible for, and another two were in hospital. Ed hadn't really had time to think about any of that but he knew the memories would always be there to haunt him.

'Shooting me isn't going to achieve anything, Johnny. The police have the ledgers now; it's all over. Shooting me is just another nail in your coffin.'

'Nobody gets one over on me! I've got a reputation round here. This is all about pride. This is personal, which I guess is why you're here now.'

Ed nodded.

'So do I get to walk out of here, or are you going to shoot me?' Ed eventually replied, remembering that Johnny was still pointing a gun at his chest. Before Johnny had a chance to answer, the door behind him burst open. Ed turned, expecting to see Bob, but stared back at Blackthorn, holding onto TJ, with a gun held to her side. Ed stared open-mouthed, and his legs began to feel hot and unsteady.

'Well well, looks like the gang's all here,' Blackthorn said unsmiling, his eyes boring into Ed's. 'Found this one coming out of Starbucks,' he said, hurling TJ into the corner of the room. Ed bristled but was in no position to do anything, as he now had a gun pointing in his back as well as his chest. Regardless, he walked over to TJ and picked her up off the floor where she had fallen and was sobbing quietly, ignoring the order from Blackthorn to stay where he was. He pulled TJ towards him and kissed her on her forehead and pulled her to him, putting a protective arm around her.

'I told you to stay in the car, you silly cow,' he said to her quietly. She said nothing, but he felt her give a small shrug.

'How very touching,' Blackthorn said. Ed turned round to stare at him and pushed TJ so that she was directly behind him. 'Makes no difference, you know. If I shoot you, a bullet from a gun this powerful will go right through and take you both out. Not that it makes much difference, really. If the bullet lodges in your spine, I'll just have to waste another bullet on your girlfriend there. Mind you, I'm surprised you want to go anywhere near her after what Denton done to her,' he said, laughing callously.

'Denton didn't get the chance to do anything. I turned his gonads into pancakes before he even got his pants off. Think he's probably going to be in hospital for quite some time. Who knows, he may even be walking again by Christmas,' Ed replied angrily. Blackthorn just laughed. Ed saw an opportunity. Perhaps he could alienate Blackthorn when he told Johnny what he and Denton had done earlier. 'That was a particularly odious thing to do, wasn't it? Torturing TJ and then leaving her to Denton, to rape and then murder. You're a sick bastard, you know that?' Blackthorn laughed humourlessly.

'I always did tell him his unhealthy appetite for the girls would land him in trouble. Looks like I was right. Any last requests before I shoot you?' Blackthorn asked, smiling.

'Miss?' Ed replied, smiling back nervously, doing his best to hide his fear 'Must be some achievement to kill two generations of the same family. One for the record books, eh?' Ed added, hoping to buy a bit of time, hoping Bob would be arriving soon to save his stubborn arse. Surely the five minutes were long gone by now? Blackthorn gave him a quizzical look, the smile dropping. 'TJ is Helen Barnes' daughter. Johnny's daughter too, come to that.'

'Well, fuck me. You're a sly little cow, aren't you?' He turned to Johnny and raised an eyebrow. 'Did you know about her?'

'Not until today,' he replied, wiping more sweat from his clammy brow.

Blackthorn turned to stare at TJ. 'I enjoyed killing your mother. Of course, I raped her before I slit her throat. Perhaps I'll do the same to you. Now I know

Denton hasn't been there. I just hope you're as good a lay as your mother was,' he said, laughing.

The first shot was to his stomach, entering at an angle, pulverising his intestines and blowing half his right kidney out of the exit hole in his back. The second shot entered just below his left eye and blew away most of the back of his skull, splattering the wall and door behind with bone and pinkish-beige brain matter. Blackthorn slumped backwards and landed heavily on the floor, blood pooling out of the two wounds, soaking into the carpet.

Ed just stared, unable to take his eyes off the ruined body of Blackthorn, watching as the blood spread out across the floor and the tissue from his brain slid down the walls like pink phlegm. A crash to his left broke his trancelike state. Johnny was lying on the floor, only his head and shoulders visible, the remainder of his body hidden behind his large desk.

For the first time since the shots were fired, Ed became aware of the smell. A heady mixture of the cigarette smoke, mixed with the acrid smell of gunpowder and blood. He also became aware of the ringing in his ears, a result of the deafening gunshots in the confines of the small office, and the incessant screaming coming from TJ, just behind him; the sounds of violence. He turned round and pulled her towards him, giving her a reassuring hug, before turning his attention to Johnny.

Ed dragged him from behind his desk and gave him a quick look over. He was sure he only heard two gunshots but now couldn't be sure if it was two or three, it had all happened so fast. Finding no gunshot wounds on Johnny, Ed reasoned that only two were fired. Ed assumed that Johnny's waxy, clammy complexion was due to a heart attack and certainly fitted with his behaviour earlier. Ed was trying to remember his first aid from the course he had attended whilst working in the city all those years ago. In his panic to do something, he couldn't remember the ratio of breaths to compressions for resuscitating a heart attack victim. One breath to fifteen compressions rang a bell, or was it two breaths to thirty compressions? So far he'd delivered none and none, and needed to act quickly. He lifted Johnny's head back, pinched his nose and blew hard. He blew again, deciding that two was better than one and hoped he'd made the right choice. Measuring down and across from the centre of his chest, Ed began pumping for all he was worth and delivering two more breaths, after thirty compressions. He listened for Johnny's breathing and checked for a pulse but found none, and began the process again.

The door crashed open, slamming into Blackthorn's pulverised skull. Dave and Bob looked around, stepped over the body, and rushed over to Ed and TJ. Dave knelt down beside Ed and checked Johnny for signs of life, and on finding none pulled Ed away, shaking his head. TJ threw her arms around Bob and wept into his chest, deep racking sobs of utter misery.

# Chapter 43

Ed and TJ were sitting in the empty club, the few remaining customers having been quickly ushered out by the police. The dancers, barman and remaining bouncers were rounded up and were being held under police guard, in the staff canteen. Ed was drinking a pint of beer and TJ was sipping on a brandy, both shell-shocked from the events earlier. They hadn't spoken, neither knowing how to broach the subject of Johnny and the fact he wasn't her mother's killer. Ed actually felt quite sorry for him, which surprised him slightly. The man had turned his life completely upside-down all for his own gain, but Ed could understand his reasons, even if they were somewhat selfish and misguided. Did his dying act of saving Ed and TJ's lives redeem him for a lifetime of crime and greed? Perhaps, he thought. Ed put his drink on the table, put his arm around TJ and pulled her towards him, and she rested her head on his shoulder. He kissed the top of her head and she looked up and gave him a 'little-girl-lost' smile.

Bob, Dave and Griggs were walking towards them and Ed groaned inwardly; this was all he needed.

'You just don't know when to stop, do you, Case?' Griggs said caustically, when he stopped in front of him.

'Just piss off, Griggs! I really could do without a lecture from you right now,' Ed replied tersely. Bob stifled a laugh and Griggs shot him an angry look.

'You know, I could throw the bloody book at you for what you've done.'

'Do it, then. A bit of time in prison would keep me out of mischief.'

'You really are something else. I thought DCI Brown here was a pain in the arse, but he's a bloody saint compared to you.' Ed looked up at Griggs, who

271

was actually smiling, and shrugged. 'Care to tell me what happened?'

'I went up to punch Johnny on the nose and he pulled a gun on me. I told him that TJ was his daughter and she was after revenge because he killed her mother. He told me Blackthorn killed her and was the real villain, dragging him into drug-dealing and blackmailing him. Blackthorn came in and started bragging about killing TJ's mother and how he was going to do the same to TJ. I guess it was just too much for Johnny to take, so he shot him and had a heart attack. He didn't look too clever when I walked in. All clammy with a very unhealthy pallor, shaking and stuff, so I guess his heart packed in. I tried to resuscitate him, but it was too late.'

'What about the guy in the gent's, then?' Griggs asked.

'He killed Barry. The one Blackthorn was trying to set me up for. I thought he deserved a bit of a slap because, so far, he's the only one who's gotten off lightly.'

'You mean he's the only one still alive.'

'Denton's still alive and Andy's still alive,' Ed replied defensively.

'Neither will be coming out of hospital for some time, though. Nice touch with Denton, by the way. I'm surprised the locals didn't tear him to pieces. I suppose I should be grateful, there's still someone alive to prosecute out of this entire operation,' Griggs said, still smiling.

'So what happens to me, then?' Ed asked, not really caring either way at that precise time.

'Absolutely nothing. You're free to go. Unless there's anything else?'

'All the CCTV tapes are in the locker in Johnny's office. You should find enough evidence on them to back up what's in the ledgers,' Ed replied, thinking he was being helpful.

'I was thinking more about the contents of the briefcase,' Griggs replied, raising an eyebrow.

'That only contained the ledgers and a smelly tuna sandwich,' Ed replied innocently, looking Griggs straight in the eyes, defying him to suggest otherwise.

Griggs nodded and stared back. 'Let this be the last time our paths cross, Case. OK?' Ed nodded.

'That was the longest five minutes of my life up there. What kept you?' Ed asked Bob, once Griggs had left.

Ed was sure Bob blushed before answering 'Your friend Pandora came back and gave me a dance. It took me a while to recover my composure,' he replied, grinning. 'She's bloody good, isn't she?' he added. Ed grinned back.

'You had a dance with Pandora?' TJ asked, Ed giving him an angry look. Ed nodded sheepishly. 'Was she better than me?'

'No, of course she wasn't. Not a patch on you,' Ed lied convincingly, which seemed to appease TJ.

'Good,' she replied, and gave him a hug. Ed looked at Bob and they both grinned at each other, like naughty little school boys.

'Right then, lets get ourselves home,' Bob said, rubbing his hands together.

The police officer at the door let them out and closed it behind them. They walked the short distance to the car park and sat in the car, relieved that the whole ordeal was finally over. Everyone was either dead or hospitalised, with the exception of Jim, who seemed to have disappeared off the face of the earth. Hopefully the CCTV tapes of the two private rooms would reveal something incriminating and he would be picked up later and charged with something, even if it was only menial.

Bob drove slowly through the congested streets, cursing anyone who didn't pull away at the traffic lights a millisecond after they turned green and shouting abuse at the myriad of cyclists, who weaved in and out of the traffic with scant regard to tax paying motorists. Eventually he made it to Waterloo Bridge, where the traffic thinned, and a few minutes later they were parked up outside TJ's flat.

TJ looked up at her flat from the backseat and made no attempt to leave the car. 'I can't stay there,' she announced timidly. 'Not after what happened.'

Ed looked at her and gave her a reassuring smile. 'Do you want me to stay the night?' he asked.

TJ shook her head and replied 'No,' looking at Ed pleadingly.

'So, want to stay at mine for a few days?' he asked. She smiled weakly and nodded.

'Are you OK to wait a few minutes, Bob, whilst TJ gets a few things together?' Ed asked, knowing he wouldn't mind.

'Not a problem, but hurry up - I want to get home, and I suppose you want to go via St Albans, to get Fat Boy?' he replied.

'If that's OK?'

'It's OK.'

'Or you can drop me off at home and I'll hire a car tomorrow and come and collect him or hire one tonight, when I get to St Albans?' Ed replied, suggesting a few helpful options.

'Ed, stop bloody burbling. I'll take you to St Albans. You can collect Fat Boy and then I'll take you home. Just hurry up so I can get out of London. I bloody hate this place, too many bad memories.' Ed leaned over and kissed Bob on the cheek for a laugh. He was still

274

shouting obscenities at him as he climbed the stairs with TJ to her flat.

# Chapter 44

The rush hour traffic was petering out, and the journey through London was bearable. Ed sat in the back with TJ, who had slackened off her seatbelt and put her head in Ed's lap and slept. Ed tried to keep the conversation going with Bob but neither was in a conversational mood, and the latter part of the journey was completed in relative silence. Even Bob didn't feel compelled to sing along to the Clash, which he had once again insisted Ed put on.

When they pulled up onto the drive of Raechael and Laura's house, Ed had to shake TJ awake. She stretched languidly and smiled, looking confused at the unfamiliar surroundings. Bob was already out of the car and had rung the doorbell by the time TJ and Ed had exited the car. Raechael answered, and threw her arms round Bob in a warm embrace. Fat Boy squeezed by them and trotted down the drive as fast as his ten year old legs would allow him, his tail wagging furiously all the way. Ed crouched down and grabbed him round the neck and made a huge fuss of him, rubbing his stomach enthusiastically when he rolled onto his back. When Ed stood, Fat Boy jumped up with an agility that belied his years and licked at his chin, unable to reach the ears that he desperately sought. Ed pushed him down and walked towards the house, giving TJ a smile of encouragement, as she seemed nervous of meeting Raechael and Laura; as he would have been, given the situation.

Ed introduced TJ to Raechael, who gave her a warm smile and invited her in. She gave Ed a slight frown, followed by an equally warm smile and embraced him, kissing him on the cheek. Ed was nervous of seeing Laura again for the first time since their amicable parting the day before. Was it only the day before? It seemed like a lifetime ago. So much had happened in such a short space of time, but it was less than twenty four hours ago.

When Ed walked through to the living room, Laura was in her wheelchair, reading. She looked up and smiled broadly when he entered, causing his heart to race. Her long dark brown hair was immaculate and cascaded over her shoulders, and she looked stunning. She was still the most beautiful woman Ed knew, and their recent parting of ways rested heavily on his heart. He gave her what he hoped was a warm smile but knew from the fleeting expression on her face that it came across as sad and forlorn.

Ed introduced TJ to Laura. TJ gave her a nervous smile, feeling like an intruder, despite knowing that her relationship with Ed was now over. Laura sensed her discomfort and gave her a welcoming smile.

'Ed told me a lot about you. It must be hard for you at the club with the situation with your father?' she said, trying to put her at ease.

TJ forced a smile and shook her head. 'Not any more. He's dead.' TJ took a deep breath to steady her quavering voice. 'He died of a heart attack earlier today.' She noticed the look of discomfort on Laura's face, and continued. 'He died saving me and Ed from being shot by the man who really killed my mother.'

'I thought that was your father?' she replied, confused.

'That's what I thought, but it was DI Blackthorn. I'm not sure if Ed mentioned him to you?' Laura nodded. 'It turned out he killed her and has been blackmailing my father ever since. I feel such a fool, having wasted years to get revenge on my father, and all along he was innocent. I know he wasn't a saint, but I just wish I'd known earlier. Then perhaps I could have got to know him as a father, rather than a dodgy gangster who ran a tin pot club in Soho.'

TJ was crying silently, tears rolling down her cheeks. Laura wheeled over to the sofa where TJ was sitting, held her hands and pulled her towards her, giving her a shoulder to cry on. Ed was watching from the floor, stroking an ever-demanding Fat Boy, and looked on in wonder at how women so easily showed compassion to each other. Ed couldn't imagine a situation like this with a close friend, let alone a complete stranger. Bob would probably say something along the lines of 'Oh well, shit happens,' and give him a manly slap on the back.

Raechael and Bob entered the room, Raechael carrying a tray of coffees and biscuits. TJ sat back and wiped her eyes and smiled, looking slightly embarrassed.

'So, who's going to tell me all about your trip to London then?' Raechael asked, breaking the silence. Ed looked at Bob and gave him a look that said he should tell her. Bob stared back at him, shook his head and gave him a sharp nod, staring at him with hard eyes, indicating he should.

Reluctantly, Ed began the second instalment of Bob and Ed's great adventure with his indignation at being treated so badly by Griggs. Raechael thought his behaviour outrageous, but laughed nonetheless. Laura remained impassive throughout. TJ sought Ed's hand when he gave an abbreviated version of events at TJ's flat, and squeezed it almost painfully. When Ed paused for breath, TJ picked up and told in great detail of her ordeal at the hands of Blackthorn and Denton. Raechael put her hand to her mouth and stared wide-eyed in horror.

'You poor thing,' she said with compassion.

'It could have been a lot worse but Ed and ,Bob arrived just in time before... well you know...' she said, tailing off.

'Ed gave his crown jewels such a kick, they came up the size of beach balls,' Bob said laughing at the memory. 'Tell them what you did next, mate,' Bob prompted him enthusiastically.

'I stripped him naked, wrote I'm a corrupt policeman and a rapist on his back, and handcuffed him naked to a lamppost,' Ed told them smiling broadly.

'You've got a real vindictive streak in you, Ed,' Raechael told him good-humouredly. Ed glanced at Laura, who turned her head away from him. To her, it was just another reason for their parting of ways.

'Well, I don't care,' TJ said. 'In my books, he's a knight in shining armour. If it wasn't for Ed, I'm sure I'd be dead now. That's why I'm here. I couldn't face staying at the flat. Not after what happened. Ed said he'd put me up for a few days.' She gave Ed a big smile and squeezed his hand. Was that a hint of jealousy he saw flash across Laura's face? Ed moved on quickly and told them of the events in the club. He gave Bob a knowing look and received a stony glare back, and decided to skip any mention of Pandora.

Ed gave them as full account as he could remember of the conversation with Johnny, before TJ's arrival at the club. He faced TJ throughout, holding her hand as the tears once again flowed down her cheeks. Ed tried to put Johnny in a favourable light, without making him out to be Mother Theresa, for TJ's benefit. She knew what he was trying to do and smiled back appreciatively. Ed hurried through the last part with very few details other than Johnny shooting Blackthorn just before his heart finally gave out.

'And that's about it,' Ed said, looking round the room and noticing Laura looking away, not wanting to catch his eye.

'So, your father was one of the good guys after all, TJ?' Raechael said. TJ smiled, knowing Raechael was doing her best to make her feel better, but it didn't help.

'I was telling Laura, I just feel that I wasted years trying to get a job in my father's club to get revenge on him for killing my mother, and that was wasted twofold because he didn't do it. Years, just wasted,' she said, shaking her head, close to tears again.

'I make that seven dead and two in hospital,' Laura said caustically. 'And there you were, telling me that you were going to be a changed man. The truth is, nothing's changed.'

'I know,' Ed replied with a shake of his head. 'I should have left it at that, but after what happened to TJ, I couldn't. I just wanted to give Johnny a punch on the nose. I had no idea what was going to happen. In hindsight, walking away would have been a better course of action, but I was fired up and made the wrong decision. What can I say? I screwed up again. Now this is finally over, that's it. I am definitely going to change.'

'Well done, Ed. You must be so proud of yourself!' Laura said caustically, adding a slow hand clap for maximum effect. Raechael stared at her angrily.

The room fell silent; even Fat Boy seemed to stop breathing. Ed looked at Laura, who gave him a hard stare, before turning her head away dramatically. To Ed, it felt as if he'd just been slapped in the face. He knew that there was an element of truth in what she had said, but thought it was a bit harsh. At that moment he knew that any chance of rekindling their relationship was over, and it hurt like hell. He stared blankly ahead, his pulse overwhelmingly loud in his ears.

'Drink up. I want to get back here before midnight,' Bob said, trying to sound jovial, aware of oppressive silence and Ed's discomfort. Nobody needed any encouragement and, in unison, downed the last of their coffee and put the empty mugs on the coffee table.

Ed thanked Raechael for looking after Fat Boy, who said it was a pleasure to have him and gave him a thin smile and a look of compassion and concern. She gave him a hug and said goodbye as if it was for the last time, and Ed knew that it probably was. Bob called Fat Boy, who followed him out into the hall, followed by TJ and Raechael, leaving Ed alone with Laura. He walked over to Laura and squatted down in front of her. At first she wouldn't look at him and Ed had to physically turn her head towards him. He didn't know what to say to her as he looked into her dark brown eyes for the last time. In the end he just leaned forward and kissed her softly on the lips and said goodbye, and smiled at her unconvincingly. He stood to leave and Laura grabbed his hand and looked into his eyes earnestly.

'I still love you,' she said, sadly.

Ed nodded. 'I know,' he replied and turned and walked out into the hall. He hesitated in the doorway and thought about looking back, but decided not to. Knowing that pleading for another chance wouldn't work, and would only make matters worse. He carried on down the hallway, leaving Laura with her head in her hands, weeping silently.


'That must have been hard,' TJ said to Ed, who was sitting next to her in the back of Bob's car.

Ed nodded, not really knowing what to say. TJ leaned across and kissed him on the cheek and rested her head on his chest. Ed put his arm around her and hugged her. 'It's been a pretty crappy day all round for both of us,' he said eventually.

TJ hugged him back and closed her eyes, relishing the feeling of total safety she felt when she was around Ed. She knew that she could never replace Laura in Ed's affection but she was determined to try; even if she was only ever going to be second best, she didn't care. Ed closed his eyes and tried to blank out his thoughts of the last three weeks. He mentally pushed them to a dark corner of his mind and filed them under shite, along with all the other disastrous episodes of his life. Within a few minutes he was snoring loudly - much to the annoyance of Bob, who was fighting his own battle to stay awake.

# Chapter 45

Bob pulled up onto the drive and stretched as much as he could in the confines of the car, relieved to have completed the journey. He didn't particularly relish the prospect of driving back tonight. He was dog-tired and wanted nothing more than to curl up in bed next to Raechael. It was the thought of that and a long weekend with her that kept him going, before having to endure the long, lonely drive back to Cornwall.

The dog reaching over the back seat from the boot and licking Ed's ears woke him up and he looked around, taking in where he was, surprised when he recognised his own drive. TJ stirred and raised her head and gave him a tired smile, her eyes barely open.

'Thanks for the stimulating conversation and making sure I didn't nod off and kill us all,' Bob said sarcastically.

Ed grunted an apology and took off his seatbelt. 'Want to come in for a coffee? Or you can stay the night if you want to,' Ed offered by way of a further apology, feeling guilty for sleeping through almost the entire journey.

'I'll grab a quick coffee, and make it a strong one. Hurry up will you, I've got a bladder the size of a medicine ball and the last thing I need is a wet seat!' Bob said, irritated at the lack of urgency from Ed.

Ed got the message, and sluggishly extracted himself from the car. He walked round and sprung the boot and let Fat Boy out, who trotted over to the shrubs that separated his house from the neighbours and urinated copiously.

'If you don't hurry up, I'll be joining him!' Bob told him angrily, making TJ laugh. The sound her laughter mellowed him slightly.

Ed fumbled in his pocket for his key and unlocked the door. It opened with a single turn, which meant that he had forgotten to lock it properly, applying the dead bolts, when he left last time. He was sure he had done as it was part of his routine, and was immediately suspicious. He dismissed it instantly, remembering the last time he had left the house he had left in something of a rush, fully into panic mode and not thinking straight. It was therefore more than plausible he had forgotten. Bob was breathing down his neck, so he opened the door and let him in. Bob hurried through to the down stairs toilet and was urinating like a horse, almost before the door was shut.

Ed grabbed the bags from the car and dumped them at the foot of the stairs. He picked up the stack of junk mail, pizza menus and local newspapers from the floor and dropped them on the armchair as he entered the living room. He turned the lights on low and pulled the curtains. TJ and Fat Boy followed him in, Fat Boy making straight for the back door, desperate to scent mark his territory again. Ed walked through the living room and dining room into the kitchen, turning on the lights under the kitchen units as he entered.

Instinct told him something wasn't quite right; even Fat Boy had stopped and was sniffing the air. Ed could feel his heart beating harder and had that feeling in his stomach, similar to having a dream where you are falling and wake up at the last minute. He turned, stared into the dining room and switched on the wall lights. Standing with his back to the display cabinet was Jim. His face was impassive, but broke into a smile when Ed turned and stared into his malevolent eyes. Ed noticed his face was still puffy and bruised from their last meeting, even in the dim light being provided by the two wall lights.

'I've been waiting for you to turn up,' Jim said, breaking into a wide grin and aiming the gun at him. Ed stared back in disbelief that Jim was actually in his house and that, once again, a gun was aimed directly at him. This one had a silencer attached, which increased its size dramatically and made it all the more menacing. He wanted to ask how he had got into the house, but it seemed a dumb question. Bob had broken into the rented cottage in the Lakes easily enough, so for someone like Jim he guessed it was just as easy. He cursed the lack of burglar alarm, but again surmised that it wouldn't have posed too much of a problem for him.

His attention was distracted by Fat Boy who was growling ferociously to his right, on the other side of the dining table. The fur on the back of his neck was standing on end and his head was pushed forward and low as he slowly edged towards Jim. He looked away, not wanting to draw attention to him, but Jim had already spotted him.

'Tell the dog to back off or I'll shoot him,' he said in an angry whisper. 'All I want is the money, and nobody gets hurt,' he added, grinning manically.

Ed didn't believe a word. 'Yeah, right. I give you the money and you're going to shoot me anyway. Then, you'll no doubt shoot the dog and TJ. You're full of shit,' Ed replied, trying to stall for time.

'The dog,' Jim said, pointing the gun at Fat Boy not taking his eyes off Ed, having learnt his lesson on how dangerous he was last week in the club.

'Fat Boy, stay!' Ed said loudly. It was enough to stop him advancing on Jim but he remained ready to pounce, emitting a low growl through bared teeth. Ed looked behind him and saw TJ, who looked terrified and was holding onto the worktop in the kitchen for support. Her lips were trembling in unison with her legs, her eyes wide and frightened. 'TJ go and get the rucksack from the hallway, please.' Ed asked. TJ stood rooted to the spot, too shocked to move. 'Now, TJ!' Ed said loudly, hoping to shock her into moving. Hopefully, loud enough for Bob to hear and work out what was going on and come up with a plan. TJ let go of the worktop and slowly edged towards Ed, heading for the living room. Jim followed her with his eyes boring into her, daring her to do something rash, any excuse to blow her away.

'And don't try doing anything stupid, like phoning the police. If you're not back here in thirty seconds, I'll shoot lover boy,' he said, giving her a twisted smile.

Ed stared back at him, wondering whether to rush him, but decided that by the time he had even moved a fraction, Jim would have shot both of them. Unseen by either Ed or Jim, Fat Boy stalked silently and stealthily, inch by inch towards Jim. Ed was looking at TJ as she brushed past him slowly, her eyes never leaving Jim. As she passed, Ed reached out slowly and squeezed her hand and gave her a weak smile of encouragement. She gave him a quick but terrified glance and turned back to face Jim, whose face was a mask of hatred.

Fat Boy seemed to sense that Jim was distracted and pounced, with a blood-curdling snarl. Jim turned in surprise and horror and aimed the gun at Fat Boy, but too late. Fat Boy flew towards Jim and latched onto his right wrist and clamped down hard, snarling and shaking it. Jim screamed in pain and fright. This galvanised Ed and he wasted no time and ran towards him, grabbing a stubby onyx urn from the radiator shelf as he hurtled towards Jim, ready to smash it into his face.

Jim stubbornly held onto the gun, despite the pain and the fact that his fingers were numb as Fat Boy severed though his tendons with his incisors and powerful molars. He reached down and with his left hand calmly took the gun from his right hand and pulled the trigger. The bullet went through Fat Boy's chest and tore through his heart, lodging in his spine. Fat Boy gave a quick yelp and fell heavily to the floor, silent and unmoving.

Ed screamed in rage and smashed the onyx urn across Jim's left wrist, with a force that he didn't realise he was capable of. The bones shattered under the impact and Jim dropped the gun, where it skittered across the wooden floor and under the dining room table. Ed was vaguely aware of TJ screaming and Bob running towards him as he brought up the urn and smashed it into the bridge of Jim's already broken nose. His head flew backwards, smashing the glass in the display cabinet behind him. Jim tried to steady himself but slipped in the blood oozing from Fat Boy's chest, and continued to fall backwards. Ed brought up the urn again and smashed it down with all his strength into Jim's upturned face. The sheer force pushed Jim further back into the display cabinet, glass and ornaments shattering, exploding everywhere.

Ed pulled his arm back for another blow, but was stopped by Bob, grabbing his wrist and pulling him back. He looked at Jim, who was twitching violently. A razor sharp shard of glass had pierced the back of his neck and was protruding from his mouth, almost completely severing one of his lips. Jim's eyes were wide and protruding as blood spewed down his chin and the life drained from him. His twitching finally abated and he slumped down, pulling the remains of the shattered glass pane with him.

Bob let go of Ed's arm and he dropped the urn on the floor, shocked. He kicked Jim's legs out the way and knelt down and dragged Fat Boy away from him, leaving a thick smear of crimson blood across the

287

wooden floor. He felt for a pulse urgently, but found none. Tears were already coursing down his cheeks, knowing that the only living thing that had loved him unconditionally was dead. Ed cradled his head in his lap and buried his head in his neck, oblivious to the blood, and sobbed uncontrollably.

TJ ran to the kitchen, and was violently sick into the kitchen sink. Bob followed her and put a comforting arm around her shoulders as she retched into the sink, leaving Ed to grieve. Bob found a glass in one of the kitchen units and poured TJ a glass of water, urging her to drink. She took it gratefully and swilled the water round in her mouth, spitting it into the sink to rid herself of the acidic taste of bile, before drinking greedily. Bob unlocked the back door to let out the smell of vomit, cordite and blood and allow the fresh night air in.

TJ looked through the dining room, tears trickling down her face as she watched Ed still cradling Fat Boy. Before TJ could move towards him, Bob grabbed her arm and shook his head and led her out into the garden.

'He needs me,' she said through her sobs.

'Just leave him for a while, love,' he said putting an arm around her. TJ nodded and buried her head in his chest and threw her arms around his waist, sniffing back her tears. Bob looked skyward, eyes opened wide to abate the stinging. He took a deep breath and composed himself. He pulled TJ off him and led her to a bench on the patio and sat her down. He then walked to the far corner of the patio, pulled out his mobile, and dialled Griggs.

Ed walked out into the garden, carrying Fat Boy, his head lolling from side to side with each careful step he took. He walked up the three steps to the lawn and carefully laid Fat Boy down on the grass in the far corner of the garden. He walked back and smiled sadly at TJ as he passed her back into the house, where he turned on the garden lights. On his return he angled one of the bright halogen lights to illuminate the far reach of the garden and a prone Fat Boy. TJ stood and ran towards him, throwing her arms around him, heedless of the blood that covered his face, hands and clothes. She looked up at his bloody face, streaked with tears, but the look of utter wretchedness she saw took the words from her mouth. Ed put his hand to the side of her face and gave her a brief smile, before walking off up the garden.

He unlocked the shed and retrieved a spade and began digging, smashing the spade into the ground and lifting out great sods of earth like a man possessed. Bob joined him and knelt down and stroked Fat Boy, who he loved almost as much as Ed did. He removed his collar and put it in his pocket and began to lay out black plastic refuse sacks on the lawn, which he had found in the cupboard under the sink. He lifted Fat Boy and placed him on top the sacks and began to wrap him up using black insulating tape, leaving the head exposed for now.

Ed was sweating profusely and still digging mechanically and relentlessly. Bob approached and looked at the hole, which was now three feet deep, and put a hand on Ed's shoulder.

'I think that's probably deep enough, Ed,' Bob said quietly.

Ed nodded and walked over to Fat Boy. He knelt down and lifted his head and kissed him, before reluctantly completing the plastic shroud and lowering him into his grave. Bob offered to fill the hole in but Ed wouldn't allow him, telling him he needed to do it. Once it was finished he leaned on the spade, utterly exhausted. TJ came up behind him and put her arms round him and rested her head on his back, which was soaked with sweat; knowing that nothing she could say would be adequate.

'Go and get cleaned up,' she eventually said to him. Ed nodded and walked back down the garden with her, TJ almost leading him along like a mother would lead a child through a crowded shopping centre.

Ed washed his face and hands and removed his blood-stained and muddy fleece, and accepted the beer that Bob offered him. He opened a drawer to his right and pulled out his emergency pack of cigarettes. Despite giving up years ago, he always had a packet for when he got completely pissed or pissed off. He handed the packet to Bob, who pulled off the cellophane and offered one to TJ, who declined. Ed finally found his lighter and lit his with a trembling hand, and handed it to Bob. The three of them walked into the garden and sat down on the bench and drank their beers.

Ed blew out a long steam of smoke. 'Fucking hell, that hurt,' he said, looking up to the star-strewn sky. TJ put her arm around his back and kissed him lightly on the cheek, not really knowing how to answer.

'At least it was quick and he didn't suffer,' Bob said, breaking the silence. 'He probably saved your life, as well.'

'I know, and I don't know if that makes it better or worse. Good job Laura's not here. I'm sure she'd have something to say on the matter.' He threw his empty beer bottle down the garden, where it bounced and rolled into the bushes. 'That was a bit unfair,' he said, to nobody in particular. 'She's dead right, though. I think I'm beyond change. Yet another bloody disaster to add to the list.'

'Don't be so hard on yourself, Ed,' TJ said, resting her hand on his forearm. 'She didn't mean what she said. Trust me, I'm a woman - I should know - it was just her self-defence mechanism kicking in, to justify her ending the relationship to herself. Anyway, Jim turning up wasn't anything you had control over. It happened.' She put a finger to Ed's lips, pre-empting Ed's next comments, and continued. 'OK. All this started in the club that Saturday night. What you did that night was what you thought was the right thing to do, which it was. None of this could have been predicted. You had a lot of hard decisions to make this week, and by and large, you made the right choices. You can't hold yourself responsible for everything that followed.'

'Well said, TJ. I've been telling him that for years but he takes everything so personally. He'd blame himself for the war in Afghanistan if he could find a tenuous link, I'm sure. Listen to the lady, Ed. She's talking sense,' Bob contributed.

Ed nodded. 'I know,' Ed replied, 'I know.'

They sat and drank and smoked in silence, until the door bell chiming startled them. Bob put a hand on Ed's chest and said he'd get it and returned shortly, followed by Griggs and Carter, who both looked extremely irate. Ed could hear others in the house and turned sharply as a camera flash went off in the dining room. He was nervous now, worrying that he was going to be up on a murder charge. If Griggs was as pissed off as he looked, he may very well throw the book at him this time and not relent, as he had back at Johnny's. He looked up and stared at him defiantly.

'Didn't I tell you just a few hours ago I didn't want to see you again?' Griggs said angrily. Ed stared back, saying nothing, assuming the question was rhetorical. 'What's your problem, Case? Do you think you're above the law or something? You can't go around killing everyone you decide is one of the bad guys. You're a walking fucking disaster! Jesus Christ, Bob, where the fuck did you find this guy?' Griggs ran a hand through his hair and turned away to stare down the garden.

Ed lit another cigarette, with a still-trembling hand, and offered the packet to Bob who accepted the offer, despite only just putting one out.

'Go easy on the lad, Griggs. He's just buried his dog,' Bob said to Griggs, when he finally turned round.

'That's easy for you to say, Brown. How am I supposed to explain this mess away? You tell me that?' Bob gave him a hard stare, which Griggs returned, with interest. 'Care to tell me what happened then, Case?' Griggs demanded, rather than asked.

'He was waiting in the house when we arrived. Pulled a gun on me and asked for the money. Not that there is any. My dog went for him and he shot him. I smashed him in the face and his head went through the cabinet, and... well you can see the result. It was an accident. I think he slipped on the blood from the dog, and the momentum impaled him on the shattered door,' Ed told him, sucking hard on his cigarette, eyes filling with tears again at reliving the recent memory.

'Were you born lucky or have you spent a life time working on it?' Griggs said spitefully. Ed chose to ignore him and ground his cigarette out on the patio, and rubbed his eyes.

'Griggs, lay off. He's just had a gun pushed in his face and he's just finished burying his dog. You've got the resources to sort this out. Christ, you make people disappear every day, and don't deny it. One dead, small-time crook that nobody will miss shouldn't be a problem,' Bob hissed at Griggs, staring daggers.

'Look, I'm sorry about what happened. It was a complete accident. I just wanted to punch his lights out and stop him shooting anyone else, OK. He killed my fucking dog. What the bloody hell would you have done in my position? Stuck your hands in the air and waited to get a bullet in your face? I don't think so. You'd have done exactly the same. If you tell me otherwise you're a fucking liar!' Ed shot back, not caring about the consequences.

Griggs turned away again and paced up and down. Carter, who had remained silent throughout, staring at Ed with little emotion in his face, turned and followed Griggs and pulled him to the far corner of the patio and began talking to him animatedly, but in a whisper. Eventually Griggs walked back and stood in front of Ed, and let out an exasperated sigh.

'I'm going to cut you some slack. Don't ask me why, but I am. I'll take care of everything and that'll be the end of the matter. But... I'm warning you. If I ever hear your name again or get a hint you're up to no good, I will personally make sure your life won't be worth living. Have you got that? And despite this sounding like a cliché; don't leave town. I will need a formal statement at some stage, OK? '

Ed stood and held out his hand and said 'Thanks,' giving Griggs a weak smile. This seemed to take him by surprise and he seemed to mellow, and shook the offered hand.

'You know the ironic thing about all this? I could use someone like you,' he said, smiling. Ed laughed

'You know the last person to say that to me was Johnny, and it landed me in all this,' Ed said waving his arms around him. 'Please don't be offended if I tell you to fuck off.'

'I didn't say I was offering,' Griggs replied, a slight smile playing at the corner of his mouth.

'Who do you work for, by the way - MI5, Special Branch?' Ed asked.

'Something like that,' Griggs replied, before walking away.

An unmarked van turned up shortly after Griggs made a phone call and the body was removed, signalling the departure of Griggs and Carter. The blood on the dining room floor was the only reminder of the night's events. Apart from the absence of Fat Boy, which Ed tried not to dwell over.

Bob came out into the garden, where Ed and TJ were sitting on the bench, staring silently down the garden, and informed them he had spoken to Raechael and she sent her condolences. Ed nodded and thanked him. He thought of asking what Laura had said but decided to leave it. Bob seemed to sense the question, even though it wasn't asked and nodded his head. Ed offered to put Bob up for the night but he declined, still desperately wanting the comfort of familiar surroundings and the warmth of a good woman beside him, curled up in bed.

Bob kissed TJ goodbye and gave her a hug, giving her strict instructions to look after Ed. TJ gave him a weak smile and thanked him for everything. Ed walked him out to the car.

'Are you going to be OK?' Bob asked. Ed nodded and gave him a quick smile. 'Call me if you need anything - and I mean anything, anytime. Got it?'

'Thanks Bob, and thanks for everything this week. It's really appreciated. I don't think I would have got through it without you. I'll be fine, honest. Shit happens and then you die, eh?'

'Yeah, shit happens,' he echoed and slapped him on the back, before climbing into his car. He wound down the window and looked at Ed. 'Look after TJ, OK? I like her and you two make a good couple. Try and make sure you don't sod it all up this time, right?'

'I won't,' he replied, smiling, pleased that he approved of TJ.

Ed waved and watched him drive off, before heading back up the drive and into the house. When he walked into the dining room, TJ was just finishing mopping the floor around the display cabinet. The ruined glass door and smashed ornaments and decanters were in a black sack beside her. She looked up and smiled at Ed, happy just to be busy doing something. Ed felt guilty about TJ cleaning up his mess but was glad she had done it; he couldn't face it. Instead he put the kettle on, and made coffee.

They were sitting on the bench drinking the coffee when Ed got up and left her there, staring after him. He returned with the rucksack and handed it to her.

'What's that?' she asked, bewildered.

'Open it and find out,' Ed told her, grinning.

TJ popped the two clips, pushed back the top pannier and loosened the drawstring. She looked inside and stared, open-mouthed. 'I don't understand. I thought you said there was no money? What's this... there must be thousands here.'

'Call it your inheritance. God knows you deserve it, after what you've been through.'

'How much is there?' she asked, pulling out one of the bundles and flicking through the notes.

'A couple of hundred shy of three quarters of a million pounds. I had to borrow a few hundred to pay Laura back. She booked the cottage on her credit card for me,' Ed replied apologetically. 'I'll pay you back, once I've been to the bank,' he grinned.

'You lied. You lied to everyone, Ed?'

'Yeah. If I'd told Griggs he would've taken it and that would be the end of it. The way I look at it, it was your father's money. He's dead, therefore it's yours. Congratulations on becoming wealthy.'

'It's blood money,' she said solemnly. 'I'm not sure that I want it.'

'If you don't take it, I'll give it to charity. It's your call. Sleep on it. This is your chance of a completely new life. No more dancing in clubs, no more struggling to pay the rent. It's not enough to retire on but you'll be able to live comfortably and take a job you want to do, rather than one you hate, just because it pays more.'

'I don't know,' she said quietly 'I feel guilty, knowing that people were killed over this.'

'Look, I know how you feel,' he said, holding her hand and looking at her earnestly. 'When my parents died, I inherited around half a million and felt exactly the same as you do now. I tried to lose it by investing in shares that were in free-fall, because I felt guilty at losing my parents and becoming wealthy. A few years later, after my wife died and a particularly traumatic period of my life, I made a decision to get on with the rest of my life. My investments had actually turned a significant corner and I was sitting on nearly three million quid. Believe me, when you get over the guilt and start living again, it's a good feeling. Trust me,' he said, giving her a reassuring smile.

'I'll sleep on it,' she said, placing a hand on the side of his face. 'Are you OK?' she asked softly.

'Me? Never better,' he replied unconvincingly, receiving a deep frown from TJ in response. 'Not really,' he added by way of stalling for time, while he thought of an appropriate answer. TJ smiled encouragingly. 'Honest answer, I feel like shit. I'm gonna miss that smelly old mutt. It's been me and him for the last ten years. It's like losing your best friend. I know he was only a dog, but...' Ed paused and wiped his eyes and sniffed loudly. 'I thought I'd lost him earlier in the year when he got stabbed. At the time that was my worst nightmare but all the time he was alive, there was hope. Now, there's nothing.' He shrugged. 'It was just a bit sudden, that's all.'

TJ held his hand and smiled, trying to suppress her tears. In the short time she had known Ed, he had always been upbeat and made light of everything. Seeing him now, looking defeated and sounding utterly broken, saddened her. 'You've still got me,' she said quietly.

'Good,' he replied, smiling broadly. TJ smiled back, hoping with all her heart that he meant it.

# Chapter 46

Despite falling into bed both physically and emotionally exhausted, Ed awoke early and couldn't get back to sleep, no matter how hard he tried. At a little after six o'clock, fed up with tossing and turning and worried that his fidgeting would wake TJ, he slipped out of bed. After a quick rummage through his drawers he found a pair of shorts and a T-shirt and put them on as quietly as he could. He stood and watched TJ, her chest rising and falling under the duvet as she slept and smiled. Looking down on her filled him with the urge to strip off and get back into bed and cuddle up against her warm, lithe body. At six o'clock in the morning he thought that she probably wouldn't appreciate it, and reluctantly pulled the door to on his way out.

Entering the living room felt strange. The eerie silence that greeted him and the absence of Fat Boy, trotting up to him for his first stroke of the day, left him saddened. He tried to push the memories of last night to one side, which wasn't easy as he walked into the dining room and was compelled to look at the shattered display cabinet. He hurried into the kitchen and made himself a coffee and took it out into the garden, not wanting to be in the house. The morning was fresh, too fresh for shorts and a T-shirt, but sitting in the garden was preferable to being inside. He knew now how TJ was feeling yesterday, not wanting to stay in her flat after her ordeal at the hands of Blackthorn and Denton. At least outside it was still relatively dark, and he was unable to see the garden and anything that brought back memories of Fat Boy. He finished his coffee quickly, wincing as the hot liquid scalded his lips, and went inside. He slipped on his trainers, put his mobile, some money and door key in his bum-bag, and headed out for a long jog.

Out of habit he found himself taking the exact same route he took Fat Boy each morning, and increased his pace to blot out the intrusive memories that flooded back. By the time he had reached the river, he was running at full pelt. Sweat and tears stung his eyes as he pounded along the riverbank, trying to purge the memories of last night. When he reached the bridge where he and TJ had stopped the last time he had walked this way, he stopped to wipe his eyes and calm down. His calf and thigh muscles were on fire and the area around the scar on his left thigh, where he had been stabbed earlier in the year, throbbed painfully. The physical pain felt good and was a welcome distraction from the even more painful memories of the last two weeks. Two weeks in which a gun had been pointed at him on no less than six occasions and he been involved in the deaths of Barry, Mo, Asif, Abdul, Pete, Blackthorn, Johnny, Jim, and finally Fat Boy. Nine lives wasted and all because of Blackthorn's greed and Johnny's paranoia; such a waste. Ed knew the memories of his experiences of the last few weeks would haunt him for a long time to come, some more than others. He took a few deep breaths and carried on at a more sedate pace and turned his thoughts to the future, not wanting to dwell on his miserable past.

By the time he had reached his front door, having stopped at the corner shop en route to pick up something for breakfast, he felt much happier at having burnt off his aggression. With a clear plan in his head now on what he was going to do next, he opened the front door.

After a well-deserved shave, finally losing the grotesque moustache he had been sporting for the last week, he showered and padded naked into the bedroom. TJ was awake and stretched and gave him a tired smile, with half-closed eyes.

'Sorry, did I wake you?' Ed asked.

'No. I was already awake,' she lied, yawning and stretching once more 'Are you coming back to bed?' she asked, with a glint in her eye.

'Nope. I'm going to get dressed and make you breakfast in bed.'

'You seem happy this morning.'

'I am,' he replied, adding nothing when TJ gave him a suspicious look.

'Are you going to elaborate on that?'

'I'll tell you about it once I've brought you breakfast.'

TJ shrugged as if she wasn't interested, but she obviously was. Ed returned the gesture and received a pout in return.

Ed stood back and looked at the two plates of breakfast in front of him, and gave a satisfied nod. For the first time in his entire life, the food looked perfect. The bacon was cooked to perfection, the sausages were a golden brown, and the eggs weren't crispy at the edges and snotty around the yolk. After spooning a large helping of baked beans onto each plate he put them on a tray with a pot of filter coffee, and took them upstairs. Ed would have preferred tea but knew TJ was a coffee lover, and he was too lazy to make both.

TJ was still in bed but Ed could tell from her damp hair, which smelt vaguely of apples, that she had showered.

'I'm impressed. I thought you told me you made a lousy fry-up?' she said, sitting up and accepting the tray.

'There's a first time for everything,' Ed said, pleased that she thought he'd made a good fist of it. Ed stripped and climbed into bed next to her and lifted up the tray so that TJ could take the second tray underneath to put her own breakfast on. He transferred her breakfast onto it and poured two mugs of coffee, placing one on TJ's tray and putting the pot on the bedside table.

'I wish you'd cover those up while I'm eating,' he said, nodding at her exposed breasts.

'They're not that bad, are they?'

'Not bad for their age,' Ed chided.

'Very funny - now eat, or I'll stick this sausage where the sun doesn't shine,' she said with a smile.

'Sounds great, but can you wait until it cools down a bit?'

'You're gross,' she replied, wrinkling her nose up.

'Like I said, there's a first time for everything.'

'You had that gay moustache too long. Anyway, are you going to tell me what you're so happy about this morning, or not?'

'When I've finished eating,' he replied, tucking into his food, enjoying the look of frustration she gave him.


They were both ravenous, neither having eaten anything the day before, and both polished off their fry-up within minutes. Ed leaned across and put TJ's empty plate and cup onto his own tray and put both trays on the floor beside the bed.

'TJ, do you trust me?' he asked seriously, 'I mean, completely trust me?'

'Of course I do. Why shouldn't I?' she replied, wondering where the conversation was leading.

'Don't know. I was just wondering, that's all. I've killed two people since the last time we were here. I thought you might have changed your mind.'

There was a pause whilst she considered the question, before replying 'Nothing's changed. You only did it to save your own life, it doesn't make you a monster or dangerous; not to me, anyway.' She gave him a sympathetic smile. 'Where is this conversation going?' she added.

'I had a good think while I was out running this morning, and I think I need to move on. I can't live here any more, not after what happened last night. Rather like how you felt about your flat, I suppose. I want to make a fresh start somewhere else and I want you to come with me. If you would like to, that is?'

'You want me to come with you?' she asked, surprised. Ed nodded. 'Answer me one question honestly and I'll give you an answer. Will I ever be anything but second best to Laura? And I want an honest answer. Don't lie to me!'

'Of course you won't be. I'd be a liar if I said I still don't have feelings for her, but it's over. To be honest, it was a blessing in disguise when Laura broke off the relationship, because it saved me from having to make a choice. Since meeting you, I've been wrestling with my conscience because of the way I feel about you. It's funny you know, all the time I was in the Lake District, I only worried about you and how you were - not Laura.' Ed gave a nervous shrug and added 'I'm not asking you to come with me just because I'm on the rebound and don't want to be on my own. I'm asking because I want to be with you.'

'So, if her operation was a success and she quite literally walked back into your life, you're not going to say thanks TJ but see you later?' she asked, staring at him as if she was trying to detect a lie.

'No. I'd be over the moon for her, but she can't accept me for what I am. Do you? Will you walk away the next time I get into a bit of bother? Not that I intend to.'

'After all that we've been through, of course not. I do think you need to change, though. You can't keep going around trying to be the knight in shining armour for all your friends and the people you meet. One day your luck will run out and you'll find someone who is just that little bit smarter, quicker or luckier than you, and that'll be that. If you want to change, then that's up to you. You are what you are, that's what makes you, you. I love you the way you are.'

'Do you? That's a bit quick, isn't it?' Ed replied half-joking.

TJ looked at him and gave him a shy smile. 'Yes,' she replied, causing Ed to grin broadly. 'When you joked about an open casket funeral, before I left for work that Friday, I thought about that a lot. I nearly cried all the way to Borough High Street. The thought of not seeing you again really hurt and I knew then that I could be a little bit in love with you. I don't want to change you but you should have a think about it, because I don't want to lose you either.'

Ed nodded thoughtfully. 'You're right. I had a good think about that when I was out running. I nearly got you killed because I took Johnny's briefcase. Fat Boy wasn't so lucky.' Ed paused and took a deep breath. TJ held his hand and squeezed it reassuringly. 'Before that, there was Jacqui. Shot because I felt compelled to protect my friends. Sometimes, I just can't help myself. From today, I'm going to make a real effort to keep out of trouble... well, as much as possible, anyway.'

TJ smiled and squeezed his hand again. 'Is my past going to be a problem?'

'No. I used to be a right bastard of a salesman. I think an exotic dancer is higher up the respectability ladder than that.'

'And you don't have a problem with my age?'

'No. Not if you're happy with a toy-boy.'

'I'm only three years older than you!' she reminded him. 'Do you still find me attractive?' Ed nodded. 'Do you still fancy me?' Ed nodded. 'And you don't think I'm too fat or too skinny?'

'No,' Ed replied laughing. 'You're perfect. So are you coming with me or what?'

'Of course I am. I just wanted to hear you say something nice to me,' she said, smiling broadly. 'Looks like I've got my tall, dark and handsome millionaire after all.'

'Well not exactly tall, dark and handsome,' Ed replied.

'Tall enough, and you'll be dark enough once you've got your hair back.'

'Aren't you forgetting the handsome bit?'

'Handsome enough for my liking,' she said, smiling. 'Do you love me?' she asked, giving Ed a serious look, putting him on the back foot. Ed smiled and looked pensive, before finally answering

'You know, someone else asked me once if I was in love and I shrugged. They asked me if I got butterflies in my stomach when I saw her for the first time each day. Then, when we were together, did I feel the urge to hold her, kiss her and hug her all the time? Finally, did the thought of never seeing that person again make me feel physically sick? If I ask myself the same questions about you, the answer is yes to all of them, so I guess I do.' TJ smiled broadly.

'Now, are you going to make love to me or not?' she asked, sliding towards him.

Ed shook his head, turned away and put the phone on the bedside table onto speaker, and dialled a number from the memory. 'Just need to make a quick call first,' he replied, much to her dismay.

'Brown,' Bob said in groggy voice, still full of sleep, through the speaker.

'Morning Bob, it's Ed,' he replied cheerily.

'What the bloody hell do you want? I've only had a couple of hours kip!' he barked back moodily.

'I thought you'd be up by now. You need a lot less sleep the older you get. TJ's been up hours,' he informed him. 'Shit, that hurt!' he added as TJ slapped him hard across his backside.

'Good. Give the cheeky bastard a slap from me too, TJ. What do you want anyway?'

'I wanted you to be the first to know - I'm emigrating.'

'Emigrating!' he said, now giving Ed his full attention. 'That's a bit sudden isn't it, Where to?'

'Cornwall, and TJ's coming with me. We're gonna be neighbours. How great is that?'

'Oh yeah, that's just fucking great,' Bob said sarcastically, before hanging up.

Ed laughed, and pulled TJ towards him.